CAT'S PLAY

A CRAZY CAT LADY MYSTERY

BY MOLLIE HUNT

Cat's Play, the 9th Crazy Cat Lady mystery
by Mollie Hunt

ISBN: 9798823943345
Independently published

Editing and Design by Rosalyn Newhouse

Published in the United States of America

Cover Art:
© 2020 Leslie Cobb www.lesliecobb.com
"Hazel came to the Multnomah County (Oregon) shelter from an animal hoarding situation. House of Dreams pulled her and brought her into their free-roam shelter. I fell in love with her while volunteering as a socializer and adopted her in October 2021." —Leslie Cobb

E1

Other Books by Mollie Hunt

Crazy Cat Lady Mysteries
Cats' Eyes (2013)
Copy Cats (2015)
Cat's Paw (2016)
Cat Call (2017)
Cat Café (2018)
Cosmic Cat (2019)
Cat Conundrum (2020)
Adventure Cat (2021)
Cat's Play (2022)

Tenth Life Cozy Mysteries
Ghost Cat of Ocean Cove (2021)
Ghost Cat on the Midway (2022)

Other Mysteries
Placid River Runs Deep (2016)

The Cat Seasons Sci-Fantasy Tetralogy
Cat Summer (2019)
Cat Winter (2020)

Short Stories
Cat's Cradle
The Dream Spinner

Poetry
Cat Poems: For the Love of Cats (2018)

Dedication

To my father, the Freemason in my life.

Acknowledgements

My father was a Freemason. What he did when he left our house in his old-fashioned tuxedo, we never knew. We did know that whatever it was brought him peace and pride. As I got older, I was able to glean more about his works within the Order and learned of the quiet good the Masons did for the community.

My father wanted to take it one step further, though. He was active in bringing people of color into the Freemasons—up until that time Black men had their own lodge.

My description of the Masons and things relating to their organization comes from the few comments my father made later in his life, as well as from the internet. If I got something wrong, the mistake is purely on my part.

Prologue

"Come along," I whispered to my companions as we tiptoed up the stairs of the haunted mansion.

"It's not haunted," I added quickly.

"Then why are you whispering?"

Why indeed? If anything, I should be excited. After all, the house and its contents now belonged to Friends of Felines. The gift would pay off bigtime for the cat shelter once the items were sold and the stipulations were met.

Besides, our guide on this house tour was a calico cat. What could possibly go wrong?

Chapter 1

Besides being a great way to meet new people who share your interests, volunteering helps increase self-confidence, self-esteem, and life satisfaction, because unlike with many paid jobs, you are appreciated!

A man was dead, and I was supposed to find his killer. No, I'm not a private investigator or an officer of the law. My name is Lynley Cannon, and I'm a cat shelter volunteer. I know cats, not murder.

The venture did start with a cat, however—Winter Orange, the dead man's cherished puss. Her wealthy cohabitor had made elaborate arrangements in case of his demise and put Friends of Felines in charge. When asked to look after the calico, I responded with enthusiastic candor. But I'm getting ahead of myself. How could I have guessed the simple request to foster a bereaved kitty would turn into tragedy?

* * *

Friends of Felines Cat Shelter was about to come into something huge. It was all anyone could talk about, staff and volunteers alike, so when Helen Branson, the shelter's executive director, called me into her office, I assumed it concerned the bequest. In a million years, I'd never have guessed what she would ask me to do about it.

I've been a volunteer at FOF for some years. It's a quiet, happy place where humans help care for and adopt out homeless cats. There is a restful routine to it: seven a.m. cats get fed; seven-thirty medications given; eight o'clock kennels cleaned, litter boxes swapped out, water bowls filled, and so on. Cats are creatures of habit, and suddenly finding themselves in a shelter blows their life-long schedule all to bits. We try our best to make things easy for them until they move on to their new forever homes.

Jasper, an elderly red tabby, had been adopted earlier that morning, and I was mopping down his kennel to make way for a new arrival when the call came.

"Lynley, you're wanted." The staff girl in her print scrubs put the phone back in its cradle and smiled teasingly.

"Is it my Prince Charming come to take me away from all this?" I joked, pushing my glasses up off my nose.

The girl rolled her eyes. I guess the idea of the handsome prince and a sixty-something cat lady who couldn't be troubled to wear makeup, let alone color her hair, seemed farfetched. "It's Helen. She said to tell you to come up and see her when you have a chance."

"Meaning right now," I translated.

"Yeah, or five minutes ago." The girl laughed. "I'll finish setting up the kennel for you."

She came over and took the cloth and pet-safe disinfectant spray from my hands, then sent me on my way. I didn't linger. In all the years I'd been at the shelter, I had never once been called to the office.

Pausing briefly in the volunteer locker room to pick up the tote I called a purse and check that my apron was on straight, I proceeded upstairs to the second floor where the corporate side of the rescue was housed. The atmosphere was subdued, the long corridor vacant, and the doors to the workplaces closed. At the far end was a balcony that looked out across the lobby. The executive office sat on the opposite side of the hall where the director could watch over the goings-on below.

The top half of the Dutch door was ajar, and I could see Helen working on her computer. In her inbox lounged a large and formidable black cat.

I felt a shiver of excitement as I gave a little knock on the jamb. "You wanted to see me?"

Helen looked up, flashing her signature smile. "Lynley, yes. Come in and sit down."

I obeyed, folding my hands in my lap like a schoolgirl, sudden memories of being called to the principal's office flitting unbidden through my mind.

Helen Branson, now in her sixties, had been with Friends of Felines since its inception some decades ago. As the place grew from a tiny volunteer-run concern to a prestigious cat shelter with forty employees and several hundred volunteers, her position had grown with it. She earned a generous salary, much of which she funneled right back into the shelter. FOF was her life; she nursed and protected it like a mama cat with kittens.

Helen leaned forward, fingers steepled and elbows on her desk. From afar, with her carefully coiffed brown curls that hung precisely to her shoulders and a touch of warm-toned makeup, she didn't look her years, but close as I was, I could see the lines. They were happy lines; I'll give her that.

Her gray eyes sparkled, and her lips curved in a wicked, cat-like grin. "You're an adventurous person, aren't you Lynley?"

It's true I seem to find myself in situations that one might consider bold or daring, and word gets around, but to have the executive director of Friends of Felines call me on it… well, that was totally unexpected. As I sat in that stiff office chair listening to Helen unfold a tale that was more fit for an Agatha Christie novel than real life, I became increasingly enthralled.

"You may have heard," she began, "the shelter is to be the recipient of a generous bequest. Extremely generous."

"There's been talk," I said tactfully. "We've all been wondering."

"There is a reason there's been no official announcement as yet." She paused for my reaction. I gave none. "The reason is this, Lynley—it's possible FOF may have to forfeit the gift."

Helen reached over and stroked the cat. "Meet Odin. He helps me think. Keeps me centered on the important things."

"Cats do that," I uttered, my mind still trying to solve the mystery of what could keep the shelter from receiving their due.

"Are you familiar with the name Roderick Payne?"

I started. "Roderick Payne, as in the notorious recluse? As in the noted millionaire eccentric? As in…"

"…the enormous Payne fortunes?" she finished for me. "That's the one. Mr. Payne has passed away, leaving the bulk of his estate to Friends of Felines. Not only is there an unfathomable sum of money, there are stocks, bonds, gold, jewelry, and a houseful of valuable items as well. Not to mention the mansion itself. Payne House, one of the largest and most notable homes in the West Hills, is also bequeathed to FOF."

"Wow!" I muttered. "That's wonderful! Isn't it…?"

"Well, yes it is. But there is a stipulation in Mr. Payne's will, one we may find impossible to meet."

"I don't understand."

Helen pried a fat blue packet from underneath Odin, wiped off a few black hairs, and handed it to me. The cover read *Last Will and Testament of Roderick Martin Payne.*

For a moment, I studied the neatly calligraphed words, impressive all by themselves, then I pulled back the cover and turned over the crisp pages one by one. When I got to the end, I gave Helen a puzzled look.

"I still don't get it. The part about caring for his cat is straightforward enough—that's standard with our Friends Fur-ever program. And the list of assets, well, it's overwhelming, but I'll take their word for it. It's this one that makes no sense." I flipped through, found what I was looking for, and held it out to the director. "What does it mean?"

"And therein lies the conundrum."

Helen rose. Moving to her front window, she gazed across the balcony down onto the kitten room in the lobby below. For a few moments, she watched the antics of the young cats at play, then she turned back to me.

"You have to understand, Lynley, we could really use this gift. It could mean the groundbreaking of the new hospital wing we've wanted for so long. And to lose it over a technicality..." She harrumphed and returned to her desk. "I don't know about the rumor mill, but only a few people have been told of the bequest itself, and even fewer about this... *twist.*" She flicked the document with a blunt-cut fingernail. "We want to keep it that way. No point in getting everyone's hopes up until we're more certain of our footing. That's where you come in, Lynley. I need three things from you."

Three things? My curiosity ramped up as I tried to envision what they might be. I had a hunch about the first two, but as to the third, I dared not guess.

"Number one has to do with Mr. Payne's possessions. I understand you know something about antiques."

"A bit. I'm no expert, but I have friends who are. I'd be happy to arrange for someone to come have a look, if that's what you're asking."

"Yes, exactly. We are thinking of doing an online auction at some point in the future, and first we need to get an idea of what is there." Her face scrunched into a mock frown. "I'm useless at that sort of thing. I wouldn't know the difference between Art Nouveau and eighties' kitsch!"

"Unless the items are terribly obscure, that shouldn't be a problem." I was thinking of my friend who ran the antique mall on 42nd street. What Gil, pronounced *Ghee* in the French manner, didn't know about old stuff you could fit into a gold 1890s sewing thimble.

"Perfect. See what you can find out and let me know."

She scribbled something on a notepad.

"Next, I was wondering if you would foster Mr. Payne's cat Winter Orange—Winnie for short. She's a calico and has proven herself to be somewhat of a diva. It will take someone with your expertise to make sure she is cared for properly. Are you interested?"

"Of course. I was about to ask Kerry if there were any cats who needed fostering. I can take her today if she's ready."

"There is a catch, Lynley, and it may be a deal breaker. According to Mr. Payne's wishes, the cat must remain in her own home."

"You mean the Payne mansion?" I spluttered.

Helen nodded. "That's the agreement. Everything Winnie needs is already there—beds, toys, food. Human meals will be provided as well, and Mr. Payne left a generous allowance for whoever takes on this job. Are you up for a little live-in cat sitting?"

I opened my mouth to say something, but no words came out. Things were flashing through my mind: *How long would it be? What about my other duties? What about my own cats—all nine of them?*

"I'll do it," I exclaimed before I could stop myself. "As long as I don't have to be there twenty-four-seven, I think I can manage. I'd probably be putting in some hours there anyway working on the estate auction."

"Are you sure? I know it's a lot to ask. And don't worry—if it gets to be too much or if something comes up, I can arrange for someone else to take over. I don't want you to feel pressured."

"Yes, I'm sure. You asked me if I was adventurous—well, I'd say this is bound to qualify."

"That will be a great relief to the staff. Winnie has been staying here since Mr. Payne's death, and to put it nicely, she's not a happy camper. Hopefully once she's back home, she will feel better. When do you think you'd be ready to begin?"

I did some quick calculations. "Is tomorrow afternoon soon enough?"

"Whatever works for you, Lynley. I'm just grateful you've agreed. You're doing us a big service." Helen picked up her desk phone and punched a number. "Good news, Kerry. Lynley Cannon is going to foster Winnie. Can you get her set to go for..." She put a hand over the mouthpiece. "Three o'clock tomorrow?"

I nodded.

"Yes, that's fine... I'll tell her."

Helen hung up, giving a sigh of relief. "You've made the foster department very happy. Apparently our little Winnie is a screamer. There's a booklet of instructions that go with her, but it's back at Payne House. If you need anything that isn't already provided, I have a number you can call. Mr. Payne wanted to make sure Winnie's sitter was cared for in every way."

Curiouser and curiouser, I thought, trying to picture myself in a mansion, and failing.

"That brings us to the last item on the list, the codicil."

I took up the will once more. "How did they put it? 'Codicil one: Stipulation to be met before the beneficiary organization can inherit, recorded on video.' There's a video?"

Instead of replying, Helen pulled a remote controller from her drawer. She clicked it, and the flat-screen TV on her wall came to life.

At first there was only flickering, accompanied by soft, classical music, Brahms if I recalled correctly. I was about to comment when someone cleared their throat. They coughed and gave another *ahem*. The picture cleared to reveal a man at a massive antique desk holding a blue folder. His face was in shadow but the tapestry behind him bloomed with rich color and light.

He began to read, an elderly voice, low but rising as he went along.

"I, Roderick Martin Payne, a resident of the County of Multnomah, State of Oregon, declare that this is a codicil to my last will and testament, which is dated as aforementioned. Whereas I now desire to make certain changes in my last will and testament, now therefore, I do hereby make, publish, and declare this as a first codicil to my said last will and testament by adding thereto…"

Payne paused, grunted, then in a flurry of frustration, tossed the folder at the camera. "Aw, heck, Debon! I can't read this stuff. It's all gobbledygook to me."

"Uh," said a voice off-camera. "Just say whatever you want, Rod. It'll be fine."

"Okey-dokey. That I can do."

Payne straightened his posture, folded his hands in front of him, and began again.

"I, Roderick Martin Payne, being of sound mind and all that legal rot, want to issue this codicil to my will. It's simple, really..."

But it wasn't. Payne seemed to feel it necessary to include his views on politics, religion, and the state of the world as a preface. As the voice droned on, my interest shifted to the picture itself. Since I could see nothing of the speaker beyond his silhouette against the bright cloth, I began to study the other things within the frame. Beside the tapestry hung a painting: an autumn hill, bright crimson and gold intermingled with dark blues and forest greens. A Tom Thomson—original I presumed. A bronze statuette of a bucking horse might have been a Remington. A glass paperweight contained an intriguing inset, a gold pyramid with an eye at the top. *Egyptian?* I wondered. I'd recently had occasion to learn a bit about ancient Egyptian relics, but those were mostly in the theme of the cat god Bast. This motif was unfamiliar to me.

My attention jerked back to Payne as he rang the small prayer bell on his desk. He giggled, seeming very pleased with himself. I didn't need to see his face to know he was grinning.

"All points of this bequest will become null and void if the recipient does not fulfill this stipulation in a timely manner. Now listen carefully. The beneficiary, Friends of Felines Cat Shelter of Portland, Oregon, will be responsible for the following: the discovery *and* the arrest of my murderer."

There was a pause, then the voice took up again, louder than ever. As he leaned in toward the camera, a beam of light hit his face, a mask of wrinkles and rage. "You got that, Helen? Find my killer or you don't get a dime!"

Helen clicked off the machine and sat back in her chair. The document dropped from my hand, and I gave a little squeak.

"What's that supposed to mean?" I blurted. "Mr. Payne knew he was going to be murdered? Why didn't someone stop it? The police? Why wasn't he given protection?"

I paused as another question came clear. "And why ever would he give the job of finding his killer to us?"

Helen put up a hand. "I can't answer any of that, Lynley. I have no idea what went on in Mr. Payne's final days nor what he was thinking when he made this record."

She paused to pet Odin, an indication of her thought process. Then her eyes fixed on mine.

"I can tell you one thing, however. According to the Oregon State Medical Examiner, Roderick Payne died of natural causes."

Chapter 2

You may have heard of Tortitude, a feistiness singular to tortoiseshell cats, but what about their near-sisters, the calicoes? Calicoes can be sassy, spunky and independent as well as sweet, loving, and loyal.

The executive director and I spent another half hour going over the details of the enigmatic bequest. We talked further about the antiques appraisal and my new foster, Winter Orange. Helen petted Odin while I asked questions. The subject of the paradoxical demand to find the killer of a man who died naturally was carefully avoided.

Helen made me a copy of the will, told me I could choose a team of helpers for the antiques inventory, then swore me to secrecy. "I'll be announcing the general points of the bequest at the assembly tomorrow. I'd appreciate it if you would keep what we've talked about to yourself until then, and subsequently not mention anything I don't touch upon in my announcement."

"Like catching a murderer? I assume you won't be making that part of the general knowledge."

"Exactly. We can't have strange rumors flying around the shelter, can we?"

"But what are you going to do? How can FOF find out about something that never happened in the first place?"

"I'm not sure yet. Our lawyers are looking into the legalities. There must be some way of circumventing such an impossible demand."

"And where do I fit in?" Did I really want to know?

Helen stood and came around to face me. "Since you'll be spending time at Payne House looking after Winter Orange..." She paused, then turned to pet Odin once more. He responded with a chirp and a purr. "I don't quite know how to put this."

"You want me to do some sleuthing," I filled in for her.

"Something like that. I don't know if there will be anything to *sleuth*, as you put it, but keep your eyes and ears open. Maybe you can learn something to help pull us out of this mess."

She gave a quick smile, then her face defaulted to her business mask. "As to accessing Payne House, we've been asked to keep the number of people to a minimum. From FOF, that will be you and your team, and by extension, your antiques fellow. Anyone else will need permission to enter." She rummaged through some papers and retrieved a list. "You will be coordinating with a Miss Whide, Roderick Payne's personal assistant. Other staff who may be present are a housekeeper and a groundsman—the estate is quite extensive, as you may have guessed. A catering service will bring your and Winnie's meals each day."

She looked up. "Sounds quite deluxe. I'm going to have to drop by when things get a bit more organized."

She handed me the page which I added to my already-extensive collection. "The stipulations of the bequest are eccentric, Lynley, but it would be such a benefit to the shelter. We must do everything we can to make it happen. I appreciate your taking this on."

Picking a business card from a ceramic holder, she wrote something on the back. "My personal number.

Anything you need, just call."

She held out her hand. I took it in a solemn shake. It was a strange thing to do, and I wasn't sure of the significance. A partnership? A pact? The feeling that went along with the gesture was obvious enough—Helen Branson and I now shared a bond. As I left the office, I took a deep breath. I had the strongest feeling my world was about to change.

* * *

The first thing I did after the momentous meeting with the FOF Director was run to the bathroom and splash cold water on my face. I had a thousand—or should I say, a *million*—questions vying for space in my head, and none of them would settle long enough for me to come up with an answer.

Focus! I sternly told my mirror-self. *You have things to do—things that require clear and level-headed thinking.*

I listed them off on my fingers like a little girl.

"One," I said out loud. "Winter Orange. I'll be picking her up tomorrow and moving into the Payne estate. I need to get ready. What does one pack for an overnight in a mansion?

"Two," I went on, so as not to lose momentum. "Gil. I must convince him to help with the estate inventory." I enjoyed the flamboyant faux-French antiques dealer and hoped he wasn't too busy to accept the job. "I won't take no for an answer."

"Three, that other thing..." Here I faltered, wrestling with a sense of apprehension. This was a weird one, and I couldn't help but be perplexed by it. Sleuthing out a killer who didn't exist was a hopeless task, but I'd give it my best. "Even if I come up with nothing," I reasoned to the mirror, "that would be a kind of something, right?"

I heard the door swing open and snapped my mouth shut, concerned the newcomer may have caught me talking to myself. Then I saw who it was and smiled.

"Hey, Lynley," said my fellow volunteer and shelter buddy Frannie DeSoto. "What's up with you today?"

I didn't quite know how to answer her since Frannie was the friend to whom I told everything, and my current *everything* would require more than a quick bathroom howdy-do.

I pulled off a paper towel and dried my hands. "You got a few minutes?"

Frannie frowned. "Is something wrong?"

"No, it's nothing like that. In fact, maybe just the opposite. Meet you in the atrium?"

"Sure, okay." Her look of concern began to fade from all but her eyes where the worry stubbornly lingered.

* * *

I beat Frannie to the little lunch area on the second floor balcony and was already at a table with a cup of cold mint tea when she came in. Underneath her green apron, Frannie was impeccably dressed in a pair of summer slacks and an Everlane organic cotton shirt. Her platinum locks curled around her face like icing on a cupcake—a new cut for her, but it suited. Though like me she was in her early sixties, she favored the age-defying tricks available to the older woman. On her, it worked. She always looked crisp, clean, and ready for anything. Though I personally couldn't be bothered with the makeup, fine clothes, and spandex undergarments, I respected her for her perseverance in the face of the inevitable.

Frannie sat down across from me and squeezed a slice

of lemon into her paper cup of ice water. "What do you think of this weather, eh? Hotter than blue blazes, as my mother used to say. Though I never really knew what *blue blazes* were. Still, I don't remember ever having a summer like this one."

"It's August," I bantered back. "What do you expect?"

She shrugged. "A nice thunderstorm would be welcome. Take some of the edge off. I miss the rain."

"Spoken like a true Portlander," I said. "I miss it too, until October comes, and it settles in for the duration."

I was small-talking and I knew it. What I didn't know was why. Frannie and I had been friends forever. We'd shared the secrets of our souls on many occasions nearly as strange as this one. Why was I finding it so difficult to tell her what was on my mind?

Thankfully it was she who started the conversation. "I hear you had a meeting with Helen Branson. Was it about the new donation? Are we getting that big inheritance everyone's talking about? Come on girlfriend—spill!"

I laughed. Her look of unabashed curiosity reminded me of a cat who has sighted something new in her world—an open cupboard door, a strange piece of furniture—and won't be satisfied until she knows all there is to know about it.

"Yes, yes, and yes," I replied coyly. "Helen is going to make the official announcement tomorrow."

"And what does she want you to do, Lynley Cannon?" Frannie gave me the eye, sensing from my behavior it was more than just caring for cats.

"She's asked me to help out with a few of the details." I rolled my eyes. "A bunch of the details, actually. I could really use your input. Would you like to help me inventory a houseful of valuable antiques and art pieces for an online auction?"

Frannie's painted lips curved into a smile knowing her feline curiosity was about to be assuaged. "Why, I'd love to. Tell me all."

I had only meant to give Frannie the briefest summary of my conversation with the executive director as per her instructions, but by the time I finished, I had practically recited the whole thing word for word. Including the live-in cat sitting of Winter Orange. Including hiring Gil to lead the antiques inventory. And including the stipulation of finding a murderer that didn't exist. There was so much I still didn't understand, and I hoped Frannie's innate levelheadedness might bring some insight. I was not to be disappointed. After a break while I sipped my tea and Frannie went for another ice water, she made her summation.

"That murder thing?" She waved a hand in the air, the light glinting off her bright blue nail polish. "Forget about it."

I sat back in surprise. "But…"

"No buts. Lynley, I know you. This is the sort of thing that drives you crazy—a mystery, a puzzle—but in this case, you can't move ahead without more information. *Lots* more information. And first you need to establish whether there's anything to it. 'Find my killer' " she quoted. "Since Mr. Payne wasn't murdered, it's got to be some sort of joke or prank. Or possibly the man was not in such sound mind as he claimed to be. Wait and see what the lawyers come up with. It may very well turn out to be a non-starter, so what's the point of wasting your time and energy?"

"But…" I began again.

Frannie reached out and patted my hand. "I know it's hard for you to let go of such a fascinating point, Lynley, but for now you should concentrate on the antiques work and your new foster cat. Leave the other thing alone."

I uttered a sound somewhere between a sigh and a huff. It wasn't what I wanted to hear, since to me, the mystery aspect of the bequest was by far the most compelling. But Frannie had a point. Chances were Roderick Payne's unfathomable demand would lead nowhere. I'd be smart to concentrate on the tasks at hand.

"You're right, Frannie," I conceded, "as usual. Humdrum, but right."

"Let's just call it practical. If the lawyers decide the stipulation is genuine, you can worry about it then." She took a sip of her water. "Though I don't really see why Mr. Payne would ask Friends of Felines to do the investigating. That's police work."

I didn't reply. I'd had a few run-ins with major crimes before and knew the police were limited, both in resources and in imagination. Maybe Roderick Payne, as a devoted cat person, put more faith in those with like minds than he did in law enforcement.

"I wish I knew more about the man," I mused. "Then maybe this whole thing would make sense. He's somewhat famous. I'll have to look him up on the internet."

"He's famous for being a recluse," said Frannie. "I doubt you'll find much there. Now that he's gone, someone will probably write a biography, but until they do, you may not get a lot of help on that front."

She gazed off in space for a moment. "I do have a thought though. You know who you should ask? Kelley Moro. She's a freelance journalist. She might have sources that go beyond the norm."

"Good idea! And she would be a perfect choice for my auction team as well. But I'm already getting ahead of myself. I need to talk to Gil first. He may have people of his own he wants to involve."

I drained the remainder of my beverage. The honey had sunk to the bottom, and I enjoyed a particularly yummy last sip.

"So that just leaves Winter Orange," I said. "I might as well go and meet her before we start to be roomies."

"You haven't met our dear Winnie?" Frannie's painted eyebrows flew up, aghast.

"No, not yet. Have you?"

"Oh, yes. She's in Tranquility Room. She's turned out to be a handful."

"Helen called her a diva. What does that mean?"

"You'll see." Frannie chuckled. "Let's just say it might be a good idea to stop by the pharmacy and buy a set of earplugs before you pick her up."

Chapter 3

Upper respiratory infections often run rampant in shelters. The viruses that cause URI are airborne, and even with air filtration systems, can be easily passed to cats whose immune systems are stressed by the sudden change in their lives.

After our little tell-all tête-à-tête, Frannie and I went our separate ways, Frannie to help with medications in the cattery, while I headed for the foster office. As I crossed the shelter lobby with all its busy, happy people coming to look at, and hopefully adopt, cats, I heard someone call my name.

"Special Agent," I said to the handsome young officer who was making his way toward me in long strides.

"Hello, Lynley. You know…" He turned his cat-green eyes on me. "You'd think after all we've been through you would start calling me by my first name."

I smiled. He had a point. Denny Paris, Humane Investigator out of Northwest Humane Society, had pulled my behind out of the flames more than once. More than twice. More than… well, you get the picture. He had saved my reputation and even my life. We were close in a way most people could only imagine.

"I call you Denny—some of the time," I laughed. "But I think you should get the respect you deserve."

His rugged face took on a slight blush, and he gazed at his shoes with that *aw, shucks* look he got when someone gave him praise. "Thanks, ma'am."

"Tell you what. You stop calling me ma'am, and I'll call you by your first name, deal?"

"Deal." He laughed. "You know I mean it with the best intentions."

"I do, but speaking as someone twice your age, take my word, I'd rather you just called me Lynley."

"Sure thing, Lynley."

We gave each other knowing smiles, then he grew solemn.

I sobered as well. "What's up?"

"I could use your help on a case."

"Of course. Anything I can do to assist the animal cops. What is it? A hoarding situation again?"

"Yes and no. There's an elderly man, Jack Hess, who has several cats. I don't know the exact number because so far, he hasn't let me into the house. He's on hospice, and the hospice people have concerns about his ability to care for them all. I know you've worked with hospice patients."

"My therapy cat Tinkerbelle and I do hospice visits, yes."

"He doesn't need a cat visit—he's got enough of that already. What I'd like is for you to go in and assess whether we need to do an official intervention, maybe take some of the cats. We don't want to interfere if we don't have to, but Hospice is worried he's to the point where he can't provide for them properly anymore. And you know what that means. The first thing to go is cleaning the litterboxes."

"Have you met him?"

"Yes, and we got along well, I thought. He's a veteran. Seems like a nice guy, pleasant. He didn't want me in the trailer, but he was polite about it. We had a good talk on his front step. It seems to me he has all his faculties, but until someone checks the state of the place, who knows?"

"I'd be happy to look in on him. Text me his information. I'll need to run it by my Hospice supervisor, but I'm sure she'll be okay with it, since they're the ones who asked for the help in the first place."

"I'll do that. Thanks, Lynley. I knew I could count on you." Denny slipped off his cap and ran a hand through his sandy mop of hair. "So what are you up to today? Picking up a new foster?"

"That's a tale all its own. Starting tomorrow, I'll be fostering the cat who belonged to the millionaire Roderick Payne before he died. It's a live-in situation so I'll be spending nights at his mansion."

"What about your own cats?" Denny frowned. "Don't you have a clowder of them at home?"

I fidgeted. "Well, yes, but I've left them alone overnight before. I figure if I get up early and race home, then make a nighttime run as well before settling in with Winnie... Oh, Denny, it's still a work in progress, but it seemed so important to Helen that I couldn't say no."

"I get it. If you need any help, let me know."

"Thanks. Her name is Winter Orange. I'm going to meet her now."

Denny gave a laugh. "You're fostering Winnie?"

"You've heard of her?"

"Heard of her and *heard* her," Denny chuckled. "You'll have your hands full with that one. She's a diva!"

* * *

I bade farewell to the special agent and continued through the shelter to the foster department. It was time I confronted this diva for myself. I'd cared for many cats in my life—Torties with tortitude, lackadaisical Maine Coons, fearful semi-ferals, high-strung Bengals. They all had their own distinctive personalities, so I was more intrigued than put off by the consensus that Winnie was trouble.

"I've come to visit Winter Orange," I said to the girl sitting behind the desk. "Lynley Cannon," I added to the volunteer's blank stare.

The vacancy turned to incredulity, then she said in an ambiguous tone, "I'd better get Kerry for you. Be just a minute."

The girl, twenty at the most, hopped to her mission. I watched as she took off into the back with a stride that defied gravity. I admit I was a bit jealous of her ability to move without creaking. But age is double-sided: though I might not be able to leap tall buildings anymore, I had gained a certain amount of serenity, self-confidence, and—dare I say—grace.

I knew it might take a few minutes for her to rustle up the busy foster director, so I sat down to wait. For a time, I perused the meager magazine collection, a month-old issue of *Catster* and a brochure for a fancy litter. I'd already read the *Catster* from cover to cover, and I didn't need a lesson on why walnut shells made the best medium for cats to do their business, so my attention moved on to other things.

I ran my gaze over a wall hung with framed diplomas of the medical staff and studied the current calendar model, a black puss sitting in a sunny window surrounded by bright red geranium flowers. Then my eye caught a page on the bulletin board that I hadn't noticed before. Though the posting was half-obscured by other flyers, I could see a photo—an intriguing cluster of assorted cats arranged on a wine-colored sofa. I was about to check it out when Kerry breezed into the room. She'd been letting her shiny black hair grow and had it bound in the cutest ponytail.

"Hi, Lynley. You're here to see Winnie, right?"

I nodded.

As she leaned over the computer and pulled up a page on the monitor, her ponytail bobbed in rhythm to the music coming from the shelter's speaker system. I truly appreciated the young foster coordinator who had the energy and boundless enthusiasm to stay optimistic in the face of a tough job.

"We'll be glad to get Winnie back home, believe me. She's been unhappy ever since she was brought in when Mr. Payne passed away. It took a while for the retrieval team to get her out of the house, which I'm sure didn't help her attitude. We're hoping that once she's back in a familiar environment she'll settle down."

I stood, stretched my foot, which had begun to fall asleep, and came over to the computer. "Tell me about her."

Kerry scrolled through the pages on her screen. "She's a seven-year-old calico. Her full name is Winter Orange Blossom Güzel."

"Güzel?"

"The note says it's Turkish for *beauty*." Kerry glanced at me and chuckled. "Payne had her DNA tested. It turns out she has Turkish Van roots. I'll include the results with her paperwork. It doesn't tell much. Ninety-nine percent of *Felis sylvestris* are basically mutts, but it's interesting all the same."

Kerry tapped another key, and the printer began to clack.

"The behavior department has been working with her since she came, but they haven't been able to make much headway. They tried to figure out whether her symptoms of extreme stress were from being in a new place or if there was more to it. According to her biography, she's never been off the Payne property, not even for vet visits. Doctors always visited her! But she was with Mr. Payne in the garden when he died. She stayed with him all night until the gardener found them the next morning. An experience like that could have affected her deeply."

Kerry sighed. "The only thing that's helped soothe her at all was putting her in the Tranquility Room by herself and leaving her alone, but that's not a solution—according to Payne's notes, she is very loving and craves human companionship. I guess we just haven't found the right human. Hopefully you'll have better luck."

I took a deep breath. "Anything else, besides that she's a diva?"

Kerry looked up in surprise. "Where did you hear that?"

"From everywhere. And that's all I've heard. Please, tell me something good."

"Well, she has no medical issues, no special diet or picky food preferences, though Mr. Payne left arrangements for her to be given some fancy noms made in the Netherlands. She doesn't claw the furniture, and she's one hundred percent fastidious—no litterbox issues. According to Mr. Payne, she's the sweetest, gentlest, friendliest kitty on this Earth. And here's a funny thing—Mr. Payne claims she's clairvoyant, that she communicated with him all the time." Kerry gathered the papers from the printer tray, tamped them even, and clipped them together with a glittery pink paperclip. "I'll let you be the judge of that one."

She placed the document in a file folder and handed it

to me. "You might want to run through this before you pick her up tomorrow. Forewarned is forearmed, so they say."

I stuffed the file in my tote beside the one I'd collected from Helen. "That bad?"

"Yes and no. If anyone can tame the savage beast, it'll be you, Lynley. Now, please follow me."

Kerry led me through the door marked *employees only* and into the back of the foster department with its kennels of cats going into or coming out of their temporary homes. I stopped to say hello to a little gray whom I recognized from her intake exam. She seemed rested and happy, all signs of her upper respiratory infection resolved. She could go up for adoption now, the potential adopter assured she was healthy and ready to start a life with a new family.

Kerry continued down a side hallway, then stopped.

"Hear it?"

I listened, and sure enough, coming from a room at the end of the corridor was the scream of a cat in distress. Or maybe it was a cat in frustration, or a cat in rage. Whatever the reason, this cat was upset and didn't care who knew it.

"Is that her?" I asked, already knowing the answer.

Kerry nodded. "Now you see why we'd like to get her out of here. She's upsetting the other cats, to say nothing of staff and volunteers who have to listen to that while they work."

"I'm sure it's not much fun for her either," I suggested.

Kerry harrumphed, then conceded, "Of course, you're right. She's obviously having a terrible time here."

We continued down the hall to a door with a plaque that read *Tranquility Room*. Underneath was taped a handwritten note, *Enter at your own risk!* From there I could pick out every screeching nuance of Winnie's protestation.

"Well, I've got to get back to the office. Go ahead and say hi, but don't expect too much. She's been singularly unresponsive to everyone so far. I really do think she'll come around once she gets back home," Kerry added apologetically.

"And if she doesn't?"

"Let's cross that bridge if we have to," she shot over her shoulder. With a flip of her ponytail, she was gone.

I hesitated on the threshold of Tranquility listening to the uproar inside. The cat sounded like she was in dire straits, but they were of her own making. I needed to remember that. I needed to be cool, calm, and most of all, confident. Taking a deep breath, I opened the door and stepped inside.

In a very large kennel was a cat unlike any I'd ever seen before. Her calico colors veritably glowed with brilliance—glossy black, pumpkin orange, and a white so bright it was almost blue. Her fur was medium length and looked silky as cashmere. I wanted to run my fingers through that luxurious coat but caught myself. Such an intrusion on her personal space would be anything but welcome.

I inched toward the kennel, making soft sounds and giving love blinks. She just stared at me—no love there. At least not yet, I told myself. Still, there was something about her eyes, something odd…

I gasped, realizing those round, wide pupil-filled orbs were of two different colors—one amber and one bright blue. With her color-splotched face, the effect was kaleidoscopic. *What a wonder,* I couldn't help but think to myself.

Winnie stopped her crying for a few moments while she studied me, then she took up again full force. I was shocked by the intensity of the sounds. More than mere unhappiness, there was an urgency behind them, a need.

"Me-ooouttt nnooowww!" she shrieked into my ears and into my mind.

Was it my imagination or had Winter Orange just spoken to me?

Chapter 4

Though few feline illnesses can survive on clothing, many cat shelter workers change their clothes when they come home from the shelter before interacting with their own cats.

By the time I pulled up in front of my Old Portland-style house, I'd begun to wonder if I was making a big mistake. A huge mistake. A mistake of gargantuan proportions! I know that some cats cry when they are stressed, but Winnie took it to a whole new level. Would that behavior cease once she was back in her own familiar surroundings, or did it go deeper? Was there trauma involved? Kerry mentioned she'd been with her beloved person when he died, and that she'd stayed with him all night long. I knew for a fact cats feel grief. Did she miss Roderick Payne? Did she know her life would never be the same?

I'd no sooner got in the door when I was surrounded by my own cats, and all thoughts of Winnie the Screamer were put on hold. Through their canny feline telepathy, the clowder knew something was up. Big Red, my shy tabby boy, immediately set to yowling, while Little, all black and a diva in her own right, competed with a loud wail. Mab, a purebred Siamese, produced cries that sounded almost human, and I wondered how long it would be before a passerby called the animal police on me. The others were there too—Tinkerbelle; Emilio; wobbly Elizabeth; rotund Violet; and Dirty Harry, the elder of the clan. Only one cat was absent—Hermione, the most recent addition to the family. Before I inherited her—*literally*—Hermione had been a single cat, and though she got along with the others, she had her own way of doing things. In this case, she was giving the meow fest a pass.

"It's okay, sweethearts," I soothed. "I'll be right back. You know the drill."

I made a bee-line for the bathroom, the cat congregation following along like a tide.

"Give me a minute," I told them, then much to their dismay, I closed the door.

Shedding my shelter clothes, I washed my face and hands. Though it's nearly impossible to transmit feline diseases on clothing, it was better to be safe, so everything except the shoes went into the laundry after each shift.

The room was sticky-hot, and I was glad for a two-minute shower and a change into the summer dress I'd left hanging on the peg. Frannie was right about the weather—this summer was turning out to be the hottest on record. Unlike places with consistently high temperatures, most of Portland's older homes, mine among them, had no air conditioning, so the best we could do was sit in front of a box fan and hope for rain.

I proceeded to the kitchen where I clicked on the overhead fan, listening gratefully to the thwump, thwump, thwump of the blades. The muggy air began to move as they gained momentum, giving at least the illusion of cool.

"It's not time yet," I told the cats who were now waiting expectantly at their food stations. "I've got a few things to do first, okay?"

It must have been okay, because one by one, the meows subsided, and the cats went off about their business. Only Violet, who lived for food as her size could attest, hung around looking wistful.

I settled down to make myself a much needed cup of tea, and while it was steeping, I opened the window, hoping for a bit of fresh air to aid the laboring fan. Greeted by something akin to an oven blast, I almost closed it again but decided that moving air, no matter how steamy, was better than stagnant.

In spite of the solace of the quiet kitchen, Winnie's wild screeches still rang in my ears. There was something about the wail of an animal in distress that tugs at the psyche, just as parents will come running to the sound of a baby's cry. Kerry had assured me Winnie was in no physical pain, but mental pain was another matter. Would I be able to help soothe her, or would she just continue to scream herself sick?

I brought my tea, a nice, calming vanilla chamomile, over to the mission oak table and pulled out my phone.

"Friends of Felines Foster Department, Kerry speaking."

"I keep hearing her, Kerry. Yowling on and on."

"Lynley?"

"She's crouched in my mind like a calico ghost."

"Winnie?" Kerry laughed. "She has that effect on people."

"It's not funny," I went on. "I can't get it out of my head. When people called Winnie a diva, they really meant *demon*, didn't they?"

The foster manager laughed again. "I'm sorry, I know it's no joke, but you're hilarious! Demon, indeed. I'll have to tell the staff."

"All kidding aside, Kerry, I'm worried. What if I can't help her, even once she gets home? It must be hard on that little body to be in such an agitated state all the time."

"The docs have been keeping a close eye on her. Her

behavior hasn't seemed to cause any adverse effects. Her blood pressure is slightly high but still in the normal range, and all her other numbers are fine as well. Her appetite is good, and thankfully she takes her eighteen hours of naptime seriously. But we can find someone else to foster her if you think it's more than you can handle."

"No, no. Helen specifically asked me to do it. I've got to at least try."

"Okay, good. It'll work out, you'll see. You've never met a cat who didn't respond to you."

That wasn't strictly true, but I accepted the compliment.

"See you tomorrow then?" Kerry said tentatively.

"Three o'clock. Yeah. See you then."

I clicked off and took a gulp of tea. I did feel better after talking. Just knowing I had an out relieved the stress of responsibility. And she was essentially correct—I had a lifetime of cat experience under my belt. There was no reason to believe Winnie would be immune to my tricksy charms.

Putting that thought away for the 'morrow, I dialed another number.

"Bonjour, Antique Row. Zis ees Gil speaking."

"Gil. Just the person I was looking for. Lynley Cannon here. Do you have a minute?"

"But of course! Always for you, Lyn-dear."

I ignored the innuendo that was just part of Gil's extravagant style. "I'm managing a project that might be of interest to you. The cat shelter where I volunteer is the beneficiary of a huge bequest, the estate of Roderick Payne. They've asked me to enlist some help in appraising his possessions. Interested?"

"You bet!" Gil snapped, losing his faux French accent in

his excitement, but only for a moment. "*The eminent Monsieur Payne owned one of the most recognized collections of Victorian Art Pottery in the country, in the world! Just to see such a thing would be marveloux!*"

"I'm not sure what compensation FOF is thinking of giving for your services. I'm a volunteer—I do it for the cats."

"*Of course, pour les chats. I also can be charitable. But maybe a good deal on a few choice items, Lyn-dear?*"

"I don't see why not, but I imagine that will be up to those in charge. I'll put in a word for you though."

"*Bien sur, bien sur.*" I could almost see the flick of his hand that surely accompanied his words. "*Eet will be fun.*"

I gave him the directions to the estate, and we set a time to meet in the morning. He couldn't wait to get inside that treasure-filled mansion, and to be honest, neither could I. Most Portland natives knew of the old "castle" perched atop the West Hills like a gothic soldier holding vigil over the town. I'd seen it from afar—who could miss it looking up from the flat plain of downtown? What that tall, turreted, slightly decaying enigma would be like up close I could only guess.

As a child, my friends and I often speculated about the true nature of Payne House. We had a handful of wild notions—a fortress where the princess was being held by an evil witch; a Frankenstein-esque chateau with a mad scientist creating monsters. Our favorite theory though, the one we always came back to, was that of the haunted manor. No one was ever seen going in or out, and at night, only one light shone in that entire huge structure, the one in the topmost turret. I suppose that could also have been where the princess was being held—who knew? I was looking forward to seeing it for myself. I had the strongest suspicion those childhood fantasies would pale against the real thing.

I heard a *yeow* as a cat landed heavily on the table across from me. The big tabby stalked over the mail and papers laid out on the oak surface, skirted my teacup with a grace unlikely for such a large boy, and put his face against mine. *Yow*, Big Red repeated.

As I glanced around the kitchen, I saw others were beginning to regroup as well. Had I really been off in my daydreams for that long? Apparently so, because many sets of eyes were staring expectantly at me as they did every evening around mealtime.

Red hopped down and joined the clowder. It used to be Dirty Harry who led the food brigade, but somewhere along the line, the orange tabby had taken over the task. Harry was getting old, I admitted sadly. He seemed content to let a new chief take his honored place.

"Okay, guys." I rose and headed for the cupboard. "You win. You know you always get your dinner before mine. Have I ever let you starve?"

Now that I was up and it was happening, a round of excited meows broke from every corner. Mab pranced to and fro, getting in my way more often than not; Little hopped onto the sideboard as I pulled out the cans, making sure I did it right; Violet lumbered to her station where she howled as if dying. Her highness would continue that ruckus until her special diet was placed before her.

Hermione was still getting used to this daily show. Suddenly cast among eight sisters and brothers, she made the best of it, neither fighting nor embracing the status quo, as if she lived in a bubble of her own. With her marbled gray and white markings and stunning blue eyes,

Hermione was one of the most striking cats I'd ever come across. Every so often I'd stop whatever I was doing to marvel at her beauty. Now was not the time, however. *Rouw,* she said sullenly from her place apart.

Nine cats with nine different diets, requirements, and in some cases, medications, took a while to get in order. By the time I'd finished, I was beginning to get hungry myself. My own repast was much simpler—a square of vegan lasagna, an apple cut in chunks, and a glass of cranberry juice. The prep took three minutes, including warming the pasta in the microwave. I carried my tray outside to the covered deck, leaving most of the cats still munching.

Though it was still only August, the garden had begun to take on a tone of the changing seasons. The daylilies and cosmos had given way to asters and hydrangea. The chrysanthemums had begun showing buds of gold, red, and bronze, while dahlias bobbed their pale pink and purple heads in the breeze. The sunflowers I'd planted along the fence blazed brightly against the blue of the sky, turning their yellow and black faces to the sun, ever the optimists of the flower world. The air too, though hot and dry, whispered of things to come. The rains of autumn would be on us before we knew it, then the wild winds of November, moaning down the wires. The dark days and long, dark nights of winter. In spite of the heat I shivered.

Rats! I said to myself. *Buck up!* But something had got me worried, and until I figured out what it was, there would be no peace.

As I picked at my lasagna, I tried to think it through. I hadn't felt this malaise in the morning, nor had it been present when I was doing my shift at the shelter. It had begun with the call into Helen's office, and the offer of the new job. But that made no sense—the estate auction was bound to be fascinating, and even though Winnie was a conundrum, I was determined to win her over, one way or another.

No, both those elements were well on their way to being resolved. They were not the root of my discomfort, which left only one possibility—the question of finding Payne's murderer. That was it, wasn't it? My mind kept running through Payne's taped demand, trying to solve the riddle, and failing. How could one find a killer who didn't exist?

Another question, equally as baffling, was why the man had left that dire duty to a cat shelter in the first place? Frannie had been wise when she told me to forget about it, leave it until there was more information, but I couldn't do that. It wasn't in my nature. Maybe it's my long association with cats, but curiosity drives me. There had to be some way of untangling this skein of mysteries, and until I figured it out, I'd be useless for anything else.

Pushing my plate aside, I retrieved a large red sketchbook from a basket on the table. I'd bought the volume in hopes of starting a journal, but after a few pages of drivel, I'd given up and began to use it for lists and random reminders instead. Now I took up the pen that was clipped to the inside cover and began to write.

The Mystery of the Murder of Roderick Payne, I penned at the top in block letters. It was a long title, but it covered the subject, so I let it stand.

One, I wrote, then hesitated. What was *number one*? That was the problem, wasn't it? I didn't even know where to start.

I doodled a small cat in the margin, hoping I'd think of something. Under the cat, I drew a curlicue of flowers, and under that, a fancy vase. Was it meant to represent one of

Payne's art pottery pieces? It hadn't started out that way, but sure—why not? Beneath the vase, I drew an oversized diamond ring—a common symbol of wealth.

After another squiggle that might be ivy, I ran out of margin. My next sketch moved to the right along the bottom of the page—another cat, Winnie. The figure with its calico spots looked more like a wolverine, but I wasn't an artist. I knew what it meant, so I skipped on to the next, a line representation of the Payne house as I envisioned it.

I really got into that little drawing, trying to recall all the dormers, flying buttresses, and colonnades from memory. When I'd finished, I found it had taken up most of the page. The drawing wasn't half bad. There was the one-story covered porch, the veranda, the balcony. And at the very top of the tallest tower was the lighted window right out of my childhood fantasies. From this, I'd drawn rays burning in all directions like a star.

I sat back with a gasp. Without words, I had come upon the solution to my query of what comes next. The mystery of the murder of Roderick Payne had something—no, had *everything* to do with that house, and it was there that I would find my answers.

Pushing the journal aside but leaving it open so I could still view my creation, I retrieved my dinner and tucked into it like a starving person. The lasagna was cold but still hearty, and the Kiku apple was juicy and not overly crisp, just the way I liked it. I took a sip of cranberry juice, then held the glass aloft.

"To Roderick Payne," I toasted, "and to Friends of Felines getting everything that's coming to them."

Chapter 5

"It may be that 'nobody owns a cat,' but scientists now say the popular pet has lived with people for 12,000 years."
—Smithsonian

The next morning just before ten, I pulled into the circular drive at the front of Payne House and sat motionless in awe. I had never seen the mansion from that vantage point before, and it was even grander than I could have guessed. Three stories of Tenino sandstone culminated in the steep swoop of a mansard style roof, complete with gables and two huge chimneys. Arched pediment windows, vignette balconies, and a million board feet of fancy moldings rose from the foundations like a wedding cake gone mad. The window trim could have used some new paint and a little repair in places, but even so, I couldn't help but be overwhelmed by the dignity of the place.

The one-story porch I'd seen from downtown continued all the way around the structure like a petticoat, coming together at the front entrance in a series of columns. Between them stood a tall, delicate man of about forty-five with bright red glasses and bright blue hair. Alongside this paradox of color and style was a younger man, one of those robust but lanky, hands-in-the-pockets, grin-on-his-sunny-face types of guys. Lover or assistant? Assistant, I surmised, since he looked to be half Gil's age.

"Gil!" I waved through the open window of my car. Pulling the emergency brake, I grabbed my bag and a tablet, the old fashioned clipboard kind that had nothing to do with technology, and went to join him on the porch.

"Lyn-dear!" Gil crooned, a big smile lighting his face. Though the antiques dealer assumed a fake identity in so much of his life, his enthusiasm and kindliness were one hundred percent genuine.

"This is my apprentice, Sanjay. Sanjay, meet one of the smartest, most savvy creatures in our fair city, not to mention she is as beautiful as a summer rose."

I blushed and laughed at the same time. "You flatter me, Gil."

"*Oui*, I do," was his sly answer.

As much as I appreciated the compliment, I wasn't up for small talk. Moving to the immense front door, I rang the bell. Almost immediately a short woman wearing a blue flowered dress and leggings appeared in the doorway. Her doughy face contrasted with the stern glare of her faded blue eyes.

"Miss Whide?"

"Lynley Cannon?" the woman replied in kind.

I nodded. "Yes, from Friends of Felines Cat Shelter." Both Gil and Sanjay were watching me, hovering with the intensity of cats observing a bug. "This is Gil Archambeau and his assistant Sanjay. We're here to assess the estate for auction."

Miss Whide stared pointedly at the men behind me, then stood aside. "Please come in. We've been expecting you."

As I passed into the vastness of the foyer, I could feel her gaze on my back. Here was a woman who didn't miss a thing.

Once we were inside, Miss Whide closed the door, and with it went the daylight, leaving only shadows and misty white shapes. It threw me off until I realized the specters were nothing more than furniture coverings. Not ghosts then, but chairs and tables, sofas and sideboards.

There was a click as Miss Whide turned on the light, a magnificent crystal chandelier that hung from the fifteen-foot frescoed ceiling. I gasped at the sight, and I thought Gil was going to faint with pleasure.

"*Magnifique*!" he was saying over and over as he drifted around the room, peeking under the cloths to see the treasures.

"And this is just the hallway!" I said, no less impressed than he.

"Foyer," Miss Whide corrected.

We continued to snoop while she stood by, solemn as a gothic statue, taking in our every move.

"Ahem," she finally pronounced. Though the sound was barely audible, all three of us turned instantly.

"You are welcome here," Miss Whide announced to her audience. "Mr. Payne was a great admirer of your cat shelter, and a great benefactor as well. It comes as no surprise he wanted all his worldly goods to go to you. He has no heirs, you see." She hung her head as if this were a sad thing, but only for a moment. "Ms. Cannon, you shall be furnished a code for the smart lock. You may come and go as you like. The rest of your group must make arrangements through you."

"Thank you. And it's Lynley. Do you live here then, Miss Whide?"

"Yes, for many years but now I'll be moving on. You can still call on me if the need arises. I'm happy to assist you in any way I can."

"Thank you," I repeated. Though her words were compliant and the tone basically friendly, her face was still stern as Grumpy Cat, and I had to assume there was more to the story.

Might she know something about the killing of Roderick Payne? I suddenly wondered. *If there were a killing,* I reminded myself. It seemed doubtful the pathologist had got it wrong. Perhaps Miss Whide could offer some insight as to what was really going on, but first, I'd need to break through that stony façade.

"Gil, come look at this!" Sanjay called, bringing me from my speculation. Miss Whide had disappeared, and Sanjay had moved into the next room. I followed his voice. A salon? A sitting room? The perfectly round chamber with walls papered in dusty rose watermarked silk was like something out of a dream, instantly transporting me to another era—one of gowned ladies and men in ruffled suits.

For a while, we explored room after room, peeking under the dust covers, each of us in our own little world. From dining hall to kitchen, pantry to parlor to a spectacular jungle conservatory, the place was filled with art, antiques, furniture, statuary, and bric-à-brac. I imagined what a fortune this would bring for the shelter, then thought of the hard work it would take to make that happen.

Finally our investigations brought us back to the foyer where a grand stairway curved up to the second story. Wide-eyed with excitement, we began to climb, Sanjay running before us like an excited child.

He'd made it up several of the wide treads when he stumbled in his haste. Grabbing for the handrail, he cried out as that section of the balustrade suddenly cracked and fell away, nearly taking him with it.

Teetering on the edge, he righted himself. "Yikes!" he

exclaimed as he watched the debris plunge clattering onto the marble below.

I ran to stand beside him but took a step back, not liking the sensation of vertigo the long, unprotected view down set off in me.

"*Qu'est que ce*?" Gil gasped.

"Darned old house is in worse shape than it looks," Sanjay swore, then sighed. "No harm done I guess, unless you count having to clean up the mess on the floor."

"We'd better get someone to check the rest of the balustrade," I said, writing a note on my tablet. I stared down at the vacant foyer. "I'm surprised the noise didn't summon Miss Whide."

Steering clear of the railings, we continued up the stairs with synchronized steps. The three of us moved silently, reverently, as if the place were a church. In a way it was, a testament to all things old and precious, and to the man who had amassed them.

Much was known about the mansion itself—that it was built in the 1800s by one of Portland's founding fathers; that it had fallen into decay when the bloodline ended with the death of a spinster daughter; that sometime in the eighties, Roderick Payne had acquired and restored it, and now it was valued into the millions. Less was known about Payne himself. He was old, that was certain, though no one knew how old. He had been ill; then he died. This collection told a further story, however. The things he had accumulated and kept so carefully were valuable, yes, but they were also beautiful and unique. It was obvious he knew what he was acquiring. Had he set out to find each piece in its own right? Aside from the art pottery collection, the Roseville, Weller, and Rookwood, there seemed to be no one preference to provenance. French porcelain, English primitives, and Egyptian relics were mixed with Navajo blankets and Indian silks. Every single item was quality, the best of the best. I couldn't begin to guess their value and was glad Gil would be there to help.

On the upper floor, we again wandered our own ways, but after a while I found Gil in one of the many bedrooms. It looked like he'd been working, pulling back the dust covers and opening cupboard doors, but now he stared out the window at the cityscape below. Coming to his side, I too took in the amazing view, the bright, glittering buildings of downtown Portland, the gray-brown Willamette River slicing through its center. Bridges spanned the waterway at irregular intervals, looking as fragile as twigs, though in reality their concrete and steel had held up for decades under the tons of crossing cars and trucks. Mt. Hood was visible on the horizon—or as my mother would say, *the mountain is out today*, equating the geographical landmark with celestial beings like the moon, stars, and sun. No snow painted its pointed peak this time of year, but it was spectacular just the same.

"Well, what do you think?" I asked the antiques dealer.

"I am speechless," he whispered. "Without words, *absolument*." He turned and grabbed my hands. "*Merci*, Lyn-dear, thank you for giving me this opportunity. Just to see this... this... *trésorerie* is more than I could have dreamed."

"It is amazing, isn't it? You've got your work cut out for you—if you accept the job, that is."

"But of course I take the job. I would be a fool not to. It will require much work however. First the inventory, then the research. The cataloging... yes, many hours, many days. Plans must be made."

"I'll set you up with the shelter's executive director.

She's the one you need for planning. I'm only the manager."

"Ah, I see. But you will help, *oui*?"

"I'd love to, if you want me. Though these things are so far out of my league," I commented, staring around the room. "I don't even know what half of them are."

I picked up a matte-blue jug from a spindly-legged bedside table and turned it over. The Rookwood mark was stamped into the clay, but alongside was the hand-etched artist's signature, denoting the piece was special if not unique. I carefully set it down again, knowing it could be priced into the thousands. "I doubt I'll be much use with the appraisal, but I can help with inventory."

"*Parfait!*" Gil exclaimed without reservation.

I loved Gil's enthusiasm for all things antique, but this time he seemed more exuberant than ever. "It will be *fantastique*!" he muttered to himself as he peered around the room once more.

"Hey, guys," Sanjay shouted from somewhere down the hallway.

"We're back here," I called.

"Sanjay?" Gil started toward the voice. "What did you find?"

"Hey," the young man repeated, excitement burning in his voice. "Did you know there's an attic?"

Chapter 6

What is it about a person's going to the powder room that intrigues our cats so? Is it the overwhelming scent of their human? The fact you're a captive audience when sitting on the loo? An act they can relate to? Scientists do not know.

After hours spent in the main house and the imprint of several hundred rare and fabulous items on my brain, the attic seemed overwhelming. Where the downstairs rooms had been orderly, well-presented, and clean, the third story was a hodgepodge of boxes, bookshelves, broken furniture, draped canvases, and other pieces beyond identification, all blanketed with a thick layer of dust. The first thing I did when I got to the top of those narrow wooden stairs was to shake my head in wonderment—the second was to sneeze. Though my seasonal allergies were mostly held in check by medication, nothing could save my nose from the barrage of particulates floating free in that still attic air.

"I'm out of here," I said to the boys. "Take your time, and I'll meet you downstairs. I need to talk with Miss Whide anyway."

Gil quipped an affirmative, and Sanjay, his attention riveted on a stack of ancient tomes, didn't bother to reply.

Retracing my steps to the foyer, again giving the broken balustrade a wide berth, I gazed around, unsure where to go. That was the last place I'd seen Payne's personal assistant, but I had no idea where she'd got off to from there.

"You're looking for me?" asked Miss Whide, appearing in a doorway as if summoned.

I whirled around. "You must be a mind reader," I gasped. "Yes, I thought we should have a chat before I go."

She stood where she was, her face giving nothing away. "Can I get you some tea, Ms. Cannon?"

"That would be nice, and please, call me Lynley. What should I call you?"

Again the sullen stare. "Miss Whide will do. Tea will be served in the sitting room. Come this way please."

Miss Whide started across the foyer but pulled up short when she saw the broken section of the banister.

"Who did this?" she demanded.

"No one did it. Part of the railing broke when we were going up the stairs. I was about to tell you."

She gave me the eye, as if I might be lying. "Was anyone hurt?"

"No, thank goodness."

"Excuse me. I need to call Cox immediately." She pulled a cell phone out of her skirt pocket, then turned away. I heard her giving swift orders, but I couldn't make out anything more.

"You should have told me the moment it happened," she chided once she rang off.

"You're right, I should have, but I didn't know where you were."

"Humph." She handed me a card, also from that extensive pocket. "My number. Call if anything like this occurs again."

"Hopefully it won't," I exclaimed. "Or is the house in

such bad repair?"

"The house is in perfect condition," she shot with such vehemence I nearly took a step backward.

She caught herself, blinked a few times, and quickly added, "Pardon my abruptness. This house means a lot to me."

"I understand," I said, though I really didn't.

Putting an end to the awkward conversation, Miss Whide led me into a small parlor that I'd somehow missed in my earlier exploration. Unlike the other rooms, this one was free of furniture coverings, and the curtains on the tall windows were open to the morning sun.

"This is lovely," I commented before realizing Miss Whide had vanished yet again.

I shrugged, wondering if I was going to have problems with Payne's assistant. It was natural that she'd take a proprietary interest in a place where she'd been employed for so many years—her life must have been totally upended by Payne's death, and now she was left with a handful of strangers come to divvy up the spoils—but none of that was my doing, and I hoped she wouldn't take it out on me.

Miss Whide returned a few minutes later with a tray of tea things. Setting it on a tiled table that seemed built for just that purpose, she commenced to pouring. "Please sit down. Do you take anything?"

I sank into a comfortable armchair by the window and watched the amber liquid stream from a porcelain teapot into a perfectly matching cup. "No, black is fine. Thank you very much."

"You're welcome," she replied. Was it my imagination, or was the ice beginning to melt?

Miss Whide passed me the cup on its paper-thin saucer

while she poured one for herself.

"This must be a difficult time for you," I put forth. "How long did you work for Mr. Payne?"

"Twenty-seven years." She perched on the edge of the window seat, balancing her teacup in the palm of her hand.

"And what will you do now, if you don't mind my asking?"

This she considered, and I wondered if I'd moved too quickly. But if I were going to bring the conversation around to the heart of the matter—Payne's death—I had to start somewhere.

She gave a sigh and chose to be candid. "Mr. Payne has done nicely by me. He has deeded me a condominium and set me up financially for the remainder of my lifetime. I will now retire, though I will continue to be available to you for whatever is required to make sure Mr. Payne's final wishes are properly fulfilled."

I didn't miss the inflection on the words, *properly fulfilled.* "I want you to know, Miss Whide," I began in my most humble tone, "we intend to respect Mr. Payne's wishes in every way possible. Friends of Felines is so very grateful for Mr. Payne's consideration, and we plan to do everything we can to honor his memory and his gift."

Miss Whide smiled for the first time, the expression transforming her face into that of a kindly grandmother with treats in her pockets and a twinkle in her eyes.

"Thank you, Ms. Cannon. That pleases me greatly."

"It's Lynley, remember?"

We sipped our tea in an almost friendly camaraderie, casting our gaze to the garden outside. The gardener had been doing his job because the sprawling lawns were mowed and the flower beds weeded. Yet in spite of the general tidiness, there was an air of desolation, as if the garden itself was mourning the passing of its master. The birdbath stood empty and dry; the Japanese lanterns strung from the covered porch to the veranda hung oddly askew.

"It must be hard for you to watch everything change."

Miss Whide was thoughtful. "There is a certain sadness, yes. The end of an era. But knowing it's going for a good cause is an uplifting factor. Mr. Payne often discussed this eventuality, so it comes as no surprise."

"Mr. Payne anticipated his death?" Was this the clue I was looking for?

"No more than anyone, I don't believe. But when one is wealthy, one has certain obligations. Death can come at any moment—that's true for us all," she said in a matter-of-fact tone. "But where most people would rather not speculate, Mr. Payne took his responsibility seriously."

"What was he like, the formidable Roderick Payne?"

Miss Whide frowned.

"I'm not trying to pry," I followed quickly. "I just think I could do a better job of dealing with the stipulations of the will if I knew more about him."

She stared a moment longer, then sighed.

"It's not that. I miss him, you know. He was like a son to me, even though he was, in fact, much older. Like some men, he always retained a boyish attitude when it came to life. A little naïve, and maybe a little bit naughty."

She chuckled, then turned her gaze to the window once more. A red climbing rose was on its second bloom, surrounding the glass like a living picture frame.

"How to describe Roderick Payne?" Miss Whide mused. "Well, he was very much an introvert. He rarely left the estate and then only because he had to for one reason or another. He often told me, 'Everything I need is right here... if only I could find it!' " She laughed. "He could be so forgetful at times. I swear half my job was telling him where he'd left things."

"That's interesting—the part about his introversion, not the part about losing things. I'd heard he was a world traveler."

"Oh, he'd traveled extensively in his youth. He had been to all the seven continents, including Antarctica. Many of the things you'll find in this house he brought directly from their places of origin. Egypt, India, South America, Europe, Iceland."

"How did he get involved with Friends of Felines? That was before my time as a volunteer."

"He loved cats. More than most people, certainly. There were many cats living here throughout the years, the most recent being Winter Orange. Little Winnie." Miss Whide smiled at the thought, and I could see she genuinely loved the feisty calico. "Winnie spent every waking hour with Mr. Payne. Followed him everywhere he went—I'd say like a dog, but of course she was much more intelligent than any canine." She gave a giggle. "Winnie even accompanied him to the toilet, he told me. And when he bathed, she would sit on the edge of the tub and groom, just like her daddy. Sometimes she would even hop in. Her ancestors were Turkish Vans, and they are known to love water."

I couldn't help but smile at the thought. A few of my own cats were extremely curious when it came to my bathroom regimen.

"Speaking of Winnie, when do you plan to bring her home?"

"This afternoon. I pick her up at three."

"Thank goodness! She was born in this house and had never left the grounds until they took her to your shelter. She was not happy to go, I can tell you that."

"I believe it! She doesn't care for shelter life, though everyone's trying very hard to make her feel welcome."

"Oh, dear. I hope it doesn't cause her any lasting suffering. It's bad enough she's lost Mr. Payne."

The teacup began to clatter in Miss Whide's shaking hand. She removed it to the table. "Poor, poor Winnie! She was never meant to languish in a cage."

"It's only for a few more hours. Maybe you can help me get ready for her homecoming by telling me about her likes and needs."

"Yes, good idea. I'll take you to her apartment—*your* apartment, since I assume you'll be her caretaker." She stared at me with such intensity I nearly squirmed.

"That's right, at least for the time being. Don't worry. I have quite a bit of experience with cats of all types and dispositions." I was just about to offer references when she relaxed.

"I have confidence Mr. Payne knew exactly what he was doing when he chose your shelter as her guardian."

The tone was perfunctory, and I didn't know whether to take it as a compliment or a statement of fact.

Suddenly a thought struck me. "What happens to Winnie when the house is sold?"

Miss Whide's face fell. "She stays with the home. Whoever buys it will take over her care. It is written in the deed."

"But what if they don't want a cat?"

"That will be up to you and your shelter," she said pointedly, "since you will be overseeing the sale."

Miss Whide and I talked for some time more, sipping

tea and discussing the inscrutable Roderick. She told stories of his exploits that ranged from humorous to mundane to tragic. The man seemed to have led quite a full life, even after he chose not to leave the walls of Payne House.

When the mantelpiece clock chimed the hour, Miss Whide looked up in surprise.

"Is that the time? I'd best quit telling tales and get on with important matters, though it has been nice to remember." She gave the briefest of smiles, then resumed her all-business attitude.

"There are two fulltime employees—Cox, the groundsman, and Alice, the domestic help. Cox will be caring for the estate until the house is sold. He also doubles as handyman. Should anything go wrong inside the house—electrical, plumbing, etcetera—go to him first. If he can't fix it himself, he will make arrangements with a professional."

"Does he live here too?"

"Yes, he has a tiny house just down the hill—you know, one of those prefab things. You can't see it from here. And I wouldn't go looking for it either. Cox is very protective of his little home."

"Protective?

"Well, to be honest, he's a bit of a grouch. Oh, he's harmless enough, but he works on his own time and doesn't like anything, or any*one,* getting in his way."

"It sounds like he and Mr. Payne were birds of a feather."

Miss Whide blinked repeatedly. "No, not at all. I'm afraid it was just the opposite. But Cox is so good at what he does, Mr. Payne made allowances."

I expected her to continue about the grouchy

groundsman, but she switched tracks.

"The other employee is Alice. She doesn't live in, but she'll be working regular hours. She'll take care of the place and deal with items that won't be going in the estate auction such as Mr. Payne's clothing, papers, and personal effects. She's a sweet girl but very shy. If you need anything of a household nature, call her cell phone. You'll find her number, and Cox's as well, at the front of the compendium."

"Compendium?"

Miss Whide gave a quick smile. "That's what Mr. Payne called it. It's a great three-ring binder filled with notes, comments, instructions—anything Mr. Payne thought an outsider might need to know. A full half of it involves the care and feeding of Winter Orange. It's in her apartment. But let me take you on the tour, and we can finish up there."

"Alright, but I've been through most of the rooms already."

She gave a snort. "I doubt that. Please follow me and I will show you what you missed."

* * *

Miss Whide had been right—though I thought I'd poked my head into every room of the house, her tour took us into at least five I'd never guessed were there. I had to wonder what else I'd overlooked in this huge, labyrinthine castle.

We doubled back to Winnie's apartment at the top of the stairs. The suite's subdued lighting gave a peaceful ambiance, the outside brilliance softly shaded by the filigree of Boston ivy that fell across the windows like a veil. The space itself was informal, with couches and cushions and no shortage of cat-specific furniture—trees and climbers of different shapes and sizes, wall steps leading to high shelves covered with rugs. A cat flap to the hallway was built right into the mahogany door.

Miss Whide nodded in approval, then moved on through an archway at the far end of the room. A single bed with a velvet coverlet, a table and two chairs, and a large television mounted discreetly above a fireplace designated this as a human space.

"Nice, isn't it?"

"Yes," I had to agree.

"Mr. Payne spent a good deal of time here—he and Winnie."

Miss Whide beckoned me to a seat by the window. On the table lay a large binder—the *compendium,* I assumed.

"How about something cool while we run through the specifics?"

I had no idea what those *specifics* might entail, but the thought of a cold drink hit the spot.

Miss Whide went to a small refrigerator "There is iced tea—home-made of course—lemonade, and soda."

"Iced tea sounds perfect." I looked around the spacious room. "I think I'll like living in the lap of luxury."

I meant it jokingly—after all, I didn't expect to be pampered during my stay, but she took me seriously. "Oh, yes, the suite is fitted out with everything you and Winnie should need to be comfortable. If I've forgotten anything, just ask."

She brought over the drinks in crystal glasses that dripped with icy condensation. A sliver of lemon floated atop each one.

"There you go, Ms. Cannon."

"Thank you. But please, call me Lynley, remember?"

"Alright… Lynley." Miss Whide seemed to think for a moment. "And my given name is Ida."

"Ida…" I tried to keep the surprise out of my voice. "That's a beautiful name."

She tucked her face into her double chin as a blush rose to her cheeks. "It's a family name, my grandmother's."

"Then it's doubly lovely. Lynley is also a family name—my paternal grandmother's maiden name. My mother was ahead of her time when it came to giving babies surnames."

Feeling like I'd accomplished something by finally establishing a first-name basis with Ida Whide, I decided to go in for the big question, the one forefront on my mind.

"I was wondering, Ida—how familiar are you with Mr. Payne's bequest to Friends of Felines?"

"What about it?" The personal assistant tensed, but I pressed on.

"His will included a stipulation that we found very strange, that we were to… let's see—how did he put it?"

"You are to find his killer," Ida stated matter-of-factly. "Is that the one?"

"You knew?"

"Of course. I told you Mr. Payne and I discussed his will many times."

"But what does it mean?" I gasped. "We're a cat shelter, not a detective agency. No one at FOF is qualified for that sort of work. To say nothing of the fact we were told Mr. Payne died of natural causes, not murder at all. Is the stipulation some kind of joke?"

"No, far from it. But unfortunately I know no more than you do. I was shocked when he came up with that notion."

"Then this was a sudden thing?"

She rose and stood staring out the window. "For about a week before his death, Mr. Payne was nervous, not himself. I asked him what was wrong, but he said I was imagining things." She whirled, setting her stare on me. "It was not my imagination! He was different—anyone could have seen it."

"Different how?"

"He was afraid of something. He called in his law firm and made the codicil. When he died a few days later, I was certain it was foul play since he seemed to be expecting it. I told the police everything, but then the coroner's report came back with a finding of natural causes. I suppose he was experiencing some sort of paranoia, a symptom of his decline. In a way I was thankful. I would hate to think there was a murderer among us."

"What were those natural causes, if you don't mind my asking?"

"Oh," Ida stuttered. "Heart failure. It was heart failure."

Heart failure could mean almost anything. Still, if there were more to it than a cardiovascular event, it should have been listed in the report. "So how is FOF supposed to fulfill the stipulation when there's no killer to be found?"

"Ms. Cannon..."

Rats! We seemed to have regressed to formal names again.

"I'm sorry, Ms. Cannon, but I just don't know."

Chapter 7

More and more people are having their portraits photographed or painted with their pets.

By the time I left Payne House, it was already past one o'clock. Gil and Sanjay had finished their initial survey sometime earlier and gone to draw up a plan and a contract to discuss the next morning. Meanwhile my head was spinning with questions, so I raced for the one place that might hold the answers—the shelter.

But answers would have to wait. Time had gotten away from me, and Helen's announcement assembly was due to begin. Though I knew what she was going to say, I was eager to see how she'd present this convoluted tale to the general public.

I made it into the parking lot with a few minutes to spare. Throwing on my volunteer apron and ID badge, I ran for the Education Hall. I felt a zing of anticipation as I entered the big room. I had the strongest feeling I was about to embark on something huge, maybe even life-changing.

Frannie was waving at me from a spot in the front row. I hustled to join her.

"Saved you a seat." She patted the metal folding chair beside her. "I was beginning to worry."

"I've been at the Payne mansion. I'll tell you all about it after the assembly, I promise."

Frannie began to object, but then Helen Branson

walked through the door, and everyone's attention, including Frannie's, swung to her. Dressed in a linen suit jacket and jeans, every shining brown hair in place, she looked undeniably the director-in-charge. Her aura exuded both serenity and strength.

She worked her way up the aisle, stopping to talk with folks as she went. When she got to me, she paused.

"Please come by my office when you get a chance, would you, Lynley?" She spoke low and directly. "I want you to meet Mr. Payne's attorney."

I frowned. "I have to pick up Winnie at three."

"I'll let them know you'll be late. It shouldn't take long."

She didn't wait for a reply but continued up to the microphone to face the row upon row of green-aproned volunteers and print-scrubbed staff. She was the absolute queen of calm, and I envied her that. If it had been me up on stage relating the weird and wonderful story of the Payne bequest, I would have turned to jelly.

"She's so amazing," I heard someone behind me whisper. Silently I agreed.

Helen flashed her famous smile, the one that got her whatever she wanted, that swayed politicians and convinced donors to hand over cash. I was ready to stand up and applaud right then and there, even though she had yet to say a word.

"Friends," she began, her warm, low voice instilling instant confidence. "Thank you for coming. There will be an official statement in the newsletter, and I'm sure you'll be reading about it on *OregonLive*—a reporter is coming by later for an interview. When something of this magnitude happens, it doesn't go unnoticed, but I wanted you to hear it from me first."

There was a buzz from the audience as everyone began to voice their speculation. Helen waited patiently for the hubbub to die down.

"As you may have heard..." There was that smile again. "...Friends of Felines is about to receive a very large estate bequest from a prominent and generous benefactor."

"So the rumors are true!" the girl beside me whispered with enthusiasm.

"You will probably recognize the name of Roderick Payne." Behind Helen, a big screen burst to life with a photograph of the Payne mansion, greeted by a round of *ooohs* and *ahhs*. "For many years, Mr. Payne has been a kind supporter of Friends of Felines as well as a close personal friend. His gifts to our shelter were numerous, and though I knew their origin, he never wanted them credited to anything other than 'anonymous.' That's true philanthropy," she proclaimed.

The pictures of Payne House had given way to ones of its gardens and view, then interior shots taken before the introduction of the drop cloths. Even I was impressed, seeing slide after slide of the amazing treasures.

Helen went on to summarize the extent of the bequest and the plans for the estate auction. When a photo of Winter Orange flashed up on the screen, she introduced Payne's lovely calico.

"Some of you may recognize this face." A smattering of laughter arose from those in the audience familiar with the difficult diva. "Winnie has been staying with us since Mr. Payne's passing, but she is going home today with her temporary guardian Lynley Cannon. Lynley has kindly volunteered to stay at Payne House with Winnie, as Mr. Payne stipulated in his will."

"Poor Lynley," someone piped up from the audience.

"Good luck with that one," another offered jovially.

"Lynley will also be acting as our estate auction lead. For that, she will need your help."

Helen beckoned me to stand, and I had no option but to do so.

"Go on," she encouraged.

I hadn't expected to be called upon to speak so I quickly improvised. "Uh, this auction will be a big event and is going to take a lot of work. I'll be asking for volunteers in the near future, so anyone with experience in antiques or online auctions, please look me up." I reseated myself with a sigh.

"Thank you, Lynley. There will be more—much more—about the auction coming soon."

Helen then lit into a eulogy for the passed Mr. Payne, extolling his virtues as a dependable devotee of cats and cat needs. The screen now showed a rare portrait of the man himself sitting in a striped canvas lawn chair with the city in soft focus behind him. Wearing a straw hat and a Hawaiian shirt, his long legs stretched out and crossed at the ankles, he looked comfortable, not at all like the man in the shadowy codicil. Winter Orange was curled in his lap, staring at the camera with her bi-colored eyes. His hand brushed her fur in an affectionate stroke. The scene zoomed inward until just the man and cat showed in the frame. It was a beautiful photo, professionally done, and I could see every hair on Winnie's sleek body, every line in the philanthropist's aged face.

Then I noticed something else. On the hand that was petting Winnie, a gold ring glittered in the sun. As the view moved even closer, I recognized the symbol I'd seen on his desk in the codicil video—the pyramid and eye.

The shot zeroed in on Mr. Payne's face. Helen began to

applaud, and the audience followed her lead.

After a respectful moment, she asked for silence. "I know there are questions. I'll answer as many as I can."

Hands went flying up all around the hall: *How much will we get? What are the plans for the monies? Will we have enough to build the hospital?*

Then someone else spoke up, a volunteer whom I had yet to meet. "Well…" she began.

"Yes?"

All eyes were on her now, cropped orange and crimson hair, a jungle of tattoos vining from her left arm to her neck.

"Well, there's been talk, speculation about this bequest and what it entails."

"Yes?" Helen repeated, but her natural and spontaneous smile now looked forced.

"Oh, my Cat!" the girl swore. "You've got to know what I'm talking about, Ms. Branson. Rumors. I've heard there are strings attached, something we have to do to get it. Something… weird."

Helen didn't answer right away, and when she did, I could hear wariness in her careful words. "There are some stipulations, yes, but nothing we can't manage. We're cat people after all!" she proclaimed to a round of nods and agreements.

The false smile still prevailed. I knew she hadn't planned on mentioning the bit about finding Payne's killer, but for her to so blatantly evade a direct question was unexpected as well as unsettling. When she'd first told me what this magnanimous bequest involved, I'd felt the stirring of concern. The fact that she was, in essence, lying to the general assembly ignited that concern into a full blown dread. What else wasn't she telling us?

I couldn't help but recall the old tale of the haunted house, the one kids had been repeating for generations:

The will stipulates that in order to inherit, the heirs must spend one night in the creepy old mansion. They start out the evening with cocktails and laughter, then stuff begins to happen. There is a noise in the attic—someone goes up to check and never returns. The lights fail, and when they come on again, another of the group has gone missing. By bedtime, the remainder lock themselves in their rooms. There is a scream! Something heavy falls from the balcony! A murder of crows fly overhead at midnight! When the agent comes to ferry them home the next morning, none are left alive.

Helen was talking again, politely skirting the volunteer's accusation with deft use of humor and diversion. Another question was asked, one far less volatile, and the talk moved on to safer subjects. Still, I couldn't shake my apprehension. Rising, I told Frannie I'd see her after the assembly and headed for the volunteer locker room, which was thankfully vacant.

I took off my glasses and sat staring into space. "There is no haunted house," I told the mirror. "There is nothing in the will about staying overnight with ghosts."

Except there was. Didn't my stint as Winnie's live-in guardian amount to the same thing? For a moment I considered opting out, letting another volunteer deal with Winnie and the scary mansion.

Someone entered the room and went to the lockers: the girl who had questioned Helen in the assembly. Redonning my glasses, I watched her twirl the padlock and click it open, then gather her purse and a pair of sandals from the cubby.

As she turned to leave, she saw me.

"Hey, aren't you Lynley, the one who's organizing the

estate auction?"

I nodded.

"I'm Skie Scarboro, and I need to be on your team."

* * *

I took Skie's information, explaining that it was still early days. The young volunteer was new to the shelter but seemed raring to go. She told me how she was mentoring to be a vet assistant and had joined a group that worked with individual cats who were having a hard time adjusting to shelter life. I had to admit she was nothing if not enthusiastic.

I guessed Skie—pronounced Sky like the firmament above—to be somewhere in her early twenties, though her choice of hair and bodily adornment might have made her seem younger than she really was. Startling blue eyes, one harboring a wedge of brown, her gaze was intent and quizzical at the same time. Her volunteer tee shirt showed off well-developed muscles, as with someone who works out a lot—that could come in handy at the Payne estate. It was a hassle to have to always rely on men for the heavy lifting.

I found myself wondering what Skie looked like in her natural habitat—rainbow yoga pants and sports bra? Black-on-black Gothic? But I couldn't think about that now. The unexpected meeting with Helen and the lawyer was already throwing off my Winnie schedule. I needed to get on with that as quickly as possible so I could collect my new foster cat.

When I arrived at Helen's office, she and the attorney were ensconced in cozy conversation. As I paused in the doorway waiting to be invited in, I got the feeling she had known him from before.

She glanced up and saw me. "Lynley, ah, good. Thank you for coming on such short notice. I alerted the foster office you might be a little late. This is Debon Kroll, one of Mr. Payne's attorneys and executor of his will. Debon, Lynley Cannon."

Kroll stood and extended a formal hand. I took it, briefly studying the angular man in the expensive gray suit. He reminded me of the cartoon character Dick Tracy from my childhood Sunday comics. The straight nose and serious brow—no fedora, but maybe he had one at home. I tried not to giggle at the thought.

"Lynley has agreed to be my right hand on the Payne situation," Helen announced. "She will lead the work on the estate auction prep, and she has consented to be Winter Orange's guardian as well."

"Wonderful," the man said. His tone was friendly, though the voice itself held a hard edge as if he had argued a few too many cases in court and now couldn't distinguish between those defenses and his everyday life. "Please don't hesitate to call me if you have any questions."

He pulled out an elegantly understated business card and handed it to me. I took it and thanked him. Questions? There were many, but I couldn't seem to put them together at the moment.

"One thing," I finally managed.

"Yes, Lynley?" Kroll replied indulgently. I had to say his twenty-four carat smile, practiced, yet genuine, was one of the best I'd seen.

"Putting on this auction is going to take a lot of work. Before we start, I'd like to be sure we'll get the go-ahead to see it through."

The Dick Tracy brows furrowed.

"What I mean is, what happens if we don't—or *can't*—fulfill Mr. Payne's impossible stipulation?"

Chapter 8

Does your sweet kitty turn into a screaming banshee when riding in a car? Get cats accustomed to car trips at an early age. Use of a pheromone spray and a thin, breathable cloth draped over the carrier can help kitty feel safe. And don't make your vet's office the only destination!

Though I hadn't got anything but legalese and runaround from attorney Debon Kroll, I decided to put Payne's killer-finding stipulation on the back burner. Buoyed by enthusiasm for both the estate auction and the new cat sitting job, I figured I could afford to let the other thing slide.

Kerry greeted me at the door of the foster office with a sly smile, as if she knew something I didn't. When it came to Winnie, that was probably true.

"Nola should have her up here any minute." Kerry grabbed a pale gray mushroom bed that was nearly big enough for me to sleep in. "This is hers as well, but we couldn't fit it in her kennel." Tossing the poof on top two cases of cans stacked on a roller cart, she added a seven-pound bag of some fancy dry food I'd never heard of. "Let us know if you need more. There is no limit to this cat's expense account."

I picked up one of the cans and read the label—all the good stuff and none of the bad. "It's supposed to be covered at the house. Helen mentioned a catering service."

Kerry laughed out loud. "I believe it! As I said, no

limit."

I heard a cat scream from the back room. Kerry heard it too and winked at me.

"Oh, my goodness!" I gasped. "Is it my imagination or is she even louder than yesterday?"

Kerry shrugged. "Good luck, Lynley. If anyone can turn the lion into a pussycat, it's you."

The door from the back banged open, and the girl I'd seen the previous day hauled in a deluxe carrier with a round bed bottom and a mesh half-dome cover. No pink plastic for this kitty! She deposited her burden beside the roller cart and backed away as if from something dangerous. I had a feeling she'd like to run if she could.

Winnie's cries had grown to such a pitch that conversation was nearly impossible. Kerry shrugged and handed me a little white bag.

"Stress reliever," she shouted in my ear. "Prescribed by her doctor. We already gave her a small dose, but you can give her another if she doesn't calm down on her own. It's mild and won't hurt her or make her sleepy."

"I hope it's not too mild," I commented, eyeing the carrier which was now shaking from side to side.

"Keep in touch," Kerry laughed. "Nola will help you out to your car."

Nola took a breath, then began wheeling the cart through the door and into the lobby. I followed with the carrier, Winnie screeching the whole time. Every person within earshot stopped in their tracks. Every head turned. Every eye riveted upon us. I knew what they were thinking: *What horrible torture is that awful woman inflicting on that poor, innocent cat?*

* * *

Much to the detriment of my nerves, Winnie screamed all the way to Payne House. Even with the car windows closed, people took note as we drove by. When I pulled into the parking area, I could only be thankful the distraction hadn't caused an accident.

Ida greeted me at the door, grabbed the poof bed, and ushered Winnie and me inside. "Is your car unlocked?" I nodded. "Then I'll have Alice fetch the rest of Winnie's things."

I gazed around for the Payne housekeeper, but she was nowhere to be seen. I had yet to lay eyes on the shy employee.

Taking no notice of the cat's protestations, Ida led the way up to Winnie's apartment. Winnie's tantrum persisted until we crossed the threshold of her room; then as if someone had thrown a switch, she went silent. Surprised but grateful, I set the carrier on a couch and zipped off the top. She looked up at me, her odd eyes squinting into a love blink, slow and sweet. Soft words came into my mind, as clearly as if she'd spoken out loud.

Thank you.

* * *

Ida had consented to stay with Winnie while I went home to finish packing and take care of my own cats. I wasn't at all sure how this new arrangement was going to work, but I'd figure it out somehow. Thankfully, Payne House was just a hop, skip, and a bridge from my own place—a ten-minute drive, because it looked like I'd be doing a considerable amount of back-and-forth travel. Nights with Winnie, then home to feed my cats, then back to Payne House to work on the estate auction. Home once more for an abbreviated evening routine, then the mansion to do it all again. How long would it go on? A week? A month? The idea had sounded good when Helen presented it, but now that I was faced with the reality of the situation, I wasn't nearly so sure.

Still, I couldn't give up before I'd even begun. Once the auction work got underway, I wouldn't need to be there as much. And I could find a standby caretaker for Winnie. Payne had specified that *someone* needed to live-in with the cat—he never said it had to be the same person the whole time.

The moment I walked in the door, the cats were upon me, greeting me as if I'd been gone forever. What would they think when I really was spending long hours away? For a while, I reveled in their attention, but it didn't last. I was distracted by the fact I had so many things to do and so little real understanding of what those things would entail. Thoughts of my third assignment resurfaced in my mind. Helen had asked me to keep my eyes open for any clues that might help resolve the find-the-killer stipulation. But what should I be looking for? That was the part I still didn't know. Though Debon Kroll had much to say on the matter of Payne's will and how it applied to Friends of Felines, the lawyer never actually gave me an answer about what would happen to the bequest if we failed to come up with a solution for Payne's impossible ask. But then I hadn't pressed him either. I'd been in a hurry to pick up Winnie, and I'd let it slide when the conversation got sidetracked. I never came right out and said what was on my mind: *What the heck's the deal?*

Debon Kroll had given me his business card and encouraged me to get hold of him if I needed further advice. I didn't know if he was just being polite or honestly offering help, but since my question about Payne's murder-slash-death had been left hanging during the conference, I felt within my rights to pursue it now.

Sitting on the edge of my bed surrounded by a group of curious cats intent on examining the various items I'd laid out for my cat-sitting stint, I retrieved Kroll's number and dialed. After a couple of rings, a woman came on the line.

"Kroll, Baxter, and Berger, Attorneys at Law. This is Felisa speaking. How may I direct your call?"

"Is Mr. Kroll available? This is Lynley Cannon."

"Mr. Kroll is out of the office at the moment. Would you like to speak to one of his associates?"

"No, I think I'd rather wait and speak to him. Can you ask him to call me?"

"Of course. May I tell him what this is concerning?"

I wasn't sure how far I wanted to go with Felisa. "I'm with Friends of Felines Cat Shelter. I have a question about the will of Mr. Roderick Payne."

"I'll forward your message, Ms. Cannon. I'm sure Mr. Kroll will get back to you as soon as possible."

Thanking her, I returned to my packing. The mysterious stipulation would have to wait a little longer.

I didn't need to take much to Payne House since I was essentially just spending the night—bathrobe, slippers, toiletries, a change of clothes for the morning. More could come later as I figured out my needs. I grabbed my red journal in case I wanted to add something to *The Mystery of the Murder of Roderick Payne* and stuffed it in on top. The idea of being alone in that huge house was compelling me more and more. The itch of fear had evaporated, and all I could think of now was exploring to my heart's content with the enigmatic Winnie by my side.

I was removing Tinkerbelle from my bag so I could

load in a book and my favorite pillow when the phone buzzed. *That was fast,* I thought to myself until I saw the caller—not Kroll but Denny Paris. Instantly I remembered my promise to look into the hospice patient cat hoarder. With all the other things on my mind, that one had slipped through the cracks.

"Hi, Denny. What's up?"

"Just wondering if you'd had a chance to talk to Jack, the guy I was telling you about."

"I'm sorry, I've been pretty busy with this bequest for FOF. I picked Winnie up this afternoon and will start staying with her tonight."

Denny laughed. *"Lucky you."*

"I don't mind. It was my choice. Actually I'm looking forward to it. I've never stayed in a castle before."

"Castle?"

"Just something I heard when I was a kid."

"Right. And you aren't nervous about being there all by yourself?"

"Not really. I'm sure a man like Roderick Payne has a state-of-the-art security service. Besides, I won't be alone. Winnie will be with me."

Again he laughed, and I laughed with him. Funny thing was, I hadn't been joking. The thought of the calico cat brought me great peace of mind, even though so far all I'd heard out of her were screams and more screams. But that wasn't quite accurate. She'd changed her tune the minute she was back safe in her home. She'd even thanked me for it...

"Well, don't worry about Jack. Sounds like you've got more than enough to do."

"I think I can still fit it in. I won't be staying at the mansion twenty-four/seven. And I'd really like to look into his situation before things get official. The hospice people have the best of intentions, but their interests are humans, not pets. Let me do a little checking and get back to you, okay?"

"That would be much appreciated. Have fun at the castle."

I rang off and finished packing, then went downstairs to the kitchen. Pouring myself some ice water from the fridge, I sat down at the table and looked up the text Denny had sent me.

Mr. Jack Hess. Reported by hospice nurse to have 'too many' cats. Concern that patient can no longer care for them on his own.

Switching screens, I punched the number for Pinkie, the volunteer coordinator for Oregon Hospice and my supervisor. Tinkerbelle and I had been going on therapy cat visits under her direction for several years, and if anyone could sort out this mess, it was she.

"Oregon Hospice, Pinkie speaking."

"This is Lynley Cannon. I have a question for you, Pinkie."

"Oh hi, Lynley. How are you? I don't have anything for you at the moment, sorry."

"It's not about a visit, at least not exactly." I explained how Denny had been called in on the Jack Hess case by one of her nurses. "Special Agent Paris has talked to the man but doesn't want to do anything official if there's no good cause. Unfortunately, since the complaint has been made, he's required to follow up. I was wondering if I could look into it, see if the patient is really that bad off cat-wise."

I could hear the clicking of a keyboard. *"I have it. Jack Hess, ninety-three, living on his own in a trailer park. Yes, here's the note from Jennine, his nurse. Pretty much what you mentioned, except in somewhat stronger terms. It says here she doesn't know how many cats there are because there are so many.*

She doesn't seem to like cats much," Pinkie commented. *"Even so, the concern is valid. I'll add your name to his chart, and you can be cat-liaison for us. Make arrangements to stop by and see what you think, then get back to me. Thanks for bringing this to my attention. I'd hate to upset the man for no good reason."*

"Doesn't Hospice have a program to care for patients' pets in their homes? That would certainly be preferable to having the cats taken away by the animal cops."

"Yes, we do. I'll look into adding Jack as a candidate."

Pinkie had a heart of gold, and I loved her for it. "I'll go by and see him tomorrow, I'm not sure what time—it depends on where he's located."

"Sounds good. I'm emailing you the details on our secure server. Take care and keep me posted."

"You too," I said as the email pinged into my box.

Chapter 9

If you are going to be away from home overnight, leave a recently-worn article of your clothing on a bed or couch to help your cats feel comfortable with your absence.

I was ready to go. My things were stowed in my little car, and all I had left to do was feed my cats before setting out for the night. I felt bad about leaving them, my sweet clowder. Though logically I knew they'd be fine without me for the next twelve hours, I still found myself worrying.

What if something happens? What if Big Red gets his claw caught in his collar again—last time he nearly went crazy trying to wrench it out. Or what if wobbly Elizabeth falls from her padded cat tree? It was only a foot above the pillow on the carpet, but with her cerebellar hypoplasia, it could be trouble.

Suddenly the what-ifs began to close in on me from every side. *What if a burglar breaks in and lets the cats out or someone gets sick or there's a fire…*

Okay, that was it—I was now officially panicked. What was I doing? I must have been crazy to take on an obligation that required me to be away from home for so much time. Though a part of me was really looking forward to my stint with Winnie, my own cats came first. Even if they survived the night without incident, what about tomorrow night and the night after that? Clearly, it was too much.

There was only one thing to do, and that was to call Helen and tell her to find someone else to take the roll of

Winnie's live-in guardian.

As I was about to dial the afterhours number she had given me, the phone rang, a call from my granddaughter.

"Hello, Seleia," I said with an instant smile.

"Oh, Grandmother!" came a stressed little yip from the other end of the line. *"Thank goodness I caught you!"*

I don't know what she expected since she'd called my cell phone which went everywhere I did, but her voice conveyed such angst all I could feel was alarm. "What's the matter, sweetheart? Is something wrong?"

"Yes! I'm in big trouble! I don't know what to do!"

The direst of circumstances promptly popped into my already-overactive mind, racing by like movie scenes. Arrested? I couldn't imagine Seleia breaking a law, at least not doing something she'd be caught for. Pregnant? Darn that boyfriend of hers—he'd promised to remain a gentleman to this eighteen-year-old girl. Car accident? Man trouble? Woman trouble? The scary possibilities were endless.

"What is it?" She'd better tell me fast before my colorful imagination moved on to kidnapping, or worse!

"It's awful, Grandmother, absolutely awful! I was supposed to move into my dorm room this week. It was all arranged. But a water pipe burst, and now they need to make repairs before they can let anyone come."

I mentally wiped my furrowed brow in relief. The change of plans might seem dire to Seleia and impact her tender first days as a college sophomore, but on the scale of adversities, it was barely a one.

"I'm sure it won't take too long, dear. I know you want to get away from home, but another week or so won't be that bad, will it?"

"That's just it—I can't stay at home either. Mother has the

decorators coming for a complete interior remodel. She's planned it for months. She and Dad are going to their place in L.A. until the job's finished. They're leaving tomorrow!"

"Can't she postpone it? No, I suppose not," I said, answering my own question. My daughter Lisa was a force unto herself, and once that force got moving in a certain direction, there was no diverting it.

I was again reminded how little Lisa and I had in common these days. But it wasn't anything new—the rift had been formed decades ago when my sweet, kitten-eyed daughter became old enough to rebel. And rebel she had, but not in the usual ways, such as a boyfriend with a motorcycle or a best girlfriend encouraging her to tipple. Those things I could have understood, having had a wild side in my own youth. No, Lisa had gone the other direction. She became distant, threw herself into her studies, high school, college, then university. She majored in art and got straight As. She cultivated her business until she made a name for herself in the chic art world. She married a respected architect, and together they had the token child but never, never any pets. Lisa had only one thing on her mind, and that was herself.

Seleia, that token child who was now a lovely young woman in her own right, had turned out the opposite of her egocentric mum. She was loving, giving, respectful, and fun. Bright, intelligent, honest, capable… need I go on? Yes, I am her doting grandma, but I'm not exaggerating when I say Seleia is absolutely wonderful.

"Fredric said I could stay with him…"

"What?" I jerked myself back from my reveries to make sure I heard right. Live with the boyfriend? Fredric was a nice young man who had, to my knowledge, respected Seleia's wishes about the bedroom, but staying together under the same roof might prove overly tempting.

"Fredric told me I could stay there," she went on, *"but, well, I don't know if that's a good idea. Grandmother, what am I going to do?"*

"I've got a thought," I put forth tentatively, then warmed to the plan. "And if it sounds good to you, you'd be doing me a huge favor. I find myself in need of a live-in cat sitter. What if you stay here and take care of my kitties?

"Why? Where are you going?"

I explained briefly about my assignment at Payne House.

There was a pause. *"Could I bring Solo? She was set to go into boarding until Mum and Dad got back, but I'd rather she didn't have to. It's going to be upsetting enough for her when I'm gone to school."*

The little white female was originally one of my own clowder but had been intimidated by the other cats and spent most of her time under the couch. The behaviorist suggested she might be better off as an only cat, a theory that was proven correct when she went to stay with Seleia.

"Of course—if you don't think it will distress her to be back among the crowd."

"I'll watch her. If she gets stressed, she can still go to the boarder, but I think she'll be fine. She's really blossomed lately."

Seleia and I were two happy campers when we rang off. She enthusiastically agreed to stay at my house until school started, resolving both my cat abandonment issues and her temporary homelessness. She couldn't come tonight, but she and Solo planned to take up residence tomorrow morning.

Much relieved, I said goodbye to my cats, promised them they would be okay without me, and left them a nice pair of well-worn sweats on the bed for their olfactory comfort.

As I went to my car, I turned back to stare at the house. To see it like that, all friendly and welcoming, gave me a sudden jab of nostalgia. I was so lucky to have it, to live the life I led. One woman and nine cats in a fourteen-room house seemed to border on decadence these days. Then I thought of the place I was headed. *How many rooms are there in the Payne estate?* I suddenly wondered.

I took a last glance at the Old Portland facade. I'd left a few lights on, and their golden glow radiated through the windows. Framed in the hallway pane was the silhouette of a cat, Little, her paw raised to the glass in a solemn farewell.

Chapter 10

Many cats love to be petted, but there is a threshold where enjoyment can turn into annoyance. Imagine brushing your hair—it feels good for a while, and then it doesn't.

I didn't think about it again until later, Little's farewell tap on the window. The sweet black cat had done it before, not often, but enough times that I should have known to pay attention. Each time she'd performed that maneuver, something odd had occurred soon after. In her canny feline way, she'd been trying to tell me something, trying to warn me. Unfortunately I rarely heeded that warning until it was too late.

Now as I sat ensconced in Winnie's cozy apartment, *Herself* on my lap purring like a happy and very normal kitty, I considered the implications of Little's signal. Last time she'd pawed the window like that, someone had died. I'd never really considered her psychic, not like Mab, my lilac point Siamese who seemed to know things that no cat should, but I couldn't deny the coincidences. And since I didn't really believe in coincidences, I should probably have taken Little's signs a bit more seriously.

Was it something about the mansion? About Payne? About a killer who may or may not exist?

Suddenly a thought hit me—if Payne had indeed been murdered, that would mean his killer was still at large.

"Rats!" I said out loud, making Winnie jump. I petted her with reassurance, and she sank back into her bliss.

Winnie had been an absolute sweetheart since her homecoming, so that was one problem solved. But now I was in a huge, strange place with the possibility of a villain lurking somewhere nearby.

"Rats!" I said again. "Rats, rats, *rats*!"

I'd been correct in assuming the Payne House was equipped with more than adequate security—locks and more locks, alarms, and surveillance cameras abounded. There was an entire chapter in the compendium concerning house particulars, including the contact information for the security company and the number for Cox, who lived just down the hill.

I'm not worried, I said to myself as I sat petting Winnie, faster and faster, until she gave me a dirty look and hopped down to check out her food bowl. When my phone rang, I about jumped out of my skin.

"Hi, it's Frannie. Hey, I'm at your front door, or I should say, the door of the gigantically huge castle of a place you're calling home for the night. I've been ringing. I know you're here. Come let me in."

"Frannie!" I sighed with relief. "Hold on a minute. I'm upstairs. I didn't hear the bell."

Running out into the hallway, then down the wide staircase, I flung open the door. Frannie was standing in the glow of the porch light, her phone still in her hand.

"Come in. I wasn't expecting you. Did you just come from the shelter? Are there any updates, anything I should know?"

Frannie wasn't paying attention to my banter as she stared around the opulent room with the look of a child on their first trip to a museum.

"This is amazing! I knew it would be, but even so… Can you imagine living in a place like this? Well, I guess you can since you're doing it, even if it is only temporary."

"I haven't spent much time in the main house. Winnie's got an apartment of her own, and that's where I'm staying."

Frannie began to tour the extensive foyer, eying the architecture and peeking under drop cloths.

"My goodness, Lynley! You must be in seventh heaven among all these glorious *objets d'art*."

"They're breathtaking, aren't they? Gil and I did a quick run-through this morning, but tonight Winnie and I have just been hanging out enjoying the quiet. She stopped all that screaming and fussing the moment she got through the door. It's like she's a whole new cat."

A broad smile came over Frannie's face. "Speaking of..."

She circled back to the staircase where Winnie was making her entrance, proceeding down the steps like a queen. The calico paused to inspect the broken balustrade, then continued her descent, coming to a halt directly in front of Frannie.

Frannie reached out a hand for her to sniff. "Hello, sweetheart. Glad to be home?"

Winnie gave a little purrumph, then smoothed her sideburn along Frannie's palm.

Frannie looked up at me in rapture. "She's lovely. I only got the briefest introduction at the shelter, and she was crying so loudly I didn't want to stress her any further by going too near."

"Miss Whide, Payne's personal assistant, said she was born here and had never been off the property until she went to FOF. Her vet makes house calls."

"No wonder you were scared, little one," Frannie told the cat. "I'd have screamed too if I'd been you."

Frannie straightened. "Do you just let her run around this huge place? Aren't you afraid she'll hide or get lost?"

"She knows the house better than I do. Payne left a book with several chapters on Miss Winter Orange. I've only begun reading it, but the first thing he said was to let her go wherever she wanted. Up until now she's been content to hang out in her room."

Frannie had started to prowl again, this time peering through doors.

"Want a tour?" I offered.

She turned to me and grinned. "I thought you'd never ask."

* * *

An hour later, we were back in Winnie's rooms sipping sparkling cranberry juice in the apartment's well-appointed mini-kitchen. Winnie had led Frannie and me on a grand excursion around the premises, though when she pawed at the door to the basement, I politely explained that was off limits, as stipulated in chapter one, paragraph seven of the compendium. We also bypassed the attic, because even though I was curious about what might be hidden in that dusty room, I'd decided Gil and Sanjay could be my liaisons for that part of the house, at least until it got cleaned up.

Though the ambiance of the apartment was comfy cozy, I was feeling ill at ease. Frannie picked up on it immediately, and with her usual empathy, zeroed in on the cause.

"Are you still worried about Mr. Payne's strange stipulation?"

Frowning, I eyed the jumbo ice cube floating at the top of my drink. "How can I not be? It's crazy. But if we don't do what he says, the bequest could be in jeopardy."

"Tell me more about the video, the codicil to his will."

I gave a nervous chuckle and took her through the details once more. "It's ridiculous, the idea that Friends of Felines should be tasked with finding his killer. Not the police, not the detectives, but little inexperienced us."

Frannie petted Winnie as she considered. "The report said the death was natural? Do you know the cause?"

"Heart failure apparently." I poked at the ice cube with my stainless steel straw, watching it sink, then bob back to the surface—the epitome of resilience.

"That could mean just about anything. I'd want to know what it was that made his heart fail."

Frannie raised a good point. "A secondary cause of death might tell us more," I agreed, "but if there was even the slightest suspicion of foul play, it should have been mentioned. And it wasn't."

Frannie gave a short laugh, but it was less the funny-ha-ha sort and more the funny-strange. "Maybe Mr. Payne expected to be murdered but died before the killer could pull it off."

I stared at my friend like a surprised cat, all big eyes and caution. She had no idea how close she'd come to my earlier fear of a killer still in the vicinity.

"If that were the case," she continued, oblivious to my panic, "would the stipulation still be binding? Would FOF still be obliged to find the *would-be* killer, or would that make the whole thing moot since no killing actually took place?"

"I don't know, Frannie. Thinking about it makes my head hurt. It seems just as likely that Payne wants us to find a person who doesn't exist—the ultimate wild goose chase,"

"You said his legal team attested to his sanity. I wouldn't be so quick to dismiss this as folly. Just because it's strange doesn't mean it's not true."

"So you think we should proceed on the premise there is a would-be killer out there?"

"Exactly. I know I said to forget about the murder, but if there's even a chance it's a real thing, we need to be careful, and the best way to do that is to find out as much as we can as to why Mr. Payne made such a request in the first place."

I considered what Frannie said, that famous Frannie logic, then sighed.

"I know it's scary, Lynley, but you won't be alone. I can stay with you if you like, and I'm sure some of your other friends would be happy to keep you company."

"Thanks for the offer, but I'll be okay. I'm only by myself at night, and the security system here could thwart a pro."

"At least you seem to have Winter Orange straightened away." Franny petted the calico cat who was now curled between us on the sofa.

I smiled. "Did you know her food is catered? They come three times a week in little packages, all labeled for the meal—breakfast, second breakfast, lunch, dinner, snack." I got up and opened the fridge to show off the stacks upon stacks of tiny paper containers. "And that's in addition to the fancy wet and dry she had at the shelter."

"Second breakfast? Like Hobbits?"

"Yup."

Closing the fridge again, I leaned on the counter. "More juice?"

"I don't think so," said Frannie. "I need to take off, but first give me a quick update on the online auction."

"I only met with Gil this morning but I'm optimistic. I think an estate auction will go well. Gil knows his business so all we really need to do is follow his instructions. It's a big job, but he's into it."

"That's good. Putting on a sale of that magnitude is going to be huge. Have you decided who you'll pick for your team?"

"Not really—besides you, that is. A volunteer approached me after Helen's presentation. Skie? Do you know her?"

"I know *of* her. She's new but already getting a reputation for being... how should I put it... in a world of her own?"

"Lots of cat people tend to be off in their own world," I countered.

"But Skie's world seems to be somewhere in outer space. Still, everybody likes her, and the cats adore her. That's all that matters at the shelter."

"I need to be careful who I chose because many of these items are valuable. It could be tempting to walk away with a few if someone didn't have a good sense of morals."

"Yes, but they'd only be stealing from the shelter. No one would want to do that, would they?"

"I hope not, but I plan to be choosy just the same."

"Well, let me know when you want me. I left my schedule open this week so I can help."

Standing, Frannie went to put her empty glass in the sink, then took up her purse. "I should get going. It's late, but I really wanted to check on you and make sure you were okay."

"You just wanted to see the house," I countered. "You can't fool me."

We both laughed, and I walked her downstairs to the

door with Winnie accompanying.

She started for her car, then turned back. "I'm still happy to stay with you if you like."

"I'll be fine. I'll call if anything comes up."

"You're probably right not to worry. Even if there is a would-be killer, there's no reason to think he'd come after you. Unless he's a psychopath." She gave a little shrug, then a wave. "Bye."

Oh Frannie, I thought with sarcasm. *You really know how to make a girl feel safe.*

I set the house alarm and headed upstairs with the cat running ahead. Winnie's room had its own set of locks, independent from the rest of the house, and once we were back, I clicked the latch. Frannie was right—if there was someone out to get Payne—and that was a big if—they had no grudge against me personally. I was a glorified cat sitter, nothing more. And unless they were some sort of psychopath, which wasn't the impression given by Payne's video, I had nothing to fear. Still, the thought made me nervous. I'd pursue it first thing in the morning. If Debon Kroll didn't return my call, I would call him again. I'd call his associates. I'd call Helen Branson. I'd call everyone I could think of, including the National Guard, until I got to the bottom of this ridiculous puzzle.

I presented Winnie her nighttime snack, a tiny package of fish and peas marked *W.O. Midnight Bite: to be given after ten p.m. if she wants it.* She wanted it and was happily munching as I got ready for bed.

I wondered if I would have trouble sleeping in the strange place, but the apartment's relaxing atmosphere and the feather-soft bed had me drifting before Winnie finished her nosh. In the quiet, I could hear crickets in the grounds outside, a sound I absolutely loved. A soft breeze wafted in through the screened windows, and combined with the air conditioning, was just the right temperature to cool away the hot August day. Only faintly could I distinguish the hum of the city below, as if I were somehow separate from its urban folly.

Before I knew it, I was asleep. I woke twice in the night—once when Winnie decided to walk on my head, and once when I thought I heard a thump in the attic above me. When I came awake to listen, however, the only break in the gentle silence was a cricket's mournful chirp.

Chapter 11

Have you put a harness on your cat, only to have her flop on her side as if dead? Don't give up! It took three summers for the real Little to take to her harness, then one day out of the blue, she was fine with it, and we went everywhere.

The next morning dawned a perfect summer day. On the fresh breeze from the open window, I could smell new-mown grass and late roses. Slipping on my glasses and robe, I went to stand beside Winnie who was staring out over her kingdom from her padded shelf. I followed her gaze to see someone on the veranda below, a man on a stepladder pruning the wisteria.

I guessed it was Cox, the mansion's groundsman, though in a tan canvas smock that came down to his calves and a broad-brimmed canvas hat, I could see nothing of the man himself. Young, old, tall, short, fat, I couldn't guess. Ida had omitted such details in her description of the surly and solitary gardener. I suppose I'd have to find out for myself.

But that would come later. First I needed to feed Winnie and plan my day. I may have been living in a millionaire's paradise, but mine was in no way a millionaire's life. I had work to do.

Since the weather report had promised another scorcher, I closed the windows to let the air conditioner do its thing. Winnie gave a purrumph of protest which cut off abruptly the moment I opened the fridge. I pulled out the package marked *W. O. Breakfast—Warm fifteen seconds in microwave, then stir.* Alongside the feline fare was an assortment of human food, and while Winnie's concoction warmed, I perused the selection, also marked with description and instructions on top. *Oatmeal with brown sugar and raisins—milk and soy milk in the door; Eggs Benedict—warm to desired.* There was French toast, blueberry cobbler, and scrambled tofu as well. I chose the oatmeal, wondering how often the caterers came to replenish, and if this were breakfast, would there also be lunch and then dinner? What happened to the meals I didn't eat? Would they be tossed? Recycled? Fed to dogs? Then I noticed a menu on top the fridge. Maybe that would explain how the food thing worked.

The microwave dinged, and I swapped Winnie's breakfast for mine. When the oatmeal was warm, I took it, along with my phone, the red journal, and a pen, to the table by the bay window. I skipped past the *Mystery of the Murder* page, and between bites of steaming porridge, I began a list.

#1, I wrote, *Pick my team.*

I scratched out the #1 and substituted a #2. In the number one place, I penned, *Take Winnie for a walk, maybe meet the groundsman.*

Jumping to number three, I jotted, *Call the lawyer—again!* I gave an inadvertent shiver. I wasn't sure why I should cringe at the thought of the confusing killer codicil—it would turn out to be either something or nothing, and I had no control over either, but it was a dilemma needing to be resolved, and that alone made me nervous. Besides, mistrust of lawyers wasn't mine alone. It dated back to Shakespeare's day and most likely before that—who was I to buck tradition?

Remembering my promise to Denny, I added a big X on the next line: *Visit Jack and call Denny with report.* I had no idea where I'd fit that into my schedule, but I'd work it out. Gil was coming at ten so maybe after I got him started I could pop out for a hospice check.

Already the list was becoming longer than the next twenty-four hours could accommodate, and apparently Winnie thought so too. Finished with her meal, she hopped onto the table and began to paw the paper, neatly hooking a claw next to item number one.

"So you want to go for a walk, do you?"

She answered by pouncing on my pen and sending it flying.

"Okay, you win. Since I'm here for you, your wish is my command."

I located her little pink walking vest and slipped it on, letting her adjust to the feel of the silk that bound her torso while I got dressed and put away the breakfast things. She seemed fine with it, no balking or playing dead. A few minutes later, we were ready to go.

Clipping the leash to the silver ring on Winnie's harness, I pushed open the apartment door and let her lead the way. She headed straight down the staircase, through the maze of rooms, and into the kitchen where she came to a halt by the back door.

She looked up at me with a me-roww. *Okay Miss Thumbs, what are you waiting for?*

Since my only knowledge of the vast grounds had been the topographic map included in the compendium and a glimpse from various windows of the house, I continued to let Winnie guide me. She moved single-mindedly across the patio, down the stone steps, and over the sloping lawn toward a small willow-shrouded terrace. As we approached, I began to hear the sound of running water and understood the allure.

The terrace itself was paved with flagstone, the trailing thyme that grew between the pavers sending up a sensuous smell as we walked. In the center of the stones was a low, cascading fountain that fed into a pond where koi drifted through water weeds. Their colors of orange, black, and white mimicked the calico as Winnie bent over the edge to stare at her fishy twins.

After a few moments in quiet contemplation, the cat began skirting the pond until she came to a small ceramic bowl built into the edge. Painted in the green glaze was an orange fruit topped by snow symbolizing a winter orange. The bowl was filled with clear, fresh water, and Winnie lapped daintily.

It was wonderful to see this lovely creature in a natural setting. It didn't take a cat psychic to know she'd been unhappy at the shelter, but I couldn't have imagined the depth of her grief until now. Where, in that foreign environment, she came off as weak, angry, and fearful, here she blossomed confident and strong. Payne had been right about keeping her at the mansion, and I would do my best to accommodate his wishes, not for him nor for the shelter's bequest but for Winnie.

When Winnie finished her drink, she became eager to move on, and I was content to have her steer me on her roundabout path wherever her fancy took her. This time she headed for what looked to be a tiny orchard. Small fruit trees of different species extended down the hill, brimming with apples, pears, and plums. The trees had been meticulously pruned and the ground underneath manicured, but a few stray fruits had fallen. Winnie sniffed at a bright red plum but found it not to her taste. I picked it up and bit into the juicy pulp with pleasure.

"What'r you doing there?" came a man's gruff voice from behind me.

I turned to see a figure standing up the hill silhouetted against the sun. In his left hand he held a lethal-looking pair of pruning shears. From that vantage, he seemed as big as Colossus and twice as imposing.

He took a few strides forward into the shadow of a pear tree and morphed into a large but normal-looking man. I judged him to be in his early forties, muscular beneath that tan coat, with a straight military bearing. Full lips frowned out from brushy facial hair. The top half of his face was shaded by his hat, but I had the impression of slitted eyes and a furrowed brow.

"Cox?" For who else could it be? "You shouldn't go around scaring people like that."

The man cocked his head, then muttered something under his breath that I couldn't make out, but it didn't sound like an apology.

"I'm Lynley. I'm here to take care of Winnie." I pointed to the cat, as if he couldn't see for himself. "I'll be staying for the next little while."

"I know who you are," he grumbled back.

This surprised me, since I myself hadn't known I was coming until two days before, but maybe he meant it in a general sense—he'd been apprised of the fact there would be a cat guardian, and one was as good as the next.

For a moment, he was silent, studying me. Then his gaze fell to Winnie who was sitting quietly at my feet grooming a white-gloved paw.

"Humph," he snorted. "Good enough. Mind yourself in my gardens."

I was about to comment on his possessive statement,

but he beat me to it.

"Not mine, ma'am. Actually more like yours. You and your cat shelter. I've got nothing against cats, mind you." He came forward and bent onto one knee to stroke Winnie under her chin. "Cats are good. I've known this one since she was born. It's just that..."

Just that what? Was this a new mystery or another part of the old one? When Cox didn't continue, I pushed. "Go on. Say what you meant to say."

"I shouldn't, ma'am. It's not for me."

"No, Cox, I'm interested. I'm not sure how long I'll be here, and I need to know what's going on."

"It's Mr. Roderick, you see. He promised me... Well, he promised I'd get something when he was gone. And, well... looks like he broke that promise, doesn't it?"

I tried to think back to the will. I hadn't paid much attention to bequests to anyone aside from FOF but recalled seeing Miss Whide's name. Had I missed Cox's, or was it not there to begin with? "I don't know. I'm sorry."

He rose and looked out across the grounds. "This was to be mine, at least part of it. The land where my house lies, and some money to keep it up too. If I'd have known I wasn't getting it, I wouldn't have..."

He faltered and looked away.

"You wouldn't have what?"

"Nothing, ma'am," he shot back angrily. "Not your worry."

"Cox, since we're on the subject of Mr. Payne's will—I was wondering..."

I'd been about to ask if he knew of the strange stipulation, but he turned away. Grumbling to himself, he headed across the lawn, snapping the clippers in front of him as if hacking at some infuriating yet invisible vine.

I shook off a jab of anxiety at his palpable rage. Though the sullen groundsman had been described as grouchy, he'd also been deemed harmless. Wasn't it natural he'd feel proprietary about the place he had worked so hard for so long? And to be promised something he didn't get would be disappointing to anyone. I'd give him the benefit of the doubt—for now.

"Well," I said to Winnie. "What do we think of that?"

"Purrumph," said Winnie. *Not much.*

I was beginning to enjoy my little conversations with the calico cat. I knew it was all in my mind, that even though her appropriately-inflected *purrumphs* and *me-rows* were a form of communication, it was my interpretation that turned them into words. Still, it was a fun pastime, and I really did believe we understood each other.

I plucked a ripe apple from a dwarf tree and popped it into my pocket, then Winnie and I headed back up the grassy incline toward the house. The mansion had been built on the crest of the hill, and from this approach the place seemed more dazzling than ever. When Winnie paused at a wooden bench underneath a vine maple, I was happy to take a seat and study the facade from this new view.

Such an architectural wonder! The covered porch that curved around from the front; the second story balcony above. I picked out Winnie's apartment a little to the side. The steep white roof set with its oval windows stared down at us like eyes.

Suddenly I noticed something else. I looked again, just to make sure. First story, second story, attic, roof. But there was another level, the turret built into the very pinnacle of the house. A strange construction that didn't really blend with the rest of the design, it had six sides and a round, pointed top like a gnome hat. I'd always assumed it was merely a decoration added for visual impact, but from this vantage point, it looked like it might actually be a room.

A shiver iced up my back, and I felt like a cat whose fur was being stroked the wrong way. What was it? How would one get there? Had Gil noticed it and not bothered to tell me? I'd have to ask him when he arrived.

Then another thought hit, and I shivered again. Could that hidden room hold a clue to Roderick Payne's death?

I glanced at Winnie. She too was staring at the turret. Her eyes were wide, and her mouth was open in a silent hiss. She perched on the edge of the bench for a few moments longer, looking for all intents and purposes like a Halloween cat, then she sleeked her fur back into place and hopped down, on the move again.

I gave a last look at the strange tower.

This isn't over, I whispered under my breath, as if the feature were a living thing.

Chapter 12

The bond between a human and their cat is strong, and none more so than that of a person at the end of life. Though it may be inconvenient for caregivers to care for cats as well as an ailing human, every effort should be made to keep them together.

I figured we'd had enough outdoor excitement for the morning, so I guided Winnie toward the house. Once she caught sight of the door, she trotted forward of her own accord. I punched the code to let us in, and we were about to head up to our apartment when I caught a glimpse of a young woman with a long brown ponytail that I presumed to be our housekeeper. She was in the pantry packing a box of home-canned goods. I had yet to introduce myself to the shy Alice so I scooped Winnie into my arms with the intention of saying hello.

Winnie had other plans. She squirmed and writhed, then gave out one of her signature screams.

"Fine," I told her. "Here you go." I unclipped the leash and set her down. For a moment she looked up at me, then she zoomed away, focused on a mission of her own.

I crossed the expansive kitchen, between the central island and the row of chrome-faced appliances, to glance through the pantry door. A tidy, narrow room, lined on both sides by shelving, now mostly bare. The box Alice had been packing sat half full on a small counter. Alice was nowhere to be seen.

For a moment, I thought she'd disappeared into thin

air; then I picked out a second door hidden in the shadows at the back of the pantry. It was open a crack, suggesting she'd gone that way. I thought about following but discarded the idea. I'd catch up with the elusive Alice eventually, but now I needed to get back to Winnie.

I wondered why Alice had been so quick to duck out. Did she have business elsewhere or was she avoiding me? I wasn't accustomed to having staff—maybe being inconspicuous was just part of her training.

I headed upstairs, skirting the break in the balustrade. I hoped it would be fixed soon. There was something about that incongruous gap with its precarious edge that made me shiver, even from the far side of the wide staircase.

When I got to the apartment and opened the door, I saw Winnie on her perch by the window giving herself a bath. "Smart girl," I told her as I slipped off her harness. "I should have come with you for all the good it did me to go after the housekeeper. Alice must have jumped down the rabbit hole," I laughed. "Well, as long as she doesn't come back with the Mad Hatter, we're probably safe. Does that make you the Cheshire Cat?"

Winnie grinned at me but made no attempt to disappear like the notorious fictional feline.

I kicked off my shoes and let my toes enjoy the plush of the carpet. I brewed a cup of coffee in the Keurig machine, then took it to the little table where I'd left my journal. I opened it to my list page, but after a cursory glance, turned my gaze to the window and the grounds outside. The green of the lawn despite the August heat indicated copious amounts of precious water, but I had to admit it was both beautiful and soothing to the soul.

Were the souls of millionaires soothed by such luxuries as a healthy lawn? I mused. I had no idea. I was one of those folk who let their bits of yard go brown in summer. Not beautiful but financially and environmentally sound in an ever-changing climate.

Thinking of my dead grass made me think of home which subsequently made me think of my cats. How were they doing without me? Mab and Violet would hardly notice, being essentially bonded to each other, but Big Red would miss me. He'd adopted me as his person from the moment I'd taken him in off the streets, and he worried when I wasn't there. Dirty Harry, my most senior senior, made a big show of aloofness but was a pussycat at heart and enjoyed his evening lap time. Little, Elizabeth, Tinkerbelle, Emilio, Hermione—they all had their routine that depended, more or less, on me.

I picked up the phone and punched the white cat icon for my granddaughter. It took a few rings before she answered, and her voice was breathless when she did.

"Grandmother, you must be psychic. I just got to your place half an hour ago, and I'm giving the cats their breakfast now."

I suddenly understood the breathlessness—feeding my clowder could be a daunting task.

"How is everyone? How are you?" I added sheepishly, not wanting her to think I put cats before her.

"They're all fine, as far as I can see. I've checked around—no messes. Can I let them into the garden? Dirty Harry really wants to go out."

"Yes, the cat fence you and your friends built for us is still working perfectly—Fredric checked it last month." I paused. "Um, have you seen him? Fredric, that is?"

Boyfriend Fredric coincidentally lived in a duplex across the street from me and often helped with chores a woman of my age would rather not have to do by herself. But his proximity was a double-edged sword when it came to Seleia. How much did I really want to know about my baby granddaughter's love life?

Seleia was eighteen, I sternly reminded myself, and turning nineteen in another month. She knew how to take care of herself.

"Fredric got called out of town to work on a television show. He's a full-fledged PA now," she added proudly. *"Production Assistant."*

I gave a silent sigh of relief. With the young man gone, the possibility of any consensual canoodling was reduced to zero.

"How is Solo fitting in with the others? Do you think she remembers living there?"

"So far so good. She's been hanging with Little and hasn't gone under the couch once. I'll be sleeping in your studio, and I plan to make that her safe space with her bed, litter pan, food, water, and toys. I'm so glad you let me have her. I really love her, and I think she loves me too."

"Of course she does. And she's flourished since being with you."

I heard a chorus of meows in the background and one especially loud screech that I recognized as Mab the Siamese.

"Lynley, I've got to finish feeding these guys before there's all-out mayhem. Can I call you back?"

"Sure. I just wanted to see if you'd made it. Don't forget to set the security alarm when you're alone."

"Don't worry. I know this house almost as well as you do."

I let her go, wondering when the kitten girl had grown up into such a responsible young woman. I'd been there every step of the way, yet the transition was so seamless I couldn't pinpoint a date.

Now that I knew everything was okay at home, it was

time to make a second call, to Jack, the hospice patient with too many cats. I didn't like calling people by phone, preferring to email or text, but there were times I had to buckle down. This was one.

I copied the info Denny had sent me onto a Hello Kitty post-it. I knew that with a single click, I could have sent it to my contacts list, but I enjoyed the soon-to-be lost art of handwriting.

I dialed, and after only a blip of a ring, a man came on the line.

"Top of the morning! Jack Hess speaking. What can I do for you?"

I never knew what to expect from folks on hospice since they are, to put it bluntly, dying. Some were morose, some just sick and in pain, and yet others had accepted their fate and intended to make the best of it. Jack's friendly tone marked him as one of those.

"This is Lynley Cannon from Oregon Hospice. I'm well, thanks. The reason I'm calling is because Special Agent Denny Paris of Northwest Humane Society asked me to check in with you."

"Ah, Officer Paris." There was a pause, and I wondered if Jack was reevaluating his initial friendliness, but then he brightened. *"Nice man. One of the good ones. This about my cats?"*

"That's right. Your nurse..." I looked at my notes. "Jennine reported she thought you might need some help taking care of your kitties."

"That was sweet of her." I looked for sarcasm or resentment in his voice but could detect none.

"Can I ask how many cats you have?"

"There are four—Horatio, Ben, and the twins Mazy and Daisy. Two boys and two girls."

Only four? I thought to myself. That was nowhere near the hoard the hospice nurse had described to Denny. My opinion of Nurse Jennine took a dive, at least when it came to cats.

Jack gave a little sigh. *"I do pretty well for them, but I admit I'm not as energetic as I used to be. What sort of help was she thinking?"*

I wasn't about to tell the poor man that Jennine's idea of help was to take the cats away.

"Would you mind if I came by and visited?" I asked, bypassing the specifics. "We can discuss it then."

Again the pause. *"You're not going to do anything drastic, are you, Lynley? Because... well, you see, I don't have all that much time left, and I couldn't get on without the Fantastic Four."*

In that instant, I made a silent pledge that I would do whatever it took to keep those cats with their person until the end. "No, of course not, Jack. I have nine cats myself and each one is a huge part of my life. I just want to see what we can do to make things more comfortable for you."

"Alright. Sounds good when you put it that way. But it'll have to be in a few days if that's okay. My son is coming from Santa Fe, and we're going to take a little trip up to eastern Washington where I was born. My neighbor's taking care of the cats."

"I'll give you a call back in a couple of days then, alright?"

"Should be. Yes, that'll be fine. And Lynley?" I heard him chuckle. *"Make sure you bring pictures of your nine cats when you come. Nine cats!"*

I laughed as I rang off. I looked forward to meeting this cat man and his Fantastic Four.

No sooner had I hung up when a bell dinged, and a voice came out of nowhere.

"Ms. Cannon?"

Once I recovered from the shock of the walls speaking to me and remembered there was an intercom, I crossed to the inconspicuous box by the door and pushed the red button. "Yes?"

"This is Alice. Your guests are here."

"Guests?" I began, but she'd already clicked off.

Not bothering to put on shoes, I stepped outside and peered over the railing. I'd hoped to catch another glimpse of the shy housekeeper, but once again, she was gone.

In the foyer were Gil, Sanjay, and a pile of equipment.

"*Bonjour,* Lyn-dear. Are you ready to work?"

"Close enough." I called down to him. "What's all that stuff you brought with you?"

"Photographic equipment mostly," Sanjay answered, glancing from piece to piece. "Cameras, lights, tripod and monopod, filters. There's a light box, to set the smaller things in—they photograph better that way."

"I have decided we begin in the parlor," Gil declared, "if that pleases you."

"You're the boss," I said. "I need to make a phone call, then I'm at your disposal."

"*Merci,* my dear. Sanjay and I are good for now."

I padded back into the apartment, back to my coffee which was now cold. Drinking it down anyway, I made the last call on my list, the one I had been dreading.

Chapter 13

Almost all calico cats and tortie cats are female. That doesn't make the males valuable, however, because they are usually sterile.

"Kroll, Baxter, and Berger Attorneys at Law. This is Felisa speaking. How may I direct your call?"

Wow! The woman could have been a recording for all the emotion in her voice. "This is Lynley Cannon again. Is Mr. Kroll available yet?"

"I'll check. Hold please."

Soft jazz came on the line, then a moment later, Felisa was back. *"Ms. Cannon, Mr. Kroll has stepped out of the office. According to his diary, he is coming to see you."*

"Me? At Payne House?"

"Yes. He should be there any minute."

"Why didn't he call me?" I looked at my phone and saw the little tape icon that signified I'd received a voicemail. "Never mind. Thank you for letting me know."

Quickly I played the message, Debon Kroll's smooth lawyer voice alerting me to his impending visit, ETA: eleven-thirty—which was now.

This time I did put on shoes. I also combed my hair and dabbed on a bit of lipstick. By the time I'd begun down the wide staircase, Kroll was coming in the door.

"Thank you, Alice," he told the housekeeper who gave the man a coy smile before she disappeared.

Debon Kroll was again wearing a perfectly tailored

suit, this one in a charcoal color with a matching tie. If it weren't for that hard look etched on his face, he might be considered handsome. *But then some people find that hard edge attractive,* I thought to myself.

"Lynley," he said, spotting me on the stairs. "How are you? Felisa said you'd called, and I've been wanting to get by the house, so when my schedule opened up this morning, I took advantage of it. I hope you don't mind."

"No, it's fine, Mr. Kroll." I didn't mention I'd only seen his voicemail moments before. "Would you like to come into the salon?"

"Yes, please. And call me Debon. Mr. Kroll was my stepfather."

As we passed the parlor, Debon looked in on Sanjay who had his camera set up and was busy photographing a collection of Chinese jade figures.

"You're already working on the auction, I see. How many people do you have in the house?"

"So far just Gil, the antique expert heading up the job, and Sanjay, his apprentice. I'll be bringing a team of FOF volunteers in the next few days to help with whatever needs to be done."

"Helen mentioned that." He gave a tiny smile, and once again I had the impression he and the FOF director were more than acquaintances. "Do you expect them to be here full time?"

"I imagine it will vary. As long as I'll be sitting Winnie, it doesn't really matter. Gil and Sanjay can come when it suits their schedule, and we'll call in the volunteers as we need them."

"At night? Will they be working at night as well?"

I scanned the lawyer, thinking it a strange thing to ask. He must have picked up on my concern because he gave a little shrug.

"I'm just trying to get a feel for the timeline. Until the estate is legally transferred to Friends of Felines, the responsibility belongs to our firm."

"I don't know about night work," I said. "I don't think so. I'm not sure how it will go. Gil has done estate sales before, so you'd be better off talking to him."

Debon seated himself in an antique straight-backed chair and I took the couch. "I'd offer you a beverage but I have no idea how to make that happen. I haven't used the main kitchen at all, and I can never find the housekeeper."

The lawyer chuckled, a dry, hollow sound. "Alice is a sly one. It's fine, Lynley. I can't stay long. I just wanted to check in to see what's going on as it relates to Mr. Payne's will. And find out why you called me, of course. You had a question?"

I felt my brow furrow as I worked to word my query. "Maybe you and Helen Branson have already discussed this, but if so she hasn't said anything to me… and it really seems like it could be a problem… and we don't want to do anything that could affect the shelter bequest… but it's a dilemma, and I don't see how…"

"Lynley, stop. What is it you want to know?"

"I'm sorry. I sort of brought it up when we were at the shelter, but I never really got an answer." I took another breath to collect myself. "I want to know what happens to the bequest if FOF fails to fulfill Mr. Payne's instructions?"

"Why would you fail? Are you having problems with Winter Orange?"

"No, she's lovely now that she's home. It's that other thing that worries me." I hesitated. "Helen showed me a filmed codicil. Basically, if I understand correctly, Mr. Payne is requiring FOF to… well, to find his killer."

"Yes."

"But he died of natural causes."

"That's what the report says."

"So… Where does that leave the shelter? How can we deal with something that didn't even happen?"

"That is a challenge," the lawyer admitted. "I've gone over this with my partners. The consensus is that it's nothing to worry about. Since there was no killing, the stipulation becomes null and void."

"Really?" I blurted.

"Well, yes," he said stiffly. "Otherwise we could not have allowed you to begin work on the estate liquidation. We are absolutely certain the transfer will go as planned."

"You're sure?"

"That is what I'm paid for," he said in a lighter tone. "Don't worry about it, Lynley. If anything comes up that Friends of Felines needs to know, I will alert Ms. Branson immediately."

"Oh, okay." Without saying it, he'd just told me it was none of my business. Alright, I could live with that, as long as the shelter wasn't going to lose out because of a millionaire's trick.

"Is there anything else I can help you with today?"

"No, that was it. You're sure this won't present a problem?"

"Very sure. Now I'd best be going. I want to stop and talk with your antiques man…"

"Gil," I finished for him. "Shall I take you back to the parlor?"

"I can find it. I've been through this house many times."

"Oh, okay." Of course, the lawyer must have visited Mr. Payne before.

As Debon Kroll rose to leave, I noticed his tie tack, gold and mother of pearl in a motif I recognized—a pyramid and an eye.

"That's an intriguing design. Does it have some significance?"

He paused. "Yes, it's a Masonic emblem. I'm surprised you aren't familiar with it. The Freemasons have been around for hundreds of years."

With that he turned and left the room. Was it my imagination, or did my mention of the tie tack have a sobering effect on the man? I'd heard of the Masons—hadn't everyone who'd read the *Da Vinci Code*?—but I knew next to nothing about them. A fraternal organization like the Elks, Moose, and Eagles—all good old boys and secret rites. There were rumors of course, iffy stuff. But in reality, wasn't it the objective of those brotherhoods to do good works, donate to charities, help children in far lands and refugees from war-torn states? Good guys, one and all.

Ultimately I concluded that how the Masons conducted themselves was yet another thing that was none of my business. Seeing it was almost time for lunch, my business was Winnie.

I was about to go check on her when I heard a crash and the sound of breaking glass, then a cough and a muffled moan.

"*Mon Dieu*!" Gil shouted from the parlor. "*Au secours*!"

Instinctively I ran toward the calamity, arriving to see Debon Kroll face down on the floor, pinned underneath a six-foot tall, seventeenth century cabinet. The sound of breaking glass had been its many-paned front panels shattering into a million pieces when it hit the ground.

"Quick! Help!" Sanjay called when he saw me.

I rushed to his side. Together, we hefted the heavy piece off the downed man, though in truth, it was Sanjay and Gil doing the lifting and me rooting them on.

"Are you alright?" I sputtered.

Debon cautiously sat up, dusting glass shards and the remnants of priceless antiques from his expensive jacket. "I think so." He rubbed his forehead where a welt was beginning to form.

Sanjay knelt to take a closer look before helping him to his feet. "You'll have a bruise there. Do you feel dizzy at all?"

"Should I call an ambulance?" I offered.

"No need, thanks. I'll be fine." Debon gave a laugh. "I'm tougher than I look."

"C'est bon," said Gil, his eyes taking in the heavy cabinet. "Such a mishap could have killed a lesser man."

Both Debon's and my eyes shot to the antiques dealer who, now that the ordeal was over, seemed a little lightheaded himself.

"What happened?" I asked, the horror of Gil's words hitting home.

"I went to open it, to look at a vase," Debon began, then he hesitated. "Excuse me. I think I'm going to sit down."

"He barely touched the thing," Sanjay continued as the lawyer sank heavily onto a chaise lounge. "There was a pop—I think one of the feet broke off. The cabinet teetered for a moment, then *blam,* down it came." He turned to Debon. "You sure you're okay, buddy?"

"Yeah, all good. But I advise you to be careful. This house is old and so was Mr. Payne. He may not have noticed things starting to decline."

"Accidents waiting to happen," Sanjay muttered.

"We've seen it before, haven't we Gil?"

"Oui, too many times," the antiques dealer softly agreed.

My phone rang, an intrusion of bells in the silent aftermath of the accident. Pulling it from my pocket, I looked at the number—no one I knew.

"Excuse me," I said, turning away to answer. I often didn't take calls from unknowns, but with the onset of my new job for FOF, there were undoubtedly going to be communications.

"Lynley Cannon?" came a man's voice on the line.

"This is she."

"This is Saul Baxter. I'm a partner with Kroll, Baxter, and Berger Attorneys at Law. I got a note you had a question about the bequest of our client Mr. Roderick Payne."

"Yes, but..." I was about to say that I'd already spoken to Debon Kroll, that in fact he and I were currently in the same room with each other, but I stopped mid-sentence. It might be illuminating to hear what Mr. Baxter had to say. He obviously didn't know his partner was there, and it could be useful to keep it that way.

"I need to take this," I said as I moved into the foyer and out of hearing range, feeling no remorse for my little charade.

"Thank you for getting back to me, Mr. Baxter. I called about the taped stipulation in Roderick Payne's will, the one requiring Friends of Felines to find Mr. Payne's killer. Since he died naturally, that stipulation would no longer be an issue, correct?"

There was a pause. *"That would have been the case, Ms. Cannon, had Mr. Payne's death indeed turned out to be a natural one."*

"Would have been the case...?" I parroted awkwardly.

"What do you mean?"

"Unfortunately," Saul Baxter drawled, *"upon further examination, it now appears Mr. Payne's death may not have been from natural causes after all."*

Baxter awaited my reply, but it didn't come. I was speechless, trying to absorb the meaning of his words.

"Ms. Cannon, are you still there?"

"I'm here, but I… I don't think I understand what you're saying."

"I'm sorry to have to tell you, Lynley, but it turns out Mr. Payne was murdered."

Chapter 14

Playing with cats and cleaning litter boxes aren't the only tasks a cat shelter volunteer can do. Volunteers may also be helpful in aiding with office chores, outreach programs, and a wide array of interesting special events.

Roderick Payne had been murdered. A second postmortem turned up signs of potassium poisoning. Potassium dissipates from the system quickly, making it nearly undetectable as a cause of death, but there are indications if one looks closely enough. Administered intravenously, an overdose of potassium is deadly. It was a pinprick wound to the right of his shoulder that got the lab checking a second time.

The news didn't surprise me nearly as much as it should have. Payne had been certain of this outcome, certain enough to announce it in his video codicil. Still, this changed everything. Payne's stipulation had concerned me from the start, but I'd always assumed there would be a workaround. Now that was no longer an option.

The whole thing was perplexing in its magnitude, but one tiny detail haunted me—the discrepancy between Debon Kroll's story and that of his partner, Saul Baxter. I'd talked to Debon only minutes before Baxter's call, and he told me the matter was null and void. He'd mentioned nothing about a second postmortem being run, let alone the revised determination of suspicious death. Had he been keeping the news to himself for some reason, or did he not yet know that was the case? Maybe he didn't want to address the inevitable questions that would come with the announcement—if there were a killer, then Friends of Felines was required to find them. *My goodness,* I thought to myself. *Where do we even start?*

That was only one of many questions that wouldn't be answered any time soon, or possibly ever. It had been a week now since the surprising news had dropped, and I'd heard nothing from either Helen Branson or the legal team. As time went by, I forced it out of my mind. No one had told us to quit working on the estate auction, and in fact, that work was accelerating. Between juggling the inventory, cleanup, and photography details, plus taking care of Winnie in a style to which she was accustomed, I had enough on my plate. I'd keep my eyes open for anything out of the ordinary, but that was about all I could do.

The ruling of murder loomed over the house like a greedy ghost. The police had come, and with them, Detective Marsha Croft whom I'd met on previous crime-related occasions. It was a brief and professional reunion, and once she determined I had nothing to do with the current crime, she went off about her business.

Winnie and I watched out the apartment window as the scene took form in the garden below. The white tent, the yellow plastic tape, the people dressed in bodysuits looking like aliens among the dahlias. *Thank goodness Payne didn't die in the house,* I thought to myself. If he had, my work would be over, or at least indefinitely postponed. And what about Winnie? She couldn't have stayed in a murder house by herself. I tried to imagine her screaming in my foster room day after day, night after night, and was grateful it wasn't to be.

Suddenly I was struck by the fragility of life. Here was a man who had amassed a fortune, yet it had taken only a little pinch of powder to end it all. Now the mansion would be sold to new owners, its contents, so carefully accumulated, distributed around the world. Winnie would go to strangers. Would they love her or merely tolerate her because she came with the house?

There was a gentle knock, and I turned to see Skie standing in the doorway. Winnie took one look at the young volunteer, hopped from her perch, and trotted over to say hello.

I joined the pair as they enjoyed their pet fest. "You've got quite a fan there."

"I love her so much!" Skie exclaimed, sweeping Winnie into her arms. "I never got to meet her when she was at the shelter. They said she was a hellion. I can't believe that, can you?"

I gave a laugh. "Oh, yes! I saw her in action. She screamed the whole time. But the minute I got her back to her home, she settled down and has been a little angel ever since." I reached out to stroke the calico head and studied Skie at the same time.

I'd picked three FOF volunteers to help with the estate sale auction: Frannie, Kelley Moro the journalist, and Skie. At first I'd resisted choosing Skie simply because she was so eager to be chosen, dogging me from the start and repeatedly reminding me she was *at my service*. I'd finally given in, though I couldn't help but wonder about her motives. Her outburst at the announcement of the bequest had been pointed. The young woman had suspicions, and rightly so, though as far as I knew, she was in the dark about the details of the bequest itself.

Per Helen's orders, I hadn't discussed Payne's odd

codicil with anyone but Frannie. I'd been ready to fend off any questions in that area, but so far Skie hadn't brought it up. Whatever drove her to tell me she *needed* to be on the team seemed to have been appeased when I picked her. Now she was perfectly content to work hard at whatever task I assigned and spend her breaks with Sanjay. The young shelter volunteer and the antiques apprentice had only known each other for the week, but love was in the air.

"So Sanjay needs you in the conservatory," said Skie. "He's setting up a special shoot—that bronze piece with the crystal detail that's so hard to photograph, and he wants to know if you have any ideas how to make it show up better."

"The French one? I can take a look, but I'm not sure what I could tell him that he doesn't already know. He's good at what he does."

"Yes, he is." Skie gave a little giggle and blush.

I grabbed my phone and the lined tablet that had become my constant companion, and we left the room, closing the door behind us. As we descended the stairs, I glanced over at the newly-repaired balustrade. The carpenters had done a magnificent job—I couldn't even tell where the break had been. I'd asked them to check the other railings throughout the house and was happy to learn the rest were sound.

Skie and I were crossing the foyer when we were interrupted by a loud banging from the front entrance. I looked at Skie and she at me. Winnie, who was catching a ride on Skie's shoulder, leapt away and hightailed it back up the staircase in a flash of colors. I panned the room to see if Alice had come to receive the noisy guest, but as usual, there was no sign of her.

Opening the door myself, I was confronted by a police officer and another man carrying a gunmetal gray hard shell case. Both produced identification.

"Officer Clyde Crowley, Portland Metropolitan Police," said the larger of the men, black haired and burly.

"Ted Callas, forensic specialist," grunted the other, the salt-and-pepper hair poking out from under his cap designating him as the elder.

"Lynley Cannon," I replied. "What can I do for you?"

Detective Croft stepped out from behind the men. "Lynley," she said with that slight accent I'd never been able to place. "I am afraid I have some bad news."

Now, it's never a good thing when a homicide detective says they have bad news, and my mind jumped all over the place. A family emergency? But that wouldn't account for the presence of a detective. Payne's murder? No, that was yesterday's headline. Had they discovered a skeleton in the tunnels? A severed hand behind one of the flowerbeds?

"We will need to check Roderick Payne's suite once more," said Croft. "Until we are finished, it will be off limits to you and your work-persons. The same will apply to the room of Ida Whide."

"Ida?" I stuttered. I could see them wanting to look over Payne's rooms, but why Ida's? "Did you find something linking Ida with Mr. Payne's… er… death?"

Croft ignored my question, as police are inclined to do, but as she pushed by me into the foyer, she whispered aside, "There may be a connection, but of course I cannot discuss it openly."

Somewhere along the line, Detective Croft had come to respect me. Maybe it was because I'd managed to offer a smattering of purely instinctual clues on a few of her cases;

maybe it was something more intuitive. Though I couldn't say we were friends, I felt a connection to the brusque homicide detective, and apparently the feeling went both ways.

On the upside of her thirties, Marsha Croft projected a formidable persona. Blunt-cut black hair, naturally smokey eyes, and her one bow to face paint, a lipstick in the blood red color my mother might have chosen when she was young. Her ambiguously stern expression matched her drab, colorless suit, but something about her stance as she stood before her officers left no doubt who was in charge.

"I need to see those rooms immediately please. Miss Whide's first. Mr. Payne's suite after that."

"Y… yes of course."

She beckoned to her company. "Now."

I sent Skie to tell Sanjay I'd be delayed and escorted Croft *et all* to Ida Whide's first floor chamber. The place had been cleared of all personal effects, leaving only a generic-looking room with no evidence of the woman who had lived there for so many years.

"I'm afraid the housekeeper's been in and deep cleaned, so I doubt you'll find anything of use. But have at it."

The men stood outside while Croft toured the room, casting a scrutinizing eye across the furnishings. "I will need to speak to her."

"The housekeeper? Good luck. I mean, she can be difficult to locate. Would you like me to text her?"

"Thank you." The detective gave the briefest of smiles and muttered something under her breath.

"Pardon?" I asked.

"Not important. I merely find it interesting that a person must use text to contact others in the same house.

But I suppose in a place this size…"

Self-conscious now, I sent the text. Alice replied an instant later that she would be in the kitchen whenever the detective was ready.

Croft took one more trip around the pristine chamber and circled back to me.

"I must ask, Lynley, what are you doing here?"

"But I've already told you," I said in surprise.

"Tell me again please. In detail."

"Well, I'm taking care of Mr. Payne's cat Winter Orange," I replied, wondering what the canny detective was up to but knowing she must have her reasons. "And I'm overseeing work on the estate auction. I guess you could call me the liaison for Friends of Felines Cat Shelter."

"Ah, yes, the non-profit that stands to inherit all Payne's worldly possessions. Did the shelter know they were in such a fortunate position before his death?"

I thought for a moment. "I don't know. I assume so, but you'd have to ask Helen Branson about that."

Croft picked up a small book of poems from a bedside table and flipped through the pages. "I shall."

"You're not suggesting FOF had anything to do with Payne's murder, are you?"

She looked at me blankly, her mouth pressed into a thin, crimson line. "I am not making any suggestions whatsoever."

Replacing the book on the table, she came toward me. "What was your relationship with Miss Whide?"

"I only met her last week when I came to stay with Winnie. She showed me the ropes, took me around, gave me the grand tour."

"How did she seem?"

"She was curt, businesslike, though she warmed up

after a while. She was saddened by Mr. Payne's death of course, but excited to be moving into her own place. Mr. Payne left her in a good position, and she was looking forward to doing things she'd never had the time or money for before."

Croft considered, then beckoned to her companions. "We will return to this room later. I want to revisit Payne's suite before we go any further. Please accompany us, Lynley."

Officer Crowley taped a seal across the door to Ida's former room, then silently, solemnly, we climbed the stairs to the second floor. Single file with me in the lead, we wove the corridors until we came to the ornate entrance of Roderick Payne's private suite. There had been police tape across it, tacked on after the initial search, but now the plastic ribbon dangled to one side.

Croft approached the door in three quick strides and touched the hapless tape. She gave me a stern glance but said nothing.

"It wasn't like that this morning," I exclaimed.

Croft eyed me. "Oh?"

"Winnie likes to come here on her walks," I explained. "I let her—but we never go in."

With a nod to Crowley, Croft quietly pushed the door ajar. I could hear noises coming from inside. It sounded like giggles.

Croft flung the door wide and moved in with Crowley one step behind. Callas set his case in the hallway and followed close on their heels. I was content to wait outside, though I managed to see enough through the door to know Payne's office study was vacant. The voices were coming from the bedroom.

Croft was across the room in seconds flat. Without

pretense, she slammed open the bedroom door, revealing a pair of very red-faced young people standing by a gigantic four-poster bed.

"We're not doing anything!" Skie exclaimed, staring at the police officers with apprehension. Sanjay blinked guiltily, his dark eyes wide with embarrassment.

"Why are you here?" the detective demanded.

"Just looking, honest," Skie began.

Sanjay stepped forward. "I wanted to show Skie something. I'd seen it before we knew about the murder and the room got closed off."

"Yeah, like the bed," Officer Clyde chuckled.

Sanjay reddened even more as he pointed to a small piece of furniture. "Actually it was the Edwardian smokers' cabinet, if you must know."

"But you could see this suite's off limits," I scolded as I joined the others. "The *Do Not Enter* tape across the door should have been a clue."

"The tape was down. We thought maybe it would be alright…"

I gave the young man a stern look.

"Okay, we were nosy. Sorry. We didn't touch anything."

Skie gave a huff. "It's really no big deal. We promise not to do it again."

"Correct—you will not," Croft huffed back. "Officer Crowley, please escort these people outside."

Crowley started toward Skie, his beefy hand outstretched. The girl took an instinctive step backward, tripped over the bed frame, and took a tumble onto the bed.

"Officer, please…" I began, about to chastise the man for being needlessly brutish, but my words were cut off by a thunderous rumble resounding from above.

As one, the six of us stared up at the ceiling. A crack had begun to form in the plaster directly over the bed. The crack split, lengthened, then split again until it resembled a gigantic spider web. Then with a crash, the whole thing fell.

Skie leapt away just in time. "Whew," she squeaked. "That was close. Why, I..." She turned to look behind her and stopped dead.

I, too, was staring at the king-sized bed. I'd expected to see a pile of plaster and maybe a bit of ancient lath, but what came to light when the dust cleared was far more grievous. In the ceiling above the bed, a six-foot-square hole had opened like a creature's maw. The opening cut all the way through the attic floorboards, the boards themselves now lying every which way across the quilted coverlet, along with a number of wooden crates that must have been stacked above. Among their spilled contents, I recognized an antique typewriter, machinery of some kind, and a collection of reference books, each as big as a family bible. Heavy, heavy items. If someone had wanted the cave-in to crush the person beneath, they couldn't have picked a better lot.

Sanjay grabbed Skie and pulled her to him. Croft wiped her eyes, for a moment looking as lost and confused as the rest of us.

I whipped off my glasses which were now coated with dust. "What happened?"

"The girl sat on the bed," Crowley gulped.

"I didn't do anything," Skie retorted, though her voice came out reedy and lacking its usual assurance.

"Of course not." Sanjay softly petted her orange hair as if she were a kitten.

Detective Croft, who had regained her confidence, took a step forward and peered up into the hole, then down at the mountain of debris on the bed.

"This..." She waved a hand to encompass the bed-to-ceiling disaster. "This was not an accident."

Chapter 15

How many cats are too many? It comes down to time, money, and love. It's easy to fall in love with multiple cats, but make sure you have the wherewithal to accommodate their lifetime needs before you adopt.

No one was hurt—this time.

If you didn't count pride, no one had been hurt when the parlor cabinet toppled on Debon Kroll either.

And though Sanjay could have taken quite a tumble when the banister broke, he was young and lithe enough to keep himself from falling. Someone older, someone slower, would not have had such luck.

After a quick check on Winnie, Detective Croft and I had moved down to the foyer, leaving Crowley and Callas to finish examining the cave-in. I'd told the detective about the toppling cabinet and the broken balustrade. She'd taken the information without a word, as if the incidents didn't surprise her. Then again, I never could tell what was going through that calculating mind of hers.

"I don't think these accidents are coincidences," I went on. "In fact, I don't think they're accidents at all. I did up until now, but whole floor joists don't come hurtling down out of the blue, even in an old house like this one. The boards must have been cut and the thing rigged to fall when someone got into bed."

I shivered at the implications, momentarily seeing old Roderick Payne pinned under those considerable pounds of rubble.

"Since it turns out Mr. Payne was murdered, can we assume these booby-traps were set by whoever killed him? Was it Ida Whide? Is that why you wanted to see her room?"

Croft smiled. She actually almost grinned. "That is what I like about you, Lynley Cannon. You are always imagining clues." She sobered. "But I do not have the luxury of imagination. I must work solely with facts, verifiable facts. We will look into this series of events. Meanwhile you must cease your work here and vacate the premises."

"Vacate?" I gasped. "But we can't. At least, I can't." I paused. "I guess the others could take a day off, but I need to stay here with Winnie."

Croft scrutinized me, then looked from side to side. "You have got yourself quite a setup here, have you not? You and the cat?"

I wondered if she was insinuating something. No telling with the canny detective—it was best just to answer her questions, honestly and completely, no matter how strange they seemed. "Yes, I guess I do. But it would be nicer if I knew the place wasn't about to fall down around me."

"My unit will make certain there are no other dangers. We will get to the bottom of this," she assured in a sudden show of sympathy. "Then you and your feline can sleep soundly, alright?"

I nodded. *That would be more than alright,* I thought to myself.

"Now I must interview the staff. Begin with the housekeeper. Would you be so kind as to ask her to come?"

In other words, I was dismissed. I can't say I was disappointed. Talking with Detective Marsha Croft always felt a little like interrogation, no matter how friendly she seemed.

I texted Alice to relay the message that Croft wanted her in the foyer, and the girl shot back an affirmative emoji. I was headed outside to find Cox when my phone rang, a number I didn't recognize. Taking the chance that the local prefix didn't indicate spam, I answered.

"Lynley?" said a voice I recognized but couldn't place. *"This is Jack Hess. You called me last week. Said you'd like to come by to meet my kitties."*

"Yes, of course, Jack. Hello." I stopped myself before asking the banal *how are you,* a difficult and disturbing question for patients on hospice, and substituted with, "I'm so glad you got back to me."

"My son went home this morning, and I'm free this afternoon, if you're not busy. I've thought a lot about your offer of help. I'm not so good at asking, but I think... Well, I guess I could really use it."

I mentally ran through my to-do list which now included dismissing the FOF team per Detective Croft's orders. Since they were friends, not employees, I predicted much explaining would be involved, the booby-trapped bedroom and the potential of other possible dangers around the house being only part of it. They would want to know what would happen now, when they could come back, and how this would impact the estate auction. Unfortunately, I had very few answers.

"It'll take me some time to wind up what I'm doing. About an hour. Will that work?"

I heard a sigh. *"That would work just fine. We're looking forward to it."*

He gave me his address which I copied into my phone.

"See you soon." He sounded a bit more chipper than when he had first called. *"And don't forget to bring your kitty pictures."*

After locating groundsman Cox and sending him up to the house to be interviewed by Detective Croft, I went to break the news to the team. I found Frannie in the parlor polishing a silver urn with a flannel cloth.

"There's been a development." I took the folding chair beside her.

"Skie told me about her near-brush with death in Mr. Payne's bedroom. She said the ceiling had been rigged to fall. Is that true?"

"It's true." I glanced at the parlor ceiling with its ornate molding and frescoes, feeling a bit like Chicken Little. "If Skie hadn't been so fast on her feet, she could have been hurt… badly."

"Oh goodness! Poor dear." Frannie's blue-gray eyes widened, long mascaraed lashes blinking wildly.

The smell of polish wafted through the air, combining with something else—dust. Could the plaster dust from the bedroom on the second floor really have made it all the way downstairs? Suddenly I felt the magnitude of what had happened and understood Croft's demand that the place be evacuated. It was more than possible we were working inside a ticking bomb.

"There may be more to these mishaps than we thought. The police have asked us to quit work until they have a chance to investigate further."

"Quit working? When? Why? How? What's going to happen with the sale?"

Yup, there they were, all the questions I knew would come. I told her what I could, which wasn't much.

"Just leave everything where it is." I nodded to the urn. "I'm sure you'll be able to come back to it soon."

Frannie set the pot on the table but held onto the cloth, as if she hadn't decided whether she was going to comply with the police order or not. "And what about you? What about Winnie?"

"I get to stay, but I plan to hole up in the apartment while they do their inspection. I'll be fine," I assured her.

"Humph," Frannie grunted, shaking her head and setting her curly locks to bouncing. "Well, you call me if you need me, okay?"

"Actually I could use your help right now. I have to step out for a while to check on a hospice patient and his cats. Would you mind gathering the team and telling them what's happening? Make sure they understand why they need to leave?"

"I can do that. Skie's gone home already—she was a bit shaken by her close call. And Gil's at his shop, so that just leaves Sanjay and Kelley. I'll phone the others so they don't come back until you say. Is Winnie in her room?"

"Yes, and I closed the cat door. She can stay there while I'm out—with the police running around, she's better off corralled."

"Probably for the best," Frannie agreed.

"Well, I guess I should go…" I muttered, but instead of leaving, I remained seated on that hard, smooth chair, absentmindedly clicking a fingernail on the crossbar. Something was bothering me, and it wasn't the booby-traps or the interruption in the auction plans. It wasn't being in the big house all by myself. There was another matter, one that hadn't occurred to me before.

"Frannie…" I said thoughtfully. "Who do you think did all this? Set the traps? It has to be someone with access to the house, someone on the inside."

Frannie took up the urn again and resumed her polishing. "On the inside?" she echoed cynically. "Which do you suspect, the gardener or the housekeeper?"

"I doubt it was Alice. She couldn't have done the heavy work. Besides, she doesn't have a motive."

"That you know of," Frannie taunted.

"On the other hand, it could easily have been Cox. He's strong enough, and he's got a grudge. Mr. Payne had promised him his tiny house but never put it in the will. Now he gets nothing. If he didn't know about the omission, he might have done it for the inheritance, and if he found out there was none, he could have done it for spite. Or I suppose it could even have been Ida, Payne's personal assistant." I recalled the talk we had the last time I'd seen her. Ida had been so happy, so enthusiastic. I could visualize her in her new condo with travel brochures spread out across the table, exotic sites bookmarked in Google. "She did receive an inheritance. Nothing like what Mr. Payne gave to FOF, but more than she'd ever had before. She would have needed help to carry off the boobytraps, but Detective Croft wanted to see her room. That must mean something."

"Hey, wait!" Frannie exclaimed as she worked away at an especially tarnished spot. "I know! Maybe the butler did it."

"There isn't a..." Then I got it. "You're teasing me."

Frannie rubbed more vigorously than ever. "Sleuthing out killers is a dangerous job, as you well know. You're going to stay out of it, right?"

"What? Me?"

"Yes, you—Lynley Cannon. You know your cat curiosity always gets you in trouble," she scoffed. "I'd imagine you'd have learned by now."

"I've learned," I grumbled. "I've learned, except..."

"There's always an exception with you, isn't there?"

I lowered my voice. "FOF needs to find Mr. Payne's killer, or we don't get a cent of his bequest."

Frannie stopped mid-polish. "Helen didn't ask you to do anything risky, Lynley. Just to keep your eyes open. Or is there something you're not telling me?"

I shook my head. "I haven't heard anything from Helen since the murder result came to light. Have you?"

"No, nothing. She still hasn't made that stipulation general knowledge. The only reason I know about it is because you told me." She went back to her chore, giving the elaborately decorated vessel a final swipe.

"Well, I guess we should keep it that way for now."

She nodded. "Finding killers is a job best left to the police, and you'd be smart to keep your curious-kitty nose out of it, no matter what that stipulation says."

She placed the urn on the table and admired her work.

"Beautiful," I commented, ready to change the subject.

"I like to polish things. The result is always so rewarding."

"That's good, because there's lots more to go."

She glanced at the cluster of sugar and creamers, tea jugs, cups, plates, and wooden boxes of flatware still awaiting her deft hand. "Something to look forward to when we're allowed to return. Let me know how it goes with the cat man. I probably won't be here when you get back."

This time I did get up, ready to head out to see Jack and his cats, but first I bent down and gave Frannie a little kiss on the cheek. "Thanks for taking care of me."

I went up to the apartment to check on Winnie and

grab my purse. The calico was sleeping like a kitten in her poof bed, so I tiptoed quietly away, trying not to disturb her. I was almost out the door when I remembered Jack's request that I bring cat pictures. There was an unlimited number on my phone, but I had something even better.

When Tinkerbelle became a registered therapy cat and we began making visits, people often asked me about the rest of my feline family. I'd put together a little photo album to show them—simpler to handle than a phone for those with physical and mental limitations. It took me a moment to find it in my tote of miscellanea, but there it was at the bottom, the perfect thing.

As I left the mansion and headed for my car, I thought how incongruous the police vehicles looked against the serene backdrop of Payne opulence. There would be more coming. Would I return to a frenzy of investigators ripping the place apart? What would they find? More dangers? More traps? Someone had put a lot of thought into the demise of Roderick Payne. Why not just stick him with the poison in the first place? Why go to all the trouble of fabricating complicated set-ups that may or may not fail?

Had the killer gotten tired of waiting for Payne to die and decided to affect a more straightforward method?

Or was it possible the trap-setter and the potassium-injector were two different people? Could we be looking for two killers instead of one?

Chapter 16

Is specific care for your cats included in your will or trust? If not, they could end up in a shelter, and not all of them are as nice as Friends of Felines.

I slipped into the comfortably worn driver's seat of my little Toyota and punched up the map app on my phone. Plugging in my location along with the address Jack had given me, I was surprised to find he lived only a quarter mile away. I set the phone in its convenient black holder to guide me through the unfamiliar area and pulled out of the drive onto the steep, winding road.

A quarter mile as the crow flies turned out to be somewhat longer by way of street, but eventually I found the place, a small trailer park surrounded by tall, old trees at the base of the hill. It took a bit more searching to locate Jack's abode, but I was pleasantly surprised when I did.

I'd been picturing the generic, poverty-stricken stereotype trailer and fearing the worst, so the vintage Airstream with its bright yellow trim came as a welcome relief. The postage-stamp-sized front yard and tidy square of grass was nicely kept. Potted geraniums bloomed in a profusion of red, pink, and magenta on the tiny porch. All in all, the impression was one of a happy home.

But that was the outside, I reminded myself, likely maintained by a gardener hired by the owners of the park. It was what I found on the inside that would tell the tale.

The door was standing open, and from the flagstone

path, I could see an elderly man sitting in a recliner, a black cat on his shoulder and a gray one installed on his lap. Climbing the three wooden steps, I knocked on the screen.

"Hi, Jack? It's Lynley Cannon. We spoke on the phone."

"Yes, Lynley. Come in, come in!" He made to rise, then thought better of it. His gaunt pallor spoke of his illness, but his face beamed with genuine pleasure that put pinpoints of pink on the sunken cheeks.

"Don't get up," I said, slipping in while watching for cats who might be inspired to make their escape. "You wouldn't want to disturb your companion, now would we?"

He reached a dark-spotted hand to pet the gray. "This is Ben," he introduced. "Horatio is the one up top. Mazy and Daisy are on their shelf in the bedroom. You're welcome to go say hello. Excuse me if I don't accompany you."

I went down the short hall to view the females, giving them a pet and a brief wellness check at the same time. The two fluffy tabbies seemed in good condition with silky fur and bright eyes. Their rotund shapes proved they were not lacking for sustenance, and their friendly demeanor showed them as happy, well-adjusted cats.

"Lovely," I said as I returned. Eying Horatio and Ben, they seemed in much the same condition, their coats sleek, their whiskers relaxed, and their eyes alight.

Horatio hopped down and came over to me as I took a seat near the old man. "Mew," he said, and I petted him accordingly.

"It's wonderful to meet you, Jack. And you know I have to ask—how is your pain today on a scale of one to ten?"

Jack was accustomed to the question—all hospice volunteers and workers asked it at the beginning of each visit, even the therapy animal teams. It helped assess a patient's condition, but moreover, it opened the conversation for the patient to talk about their health if they felt like it. I had been trained to answer questions and call in the nurse if needed, but thankfully none of that was necessary with Jack since his answer was low on the scale.

I gazed around the neat little room. The furnishings were sparse, but several bookcases were filled with books of all types and ages as well as knickknacks and a few nice collectibles. Everything seemed clean except for the floor which could do with a vacuum where litter had been tracked and crumbs had fallen around the recliner chair.

"Have you lived here long?"

"Oh, about ten years now. Came when my wife passed away. Sold the house and most everything in it. Picked up the cats and moved, just like that." His attempt to snap his fingers failed to make much of a sound, but the meaning was clear. "They were different cats then," he added.

"Have you always had cats?"

"Ever since I was a boy. One time me and my wife had ten at once!" He laughed at the memory. "That was too many really, but we gave them good care. Happy kitties, one and all. I couldn't do that now though. The Fantastic Four keep me busy enough."

I sniffed, detecting a mild odor of cat urine and unobtrusively looked around for a source. Jack must have caught my intent because he gave a sad little chuckle.

"I'm afraid I haven't got to patrolling the commodes today. It's getting hard for me to bend over without feeling dizzy."

"Oh, dear, dizzy is no fun. Does your nurse know

about that?"

"Jennine knows. It's my medication. I just have to be careful. And try not to bend over much."

I smiled. "Well, Jack, good news! I think we can help you there."

Jack and I talked for a long time, about the disease that was killing him, about the plans he'd made for his cats when he was gone. He was excited to hear about the *Pet Peace of Mind* program that brought in volunteers to take care of hospice patients' pets. He consented to having someone come by a couple of times a week to clean the boxes and any inadvertent messes, restock, wash food and water bowls, and otherwise cater to his kitties' needs. I wouldn't be able to do it myself, but Pinkie could easily find a volunteer for such a nice, straightforward assignment. Once that was established, Nurse Jeannine should have nothing feline to complain about, and the cats could remain safe at home.

Jack was thrilled to see my little book of cat pictures, admiring the clowder as if they were his own. While he pored over each and every one, I cleaned the boxes and tidied up the food stations. The Fantastic Four were very interested in what I was doing and followed me around the house like a little parade.

When I was ready to go, Jack insisted on escorting me to the door. Holding the railing for support, he hobbled out to pluck a faded bloom off a brick-red geranium. I watched to make sure the old man didn't topple as he bent to the potted plant. When he was safely up again, I started for my car but paused to take one last look at the homey scene—the shiny silver Airstream, the garden with its potted plants, the smiling old man. My gaze shifted wider—the shade trees surrounding the park, the backdrop of the green hills behind.

Suddenly I saw something I hadn't noticed before.

"That's Payne House!" I exclaimed as my eye flew to the mansion perched on the hill directly above. "You can see it from here."

Jack followed my gaze. "Oh, yes. That old place."

Surprisingly, I could pick out details of the house and grounds. "It's closer than I thought. Why, I can even make out the police tent in the garden where Mr. Payne died."

Jack shot a look at me. "Police?"

Rats! Me and my big mouth. Not that it was a secret, but I didn't feel the Payne murder was something to discuss with someone so very close to their own death.

Jack didn't seem concerned, however. If anything, he was intrigued. "Police means foul play. Was the old bird murdered?"

"It's what they're thinking."

"Interesting. Do they know why?"

"I really couldn't say," I told him—an ambiguous reply but an honest one.

"No, of course not. But I can't be surprised. He was an odd duck."

I watched as a police van pulled into the drive and disappeared around the side of the house. *Thus it begins,* I said to myself. Then I registered Jack's statement.

"Mr. Payne was odd? How do you mean?"

Jack dismissively waved a hand. "Not that I ever met the old boy. No, I just sort of spied on him from time to time." He gave me a little wink. "Well, why not? Up there in his fancy house—it didn't do him any harm."

Jack grasped the handrail and lowered himself onto the step. "I have a telescope, for looking at the stars. Not a whole lot to do when you can't go anywhere, you see. And every once in a while..." He nodded from side to side in a playful manner. "...I look at other things too."

"What did you see?"

"Nothing bad, mind you," Jack declared. "I'm no voyeur, so don't be thinking that. But it was hard not to notice. And then once I did, I couldn't help but wonder what it was. So whenever it happened, I'd get out the old scope and take a look-see. It stopped when he died, of course. I never did figure it out."

"What, Jack? What didn't you figure out?"

He pointed to the mansion. "See that tower—the one that looks like a keep on a castle? Well, some nights, there'd be funny lights coming from out of it, a bright one shooting straight up and another, flashing from the windows. It was peculiar, reminded me of the coded messages we sent when I was in the war. But if they were code, I couldn't crack it." His hand dropped and he shrugged. "Who knows what rich people do? Or why?"

Coded signals from the turret? I had to wonder if Jack were making it up. My instinct told me he wasn't. "How often did this happen?"

"Once a month."

I was surprised how quickly he answered. "You sound very sure of yourself."

"I should be." He snickered. "I keep a log."

Pointing a long finger at the door and the table beyond, he said, "See that little blue book? I write everything down in there. Not that I have memory problems," he added quickly, "but when it comes to details, one can recall only so much. Got all the dates and times if you're interested."

Sure, I was interested, but I didn't feel like getting into it right then. I knew where the blue book was if I needed it. "I'm good, thanks. It is curious though. And you have no idea what it meant?"

"Not a one."

The Fantastic Four had begun clamoring at the screen door, unsure why their person was on the other side.

"I'd better get back in there before they tear the place down. They worry about me when I'm out." He laughed. I was still staring at the turret, trying to imagine what could be the source of the strange flashing lights. "Lynley?"

"I'm sorry. I was just thinking." I turned my full attention back to the old man. "Thanks for seeing me. Someone from hospice will contact you soon about helping with the cats."

"Thank *you*. It's such a relief to know they won't take them away from me."

"I promise that won't happen. You can call me anytime if you have questions, but I imagine things will work out fine."

I waited to make sure Jack got back to his chair without any mishaps or kitty escapes, then went to my car, but I didn't take off right away. From where I sat, I could still see Payne House crowning the hill like a lookout. Gil and I had searched for an entrance to that mysterious turret but without success.

Now I'd need to look again. Something had been going on up there, something a savvy army veteran with a high-powered telescope and an inquisitive mind had deemed as *peculiar*.

Chapter 17

Are cats really little four-legged detectives? Cats' curiosity, combined with their superior eyesight and sense of smell, make them perfect sleuths, but unfortunately for us, they seek only those things that are of interest to them.

A few more days went by, and the forensic team moved out of the garden, leaving only a haphazard square of crime scene tape to mark the place of Payne's passing. It was a small dell, surrounded by crocosmia, their bright orange spears and deep green spikes shielding the spot from unwanted eyes. I'd passed by it before I'd known its significance, then afterward. Picturing him there with Winnie sitting sentry was heartbreaking; I doubted I would visit that pretty little hollow again.

Detective Croft and her investigators had wound up their work inside the house and deemed it free and clear of further booby-traps. Payne's and Ida's rooms had been fully examined and the restrictions dropped. The volunteers were allowed to return, and work on the estate auction went back to normal.

On the subject of Payne's stipulation, there was no word. Helen went along as if it didn't exist, so I did too. I felt reasonably assured we'd get around it somehow—at least that's what I told myself. The thought of putting all that time and effort into readying for the sale, only to have it yanked away from us and given to the next in line to inherit, was more than I could bear.

Who is the next in line? I wondered. Ida said Payne had no family. Would it be another charity then? A school? A museum? His fifth-grade music teacher? None of those possibilities seemed likely to have killed him for it.

Rats, there I went again, my mind wantonly slipping to the murder. *None of my business*, I reminded myself sternly.

I had already put in a long day. After seeing to Winnie's requirements, I'd gone home to check in on Seleia and my own cats, dropped by the Pet Pantry to pick up cat food and toys, and made a quick trip to the shelter to visit the cats I'd been working with before the Winnie affair came up. Now it was late, but my day wasn't over yet.

Gil had gone back to his shop to attend to business there, and I'd sent the other volunteers home, but Skie and Sanjay had stayed behind to put in a few extra hours finishing up in the basement, a thankless job of picking the few saleable gems from a boatload of garbage. The three of us were taking a well-deserved break on the veranda as the twilight deepened. In spite of the day's spiking temperatures, the night was soft as cat fur and just as soothing.

"I've done my share of antique and collectible shows," I said, reminiscing on my earlier days as a collectibles dealer, "but this is something else! I really had no idea how much work went into an event of this scale." I took a sip of my iced tea. "I would never have guessed there could be so many details involved in an online affair."

"I'd never have guessed one guy could have so much valuable stuff," Skie put in. "Can you imagine how much money he must have spent on it? Probably could have fed a small country."

I smiled. "I take it you aren't a fan of the wealthy."

"It's hard to be a fan when you work for minimum

wage and every dollar is precious." She looked at me, all righteous innocence, her orange and red hair flaming in the setting sun. "How he can have all this when so many are struggling... Well, it doesn't make sense."

I'd wondered the same thing myself many times during my sixty years on this planet, but it wasn't a question that would be answered in my lifetime. "At least now it's going to a good cause," I said optimistically. "The cats at our shelter."

"Yeah," Skie shrugged. "I guess Mr. Payne was an okay guy at heart."

"It's not just a matter of rich people giving their money to those who don't have it, you know," said Sanjay. "Even if they wanted to, our society isn't set up that way."

"I guess. But how did we get like this in the first place? Some cultures share what they have with each other."

"And some societies are even worse than ours, with whole social classes trapped so deep in poverty they can never get out. At least here, everybody has a chance to make something of themselves."

"Like become a celebrity influencer or a sports icon?" Skie scoffed.

"Sure," said Sanjay, "but other things as well. Doctors and artists. Spiritual leaders..."

Skie gave a harrumph. "Politicians? Arms dealers?"

"Advocates?"

"Used car salesmen."

"Cat people," Sanjay definitively stated.

As Sanjay and Skie argued amicably about the state of the world, my mind wandered. The sun was setting, the last rays hitting the roof of the house. *Hitting the turret,* I corrected. As I watched the dazzle reflect off the narrow windows, I thought of Jack's story about the telltale lights.

"Hey, guys," I interrupted. "Do you want to do something fun?"

Both Skie and Sanjay stopped mid-sentence and turned to me in surprise.

"Like what?" Skie asked suspiciously.

"See that turret up there?" I pointed unnecessarily to the place, lit up like a flame. "We need to find a way inside."

"But we've already looked, Lynley," said Sanjay. "There isn't one. Didn't we decide they built it for show?"

"Yes, but that was before I found out things happened up there. Or at least they did when Mr. Payne was alive."

I explained about the beam and the coded lights Jack had picked up with his telescope. "So there has to be a way. It's probably hidden, which makes it that much more imperative we find it."

"So an old guy who never leaves his trailer told you he saw lights in the sky?" Skie laughed.

"In the turret," I corrected.

"Lynley, really! And you believe him?"

"Yes, I do. Why shouldn't I? He's perfectly lucid. It's his body that's failing, not his mind."

Skie sniffed. I understood. To the young girl, I seemed old, which made someone twenty years my senior ancient beyond comprehension.

"I wouldn't mind giving it another try," said Sanjay. "Anything to keep me out of that basement for a while longer."

"And if we do get in," I added with a sly smile, "who knows what treasures we might find?"

"Okay," Skie conceded. "Sure, why not? Let's see if we can locate the magic tower." Then she chuckled. "Maybe we'll see a ghost."

* * *

We talked for a bit longer, so by the time we made it up to the attic, it was full dark. The single light bulb cast only a limited glow across the vast, long room. Though the set of oval windows at the far end had been opened, the air was stifling hot and close. There was a smell to it that anyone who has lived in a house with an attic would recognize—a dry, dusty scent with hints of mothballs, old fabric, wood finish, decay, and mouse.

"Whoa!" Skie blurted as she topped the stairs. "This is crazy."

"Your first time up here?" Sanjay took her hand. "You should have seen it before we cleaned it up!"

"And you did a good job," I commented, gazing around at the space. "With all the stuff cleared away, we've got a much better chance to find what we're looking for."

Gil and Sanjay, with the help of the volunteers and a bit from the police, had made great strides since I'd last been up. Though the place never would be pristine, my lungs were no longer clogged with ancient particles of who-knew-what, and I felt no hint of an allergy flare. Most of the boxes had been removed elsewhere and those that remained were stacked neatly against the walls. I was happy to see a sturdy piece of plywood fitted across the hole above Payne's bedroom.

"Where do we start?" Skie posed. Her voice was low, and I thought I caught just the hint of reluctance, as if she might be having second thoughts. I sensed it too, an otherworldly atmosphere that brought to mind all those stories about monsters in closets, fiends under the bed, and things going bump in the night. That last one felt a bit too close for comfort since I'd been hearing those nightly bumps ever since I'd come to the house.

I shivered in spite of the heat. "I suppose we just... look."

Sanjay had set his phone to the flashlight app and was already moving into a corner, playing the beam across the vaulted wall. I walked the other direction, toward the windows. Skie stood frozen underneath the light bulb.

Suddenly she screamed. "There's something in here with us!"

I shot a look back just in time to see a cat slip behind an antique chest.

"It's just Winnie. But how did she get up here?" I mused. "I thought I closed the door when I came through."

"Maybe she opened it with her paw," offered Sanjay. "Or maybe it was Skie's ghost who let her in."

"Stop that," said Skie. "I'm not scared," she added, the fear still resounding in her words.

"Sorry, love." He made his way back to the frightened girl and put an arm around her. "We don't have to do this if you don't want to."

"No, I'm good. I'd like to see what's in the turret if we can figure out how to get up there." She took a deep breath, smoothed back her spiked hair, and headed boldly into the shadows toward where Winnie had disappeared.

I wondered if I should take the sly cat back downstairs, but Payne's instructions were to let her go her own way, which included the attic. A scattering of cat toys strewn across the floor were evidence this wasn't her first excursion, so I dismissed the idea and went back to my search.

Fifteen minutes later, we still hadn't turned up anything useful. No hidden stairways or buttons that opened doors built to look like bookcases. The plaster walls were old and cracked but lacking any suspicious gaps. The floor was made up of long plank boards, no Persian carpets with square-cut trap doors hidden underneath. Besides, we wanted to go up, not down

Then I heard a long meow from the very farthest end of the attic, an annex room.

"Winnie?"

A louder meow came from beyond the feeble glimmer of the low wattage light bulb, followed by one of her signature wails.

"Goodness, is that our Winnie?" Skie asked in surprise.

"Oh, yeah," I sighed. "That's our Winnie alright."

"No wonder she got a bad rep at the shelter."

I nodded. "Now you understand. She's a Dr. Jekyll and Ms. Hyde kitty."

"Or maybe Aziraphale and Crowley," Sanjay translated into a more modern allegory. "The demon one," he added. "Not the police officer Crowley."

I followed the cries to a small room partitioned off from the larger space. This area had not yet been tackled by the cleaning elves, and as I shone my beam through the door and around the stacks of wooden crates, I found the calico perching on the highest one, the spidery ceiling only inches above her ears. Her paw was raised, and she was staring at me as if she were trying to tell me something.

She yowled again. This time I swore I could hear the word come out of her little cat mouth! *Here!*

Both Sanjay and I had gone over that area during our previous search, including the place Winnie now found so fascinating—we'd come up with exactly nothing. Still, Winnie's behavior indicated we must have missed a clue, and she wasn't going to let us get away with it.

The cat ended her triad with a tiny mew. *Here…*

"What is it, sweetie? Is there something you want me to see?"

She gave a series of chirps, and touched the low ceiling with her paw. *Here. Right here.*

I might have felt silly following directions given by a cat had I not been such a believer in the power of feline insight. Cats had senses that went far beyond our poor human ones. Whether you want to call it intuition, instinct, or plain cat magic, it all came down to them knowing things about the world around us that we humans just don't get.

Sanjay and Skie joined me in the small room, and now three beams played across the cat, the paw, and the ceiling. I stepped forward, gave Winnie a pet, then turned my attention to the spot she'd pointed out with such enthusiasm. As I focused the light, I saw something I hadn't noticed before.

There, sticking out from between two of the ceiling boards, was the tiniest edge of yellow fuzz. I touched it lightly and felt the springiness of rope. Cautiously I drew it out, the frayed end of a foot-long length of hemp.

I felt resistance and stopped, peering up between the timbers. I couldn't see what it was attached to—maybe nothing at all. But then again, this could be exactly what we were looking for.

"Here, let me see." The young man stepped in and began running his fingers around the low ceiling, spiraling out from the rope. A minute later, he shrugged. "I can't feel a seam. But there has to be a reason for it. I say let's pull it and see what happens."

Meanwhile, two things were occurring on the periphery: Winnie was batting at the rope with the intensity of a tiger on prey, and Skie had shrunk into something more resembling a scared little girl than the assertive woman I had come to know. Though both these details registered in the back of my mind, my attention was solely fixed upon the ceiling.

"Go ahead, Lynley," Sanjay whispered. "Do it."

I retrieved the rope from Winnie and pulled. Nothing happened so I yanked harder. With still no result, I wound it around my wrist, stepped back, and gave a huge tug.

In a burst of noise and dust, the thing gave way, sending me staggering backwards into a set of wooden crates that tumbled to the floor, taking me along with them. At the same time, a large panel of ceiling fell away, dropping down on brass hinges and hitting Sanjay squarely in the face. He also fell. The only one of us left standing was Skie.

"Oh, my Cat!" she cried, running first to Sanjay and then to me. "Are you guys alright?"

"I'm okay," I muttered, straightening my glasses and pulling myself up with the aid of one of the crates. "Sanjay?"

"Yeah, I'm fine." He, too, rose. Wiping blood from his nose, then looking at his reddened hand, he added, "Or maybe not."

"We'd better get you downstairs. There's a first aid box in the kitchen."

"No." He pulled a bandana from his pocket and held it to his face. "It's nothing. We've come this far. I want to see what it was I got injured for."

I looked at Skie, forlorn and scared. In spite of her terror, she echoed, "We've come this far."

The three of us stared up at the hole. I could make out nothing but featureless black.

"Look, there's another rope," said Sanjay.

The young man stood on his tiptoes and felt around the edge of the opening, dislodging a second cord. Unlike the old hemp one, this line was made of silk with a carved wooden ball at the end.

Swinging lazily from side to side, it dangled seductively from the darkness.

"Stand away," Sanjay commanded as he took the ball in his hand.

"Are you sure?" Skie whispered.

He nodded, then slowly, cautiously, he pulled.

There was a creaking from up in the shadows and the grating of old hinges. The noises grew louder as Sanjay increased his force. Then I heard another sound that I couldn't identify, a low moaning like someone in pain. Whatever it was, it set my teeth on edge.

I was about to ask if the others could hear it too when, with a final scream of metal that overwhelmed all else, a polished oak ladder came thundering down upon us.

Chapter 18

A cat can fit through any hole larger than its head.

"Oh, Cat!" Skie exclaimed as the dust cleared.

"Will you look at that!" Sanjay took a step closer to inspect the new thing taking up the entire middle of the small room, a heavy, counterbalanced ladder that led up to whatever was above.

"Winnie!" I cried. "Did anyone see where she went?"

Both Skie and Sanjay gaped at me, then began staring around the room.

I jumped to the spot where the incongruous set of steps had settled and sank to my knees. I was afraid to look but I knew I had to. If Winnie had been underneath… If she was in the way when it landed…

"She probably ran off when the ladder came down," Skie offered. I appreciated her attempt to make me feel better, but I'd rather she concentrated on finding the cat.

There was a narrow space between the bottom tread and the floor, but I could see nothing in that one-inch shadow. A light bloomed over my shoulder—Sanjay's flashlight app. As he shined it into the dark corners, I held my breath. Though I'd feared the worst, the space was bare.

"I guess you're right," I told Skie. "She probably hightailed it back to her room when things started crashing."

"Smart girl," Skie muttered to herself.

Sanjay's interest had turned from the cat to the hole looming above us. A secret stairway had just fallen out of the ceiling, and he was not about to let that go unexplored.

Edging to the bottom step, he pointed the flashlight into the dark. "Should we go up?"

"I don't know…" Skie hemmed. "Can we trust it? It could be dangerous."

He set a foot on the first tread. "Dangerous, how? It can't be any worse than having a hatch hit you in the face."

"I don't know. The floor might be rotten," she fussed. "Or… spiders."

"Maybe we should leave it for the morning," I conceded, "when there's more light. It's not going anywhere."

"I guess," Sanjay acquiesced, staring wistfully at the trap door.

I turned to go. "We've had enough adventures for one night I think."

A loud mew broke from the shadows, and a calico blur shot up the ladder into obscurity. The three of us watched with our mouths open.

"Winnie!" I lunged after her, staring up at the hole from the bottom step.

"I guess that seals it." Sanjay smirked. "Now we have to go."

"You're happy about it!" Skie accused.

"Why shouldn't I be? A hidden turret in a hundred-year-old castle? Don't you want to know what's been there all these years?"

"Not really," Skie grumbled.

"What's up with you, Skie? I thought you were the adventurous type?"

"I am!" she declared, then she looked away. "Just not

in the dark."

"You don't have to go," I told her. "It's fine. But I've got to retrieve Winnie. Even if the place doesn't turn out to be dangerous for us, it might be for her."

As I stared into the shadows, a calico face materialized, and the cat in question trotted down the steps to wind herself around my ankles.

"Okay, she's back." Skie edged toward the door. "Now let's go downstairs. Whatever is up there has waited all this time. It can wait a few hours longer until daylight, and maybe for Gil to come along too."

"Gil's a big guy, but he's more scared of spiders than you are," said Sanjay. "Besides, I'm curious. Like Lynley said, you don't have to come. Go on back down and I'll meet you after. I can fill you in about all our great discoveries."

Skie harrumphed and swung away, but she didn't leave.

Winnie hopped onto the first step, then gave me a *come hither* look. She hopped up one more and repeated the gaze. On the third tread, she gave a full-throated meow. *Get your butt up here right now!*

"Well, I'm curious too," I admitted, "and Winnie wants me to go." I gave Sanjay a sly smile. "Shall we?"

* * *

Winnie led the way up. I came next with Sanjay behind me. Skie stood poised at the bottom, still deciding whether she would rather accompany us or stay in that dark attic annex all by herself.

We'd made it about halfway up when the moaning began, the same eerie sound I'd heard right before the stairway fell.

"What is that?" Skie hissed.

I hesitated, my hackles rising like a frightened cat.

"Just the wind," said Sanjay, though he sounded unsure.

"Yeah, the wind," I repeated. Was I trying to convince Skie or myself?

For the first time in years, the image of my childhood's haunted mansion came back to me full force.

"Come along," I whispered, continuing up the steps but now on tiptoe. I added stubbornly, "It's not haunted."

"Then why are you whispering?"

Pausing, Sanjay shined his light through the hole. An arched ceiling, nicely painted. No cobwebs, and nothing that could account for the moaning—at least not so far.

As we got to the top, Winnie dashed ahead. I quickened my pace. Sanjay was close behind me, his light flashing around like a firefly. I kept eyes trained on Winnie, not wanting to lose her again, so when the young man gasped, I had yet to see why.

"Look at this!" He was turning in circles, running the light over the hexagonal space and the furnishings within.

"What is it?" Skie called from below. "Are you alright?"

"We're fine. It's just a room. An amazing room," he added.

Suddenly light blazed from above, revealing Sanjay standing at a modern-looking wall switch. "That better?"

I took a deep breath, only then realizing I'd been holding it. "Much."

"Skie, you have to come look at this," Sanjay called down. "The light's on now. No dangerous floors, and no spiders."

Hesitantly she ascended to join us, her reticence

morphing into curiosity and then excitement as she got a good look.

"What is this place?"

"I..." I stared around at the impossible sight, but I couldn't give her a definitive answer. "I have no idea."

Sanjay was already snapping pictures with his phone. Skie stood as if rooted, peering from side to side. Winnie stalked across the floor and hopped up onto something I could only describe as an altar. There she sat, surveying her queendom.

The space was bigger than it had looked from the ground. Six high but narrow windows defined the hexagon. Where in the darkness, stars had shone through brightly, now the panes were black mirrors, wavy reflections of the interior—and of us.

Between the windows were floor-to-ceiling shelves containing books and other items. Much of the display incorporated a now-familiar motif, the pyramid and eye of the Masons. My fear that the room was abandoned, rife with dust and bugs, couldn't have been more wrong. Someone had cared for it, cleaned it, tidied it, and kept its many bits in pristine condition. Ida? Alice? Roderick Payne himself? A catnip mouse lay upon the antique rug. I glanced at Winnie who was still mimicking a statue of the cat goddess Bast. I felt relieved that this too, though secret to the rest of the world, had at one time been part of her domain.

My gaze moved to her altar-like perch, a toned wood cube about three feet in height. At each of its corners were little pointed protrusions, reminding me of horns. Atop it, besides Winnie, was an ancient-looking book, open to the center. A pair of tools, a compass and a square, had been placed across the text. These were gilt and ornately decorated, and I doubted they'd ever seen a lick of the work for which they'd been designed.

I turned to Skie who was on the opposite side of the room, examining a massive desk that held a computer and a carved wooden gavel. She picked up the gavel and slapped it into her palm.

"Is it some sort of court?"

"It's Masonic," said Sanjay, "you know—the Freemasons, Knights of Templar, the Illuminati?"

"Not really," Skie replied.

I stared at the young man. "It sounds like you do."

He nodded. "A little."

"Tell me about them."

"What would you like to know?"

I shrugged. "Pretend I know nothing, which is next to the truth. Give me the elevator pitch."

"Okay, I'll try." He cleared his throat. "Freemasonry began as a guild of skilled builders and can be traced back to Europe in the Middle Ages. They're one of the oldest fraternal organizations in the world. Masons believe honor and integrity are the keys to a meaningful existence, and that everyone has a responsibility to be a good citizen, living a virtuous and socially oriented life centered on faith in a Supreme Being."

"A religious sect?" Skie spat.

"Not really. According to their principles, no one has the right to tell another person what they must believe or think, and that includes religion. Mainly they want to make the world a better place for all."

Sanjay picked up a small carved bust of George Washington, and held it out to us. "I bet you didn't know he was a Master Mason. And Benjamin Franklin was a founding member of the first Masonic Lodge in America.

Presidents Franklin D. Roosevelt and Gerald Ford were Masons too, as was Prime Minister Winston Churchill. Mozart, Davy Crockett, Duke Ellington, Nat King Cole, Henry Ford, Paul Robeson, Buzz Aldrin…"

"I get it, Sanjay," interrupted Skie. "They're the good guys."

"How did you come to know so much about the Masons?" I asked.

"My dad's a Mason. He wants me to join, but so far I haven't had the time for such an important commitment."

I cast my gaze around the room once more, pausing when I came to the bulky desk. Besides the computer, there was a small but spectacular bronze of a bucking horse, a glass Masonic paperweight, and a bell. Behind the desk hung a silk tapestry, and woven within its pictorial scenes I recognized an apron, a set of builder's tools, and the ever-present pyramid and eye.

"This is where Payne filmed his codicil," I exclaimed. "The stipulation about FOF finding his killer." I pointed to the armchair directly in front of the wall hanging.

"What codicil?" Sanjay snapped, turning to squint at me. "What stipulation? I've heard nothing about this."

"I have!" exclaimed Skie. "Or at least the rumors that there's more to Roderick Payne's bequest than Helen's been telling us." She came and stood squarely in front of me. "I get why she kept secrets, but you, Lynley… Don't you trust us?"

I hesitated. What could I say? I'd put my foot in it, and now I had two choices: I could lie, or I could tell the truth. Since lying carries its own karmic consequences, I decided it was time to come clean.

"You're right, Skie. There is something else."

"I thought so!" Skie slapped the gavel into her palm

once more. "I thought something was going on. Come on, Lynley, we have a right to know."

I sighed. "Yes, you do, but it's complicated."

"Take your time," Sanjay said, but not in a nice way. His was a command, for he too wanted the truth.

"Shortly before his death, Roderick Payne filmed a video codicil to his will… right here." I moved around the desk and took a seat in the chair, placing my arms on the antimacassars, just as he had done. "He added a stipulation, and it's a strange one. He said that in order to inherit, Friends of Felines must find the person who murdered him."

Both Skie and Sanjay went silent. Skie was the first to work it out.

"But until last week, the cops thought Mr. Payne died of heart failure. What you're saying would mean he knew someone was going to kill him before it even happened."

Sanjay frowned. "Why would he ask a cat shelter to investigate?"

"Because he was an eccentric old coot who was accustomed to getting his way?" I offered.

"Seriously, this is ridiculous," said Skie.

I shrugged. "I agree, but he and Helen Branson had history. He trusted her where he didn't the police." I sighed. "But you see, that's the problem. There's no one at the shelter who does that sort of investigative work."

"So no inheritance?" Skie exclaimed.

"Not unless the killer is outed by someone from FOF or the lawyers come up with a loophole. At least that's the way I understand it. Helen knows more, as of course do Payne's attorneys."

"Catch a killer?" Sanjay sank into one of the antique straight-backed chairs that ringed the wall. "That's never going to happen."

Skie tossed the gavel onto the desk. "Then why are we doing all this work if we're not going to be allowed to see it through?"

"We'll figure it out, I'm sure." I gave Skie a reassuring smile that probably came off more like a grimace. "We know Payne wanted his estate to come to us, so there's got to be a way to make it happen, even if we can't solve the crime. And meanwhile, we'll keep at it. That's what Helen wants, and Debon Kroll agrees."

Winnie hopped from the altar onto my lap and settled in, burying her black nose underneath the white of her breast.

"We'll find a way," I reiterated to the forlorn pair. "FOF will get its inheritance, even if I have to find the killer myself."

For a few moments there was complete silence, then as if in response to my bravado, the weird moaning took up again. It seemed to come from all sides, more intense than before, a howl like the wind but not the wind since the night was still as stone.

My blood ran cold as I tried to pinpoint a source. Sanjay was looking too, but Skie was already halfway down the stairs and not slowing. As the sound grew louder, taking on the keening of old-time horror movies, I admitted she had a point. Instinct drove me, the primal terror of the unknown, the dark, the paranormal. I grabbed Winnie to my chest and followed Skie's lead. Sanjay hesitated for a moment, then hurtled after us.

We bolted from the annex, through the attic, and down the stairs into the hallway. I slammed the door shut, then paused, panting.

Winnie pushed out of my arms and dashed for her

room. Skie, Sanjay, and I continued downstairs to the foyer at a more sedate pace, then back out to the veranda where we took up our iced tea glasses with a silent vow not to mention the moaning ever again.

Later that night as I lay in bed listening to the sounds from the floor above, I couldn't decide whether knowing about the turret made me feel better, or if the rhythmic thumping that echoed from that hidden site now seemed more menacing than ever.

Chapter 19

Keep cats inside during extremely hot weather and make sure they have plenty of fresh water available.

Summertime in Portland seemed to be getting warmer each year. Some said it was a normal cycle; others claimed it was climate change. Whatever was causing it, I found it intolerable. Eighties, I could handle; nineties were pushing it; but when the temperature climbed to over one hundred degrees Fahrenheit, I turned into a puddle, a blob of melted goo, with only one goal in life—to find relief from the oppressive heat.

Today was one of those days. It had started out hot at six a.m. and was getting hotter by the hour. Among the updates Roderick Payne had made to his century-old mansion was air conditioning, but even so, the torridness was a tangible pressure.

I was sitting in the conservatory, drinking my third coffee of the morning, something unheard of for me, a one-cup kind of gal, but after the revelations of last night and the questions that plagued me, I was searching for a remedy. Caffeine seemed closest at hand.

Winnie had accompanied me into the greenery-shrouded room and was now exploring the giant ferns and exotic climbers—her own jungle and she, the mighty lioness. At first, I'd worried that the exotic plants might be toxic to cats, but a note in Payne's compendium assured me that only harmless plants grew there.

Just as I was considering whether I should finish my cataloging or go back to the apartment for a nap, one of my volunteers walked into the room.

"Kelley," I greeted the tall young woman. "Are you looking for me?"

"Hi, Lynley. Yes and no." She came forward and took one of the white wicker chairs. "At least not about the estate inventory. You asked me to do a little checking into the reclusive Roderick Payne. It took some digging, but I think I came up with a few items of interest."

Besides being a Friends of Felines shelter volunteer, Kelley Moro was a freelance journalist with a cat's inquisitive nature and the persistence of a terrier. With her long, blonde hair and emerald-green eyes, the willowy woman could insinuate herself into just about any environment, to weasel, flirt, or eavesdrop until she got her story.

My mood brightened. I wasn't sure what I hoped to learn—maybe something about this cloistered millionaire that would make sense of his crazy legacy—but it was obvious from the crafty look on the pretty face that her news was bound to intrigue.

"As you know," Kelley began with a sly grin, "Roderick Payne was notoriously solitary. He never married, and I found no information on an intimate relationship of any kind. If there was one, he kept it way far out of the public eye."

"Friends?" I offered. "Associates?"

"Nada, at least nothing I could turn up from the archives. By all accounts, Payne was a modern day hermit."

"Where did his money come from? He must have had business contacts."

"Most likely, but that was decades ago. He made his fortune early in life through hard work, persistence, and amazing luck. It was some sort of import-export business, and he traveled all over the world. Which explains this exotic hoard." She waved an all-inclusive hand. "He kept the best for himself."

"He was an antiques dealer?"

"Antiques, antiquities, and anything else that could make him money. That part of his life is somewhat vague. He established a corporation which is where the big bucks came from. Then when trade restrictions got tighter and laws, more strict, he sold out at a huge profit. Some careful investing, and a lot more luck, and there he was, one of the great American wealthy. He bought the mansion, moved in, and essentially never left again."

"Interesting. But it doesn't really help me with..." *The stipulation,* I almost said, but I caught myself, unsure how much I should tell Kelley about the real reason I wanted the info. So far she hadn't asked, but I knew that would come.

Maybe sooner than I'd hoped. Kelley's fine eyebrows rose. "Help with what?"

For a moment, all I could do was stare at her and wonder if she could read minds, then Frannie appeared in the doorway with a tray of refreshments, and I was saved for now.

Frannie wore a frilly blouse and a cute set of shorts. With her perfect white-blonde coif and nicely made-up face, she could have doubled as a waitress from days gone by.

"Nice legs," I commented, trying to conceal my relief at her opportune interruption.

She struck a model pose. "Pretty good for sixty, eh?"

Even Kelley had to agree it was.

"I come bearing gifts." She held out the tray—fruit, a large pitcher of iced tea, and enough glasses for an army. "Mind if I join you?"

I scooched over on the little wicker bench. "Please do."

Frannie placed the tray on the table and sat down with an *oof*.

"I thought this might take the edge off the heat." She held up the glass pitcher, its dark red contents brimming with ice. "Hibiscus honey. Can I tempt anyone?"

I looked at my half-cup of lukewarm coffee sludge and quickly agreed. Kelley also accepted the offer of the cool beverage.

"Kelley was just giving me a little history on Roderick Payne," I told Frannie.

"Wonderful! Do you think it will help you figure out who killed him?"

I shot Frannie a black look.

Her hand flew to her mouth. "Oh, sorry, Lynley. Did I spill some beans?"

"What's this?" Kelley skewered me with her green gaze. "You're looking for clues to the murder? Aren't the police supposed to be doing that?"

"Well, yes, normally," Frannie said. "And I'm sure they're working hard," she added when I nudged her with my elbow.

Kelley frowned. "Okay, hold on. I sense something going on here that has nothing to do with Payne's biography." She gave me a pointed smile. "I'd sure like to know what it is."

I suddenly felt like the cat caught licking the butter dish.

"Well?" Kelley pressed.

A figure materialized out from behind a giant parlor palm. "Are you going to tell her, Lynley?"

"Skie," I stammered. "I didn't see you there."

"I'm meeting Sanjay for break." She came around and speared a piece of cantaloupe with a long-tined fork, biting into the cool orange fruit with delight. Then she pointed the implement at me. "But go on. You were about to explain something to Kelley, weren't you?"

I looked at Frannie and she at me.

"Sorry, me and my big mouth."

"No, Skie's right," I conceded. "I think it's time. Helen may not have given the official go-ahead, but Helen isn't here, working in the thick of things like we are."

"Helen Branson?" Kelley asked. "What's our dear director keeping from us now?"

"Skie already knows part of it." I turned to the orange-haired volunteer. "But there's more. I got the news this morning." I bowed my head. "And I just can't carry it alone."

I paused, hearing the approaching chatter of Gil and Sanjay as they made their way through the potted plants from the outer door. They hesitated when they saw four pairs of female eyes staring straight at them.

"Hey, guys." Sanjay came over and stood next to Skie. "Wow, is it a party?"

"*Bonjour*, all. May I sit?" Gil asked.

"Of course," said Frannie. "We were just having a bit of refreshment. Help yourself."

"*Merci, oui*." He poured a glass of the red-colored tea and relaxed into a wicker lounge chair, stretching his long legs in front of him.

"You're just in time," Skie said to Sanjay, as they made themselves comfortable on a loveseat. "Lynley was about to let us in on a secret she's been keeping." Her eyes turned full on me, a pair of blue spotlights boring into my mind. "Another one."

"A secret?" Gil smiled cunningly. "*Ooo la la*, what fun."

"Well, this may not be quite so fun as you imagine, Gil," I said slowly.

Gil's smile evaporated. "Oh?"

Once again, I felt the pressure of everyone's attention. When Winnie returned from her adventure and hopped up on my lap, I took it as a sign.

She smoothed her cheek across my hand, then she, too, looked me in the eye.

Purrumph! *Tell them!*

So I did.

* * *

"Some of you already knew about Mr. Payne's stipulation that tasks Friends of Felines with finding his killer," I said, once I'd explained that part of the story, "but what I only just learned this morning is that Helen has officially asked me to investigate Mr. Payne's death."

I paused to let that news sink in. "I told her I wasn't a detective, but she's desperate. The lawyers haven't come up with a way to circumvent the stipulation. And it won't work if the police make an arrest. It's up to me."

"Why you?" asked Skie. "Are you some sort of Miss Marple?"

"I have had some experience with murder cases in the past," I said ambiguously.

"She sure has," Frannie attested. "More than her share."

"What can I say?" I smiled self-consciously. "I'm a cat person—naturally curious."

That got its usual round of laughter, all except for Kelley who was actively watching a droplet of condensation make a glittering path down the side of her glass.

"But it's not," she contemplated.

"Not what?"

"It's not just up to you, Lynley. You've got us."

"She's right." Skie bobbed her head up and down, sending the orange spikes flopping.

There were murmurs of agreement from all sides, with the notable exception of Gil who was busy putting together a skewer of fruit.

"Where do we begin?" Sanjay asked conspiratorially. "I've never done any sleuthing before."

"We begin with the background," said Kelley, "then lay out the facts, just like I do when I write a feature article. Go ahead, Lynley, tell us what you know."

I spent the next few minutes bringing everyone up to date. Frannie was already in on the story; Skie and Sanjay knew most of it as well; but the whole thing was news to Kelley, and to Gil.

Kelley assimilated what I'd told her. "Now give us the pertinent points as you see them," she instructed.

"Alright. Point one: Mr. Payne was murdered. We don't know why or by whom. What we do know is that somehow he predicted the crime before it happened.

"Point two: Mr. Payne was a serious recluse and had been for decades, so that seems to leave a very small suspect pool."

"Of whom we know absolutely no one," Frannie said morosely.

"That's not quite true. Which brings us to point three, the fact that whoever did it must have had access to the house, because only someone on the inside could have rigged the booby-traps."

"You're assuming the traps were set by the killer," said Sanjay. "But what if they weren't? The actual killing happened outside the house, on the grounds. Anyone in the city of Portland could have gained access there."

"Are you saying there might have been two people trying to do in poor Mr. Payne?" queried Frannie.

Sanjay shrugged. "I'm just saying it's possible."

"It is possible," I agreed. "But either way, there has to be a motive. Maybe we should start with that. If we can figure out why someone would want Mr. Payne dead, it may point to a culprit."

"Money?" Kelley suggested. "He was rich."

"Inheritance? That would make sense except his will gives most all of his assets to Friends of Felines. Helen Branson might do harm to someone she caught abusing an animal, but she'd never kill for greed, no matter how righteous a cause."

Skie frowned. "Someone else at FOF, maybe thinking they were doing the shelter a favor?"

I sighed. "But no one knew about the bequest until after Mr. Payne died. He'd been very secretive about his gifts to the shelter. Even his monthly contributions were donated anonymously."

Kelley gazed out to the garden. "Someone might have known—someone with inside information. Or they could have found out by some means we haven't thought of."

"I suppose," I admitted. "But hard to confirm. I personally can't imagine anyone at the shelter killing another human being in cold blood. Let's put that one aside for now."

"What about someone who imagined they would

inherit?" Frannie queried.

"Payne didn't have any living relatives," said Kelley. "I checked."

"Mr. Payne may not have had family, but maybe a different kind of relationship? Friend? Employee?"

"The groundsman Cox was led to believe he was going to get something upon Mr. Payne's death," I said. "Payne promised him his tiny house and a sum of money for upkeep, but he never put it in the will."

"Mr. Cox must have been disappointed when he found out," Frannie commented.

"More like angry," I huffed.

Sanjay looked up. "Angry enough to kill?"

"What good would that do if he wasn't going to get anything out of it?" said Skie.

I nodded. "I don't think Cox knew about the omission until the will was read. But to kill in anger? Neither the booby-trap scenario nor the injection of potassium were hotheaded actions."

Skie reached over and speared a watermelon chunk. It looked like a good idea, so I did the same. There's something undeniably *summer* about watermelon, and though the olden days of spitting seeds into the river have passed with the advent of the seedless varieties, the flavor remains a special treat.

For a moment I was transported to childhood, long before I knew of all the strife in the world, long before I was faced with hatred, greed, and murder. I tried to float away on that happy memory but found it impossible—there was too much going on in the here and now.

"What about the other employees?" asked Kelley.

I wrestled my thoughts back from summers past. "I'm not sure about Alice the housekeeper, but Ida received a condo and a pension. She was very pleased with her gift, but she loved the old man—she would never have hurried his demise, even if it did mean she'd be set up for life."

"Are you sure?" put in Frannie. "Your Detective Croft must have thought something was up when she searched her room."

"I suppose. But Ida seemed honestly indebted to Mr. Payne, and we haven't heard anything about her since. Not that we would necessarily—the police are notorious for keeping secrets."

"So that brings us back to Alice," said Skie.

"That Alice is an odd one," Frannie mused. "She hasn't said two words to me since I've been here."

"That's nothing," I scoffed. "She's avoided me from the very start. I found it strange at first, but then I got used to it. But maybe there's more to her reticence than bashfulness.

"I've never talked to her either," said Kelley "It might be something to consider."

Sanjay sat forward, elbows on his knees. "I've talked to her. Why not?" he added when I turned in surprise. "She and I've had plenty of conversations. She's really nice. Payne left her a small endowment as well. She seemed pleased."

"How much?" asked Kelley.

"Not enough to kill for."

"That sum can be less than you'd think," Kelley remarked. "It all depends on what you want versus what you have."

"You don't think she could have done it?" I asked Sanjay.

"Naw, of course not."

Kelley had that faraway look in her green eyes again.

"Then why is she avoiding Lynley, Frannie, and me?"

"Maybe she likes boys better than girls," Skie joked.

"I'm just a likable person," boasted Sanjay. He spread his arms wide, then blew a few kisses into the air.

"This is not a game!" Gil burst out with sudden vehemence. "This person has killed once and could kill again if provoked."

All eyes swung to the antiques dealer, who had, so far, been uncharacteristically mum. In his urgency, I noted he had forgone a bit of his French accent.

"You're right, Gil." I turned to the others. "And it's true, if we go poking our noses into murder, we are treading on dangerous ground."

"Well, I hope you heed your own words, Lynley," said Frannie. "You're the one who likes to prance into danger without a second thought."

"Oh, I always give it a second thought, believe me."

"You're right, of course," said Kelley, "but talking can't hurt. If we could come up with some leads or directions, then put the detectives onto them, it would be almost like solving the crime ourselves. Possibly enough to satisfy the stipulation."

I nodded thoughtfully. "That makes sense. But let's just keep this to ourselves for now. I don't want the whole shelter running around with deerstalker hats and magnifying glasses."

Skie gave me a questioning look.

"The Great Detective Sherlock Holmes," Frannie translated for the girl. "She doesn't want everyone acting like amateur sleuths."

Sanjay had been staring out the window at Cox who was watering the roses with a vengeance. "Maybe it has something to do with the Freemasons" he speculated.

"The Freemasons?" Gil echoed.

"Oh, yeah!" Skie exclaimed. "And the secret room."

That got everyone's attention in a heartbeat.

"A secret room?" Gil's head spun around to face his apprentice. "You discovered the secret room?"

"It's in the turret. We'd missed it before, but last night Winnie led us right to it. I was meaning to tell you..."

Gil leapt from his chair, bumping the wicker table and setting the tea glasses clattering.

"Show me!" he commanded. "Show me now!"

Chapter 20

Cats can't see things that are right under their noses—literally.

"Show me this room!" Gil repeated.

"Don't get your panties in a knot," said Sanjay, though he didn't waste any time jumping out of his seat at his employer's command. The others followed suit—who doesn't want to see a secret room?

"The attic," I said. "The access is in the attic. We discovered a ladder that goes up from there into the turret. Actually Winnie found it. I have a feeling she knew about it all along. The room is filled with what Sanjay says are Masonic items—a sort of an altar, chairs around the walls, a big desk, tapestries. All sorts of stuff."

No one was listening to my chatter, too busy talking amongst themselves, so I gave it up. A picture is worth a thousand words, I reminded myself, and a real-life look-see beat a photograph by miles.

The group headed for the top floor, Winnie running on ahead. Gil came next with Sanjay and Skie just a few steps behind him. Kelley had paused to grab a camera out of her bag but still managed to keep up. Frannie and I lingered at the rear.

Ascending into the scorching attic was like entering a fire zone—the air conditioning may have worked its miracle throughout the main house, but it didn't extend to that area, and the temperature in the stuffy, close room must have been well over a hundred degrees. In spite of the heat, we crowded in, and aside from a few gasps and groans, all attention was set singularly on the new find.

Since Skie, Sanjay, and I had basically run away the night before without putting away the ladder or closing the trap door, Gil had no difficulty locating the otherwise-elusive entry. He stood at the base, staring upward in the classic pose of an explorer. With a ray of sunlight from the bright turret streaming down upon him, setting his blue hair alight with sparks of gold, he might have been a mythical god.

Then he turned to us, to me. His face soured, and all resemblance to the transcendent vanished.

"No one must enter," he commanded in a purely local accent instead of the French one. "This area is now off limits."

He hefted the ladder upward, letting it slide back into place on its counterweight, then slammed the trapdoor shut with a bang.

"But… why?" Skie stuttered.

Gil's tone softened. "I must get an expert to evaluate the contents, Skie. Someone who is versed in Freemasonry must make an assessment before we can take this further. The place may hold valuable items. Items that are sacred," he added, "and must not be defiled."

"Everything in this house is valuable," Skie retorted. "Why should this be any different?"

"I think it has to do with that *sacred* part. Isn't that right Gil?" I turned to the man, my senses tingling. "Do you know something about the Masonic Order?"

"*Mais non*, Lyn-dear." His look was all innocence, and his accent was back with a vengeance. "*Je pense que* we should be careful, is all."

Kelley snapped a couple of photos of the trap door

area. "Careful of what?"

For a moment, Gil hesitated. A droplet of sweat began to roll down his face. Temperature, or tension? "I am in charge of the appraisals, *oui*? I say we wait. Must I install a lock?"

"Of course not," I replied, feeling my own trickle of cold sweat ice down my back. "No one will bother the place until you give us the go-ahead."

"*Bon*. Now shall we retire to a cooler atmosphere? *C'est pas froid ici!*"

He was right about that, I thought to myself, translating his comment with the dab of French I'd learned in grade school. *It is not cold here.*

* * *

With the turret declared off limits and the attic hotter than Hades, everyone went to work elsewhere, thankful to get back to the air-conditioned portions of the house. If they were reflecting on the revelations of Payne's stipulation and the mysterious secret room, they didn't seem inclined to discuss it, which was fine with me.

I was seated on the stairs with Winnie by my side, pondering my next move and thinking about Gil. I'd never seen him so angry before, though truth be told, up until this venture our relationship had been rarely more than glib banter at his antique shop. Still, I thought we were friends. I couldn't guess what had made him snap like that—it was so contrary to his usual demeanor. The heat? The pressure of the big job? Something in his private life that had nothing to do with the estate sale or us? Everyone had a breaking point. He'd probably waltz back in any minute, his old colorful self again, and all would be forgotten. I hoped so. This new stern, controlling Gil was not someone with whom I wished to work.

My hopes were dashed a moment later when the antiques dealer came stomping into the foyer. With one look, Winnie scorched up the staircase to the sanctity of her room.

"Zut alors!" Gil grabbed his bag from the side table and was about to head out the door when he noticed me. He gave a little jump of surprise, then sighed. "Oh, Lyn-dear. I did not see you there."

I rose and stood gripping the smooth wood of the balustrade. "Are you leaving?"

For a moment, he was silent. *"Oui."* Another sigh. "Forgive me, *s'il vous plaît*, but I must go out for a bit. I will return soon."

"Gil…" I hesitated, unsure what I wanted to say. "Is everything okay?"

"But of course!" he shot back far too quickly. The pasted smile that went along with the statement did nothing to ease my concern.

"You know you can talk to me." I went over and put a hand on his arm. He seemed to fold in on himself at my touch.

"I'm sorry, Lyn-dear. I think the enormity of this task is getting to me. Such details! Such responsibility! *Zut alors!"*

"You're not alone in this, you know. We're all here for you. And I can get more volunteers if you think that would help."

"Mais non!" he said quickly. "More would just be in the way."

"Is this about the turret? The Masonic things we found?"

Whatever emotions Gil had been feeling, his face now blanked into stone. *"Pardon* but I must go."

He made to leave, then turned suddenly and looked me in the eye. "Lyn-dear, you must promise not to go snooping in that room again."

I took a step backward. "No, of course not..."

"Because I know you." He gave a short and unconvincing laugh. "You have the *curiosité d'un chat*."

"Curiosity of a cat," I translated. "Yes, you're right, but I'll do as you ask. I would like to know more about it though," I added. "Maybe when the expert comes, I can tag along? Is that where you're going now? To get someone?"

Gil gave me a look of utter grief, then spun on his heel and rushed out the door.

The blast of outside heat combined with my concern over Gil's aberrant behavior left me lightheaded. I sunk back down on the step and gazed around for Winnie, but she was long gone.

"Ahem."

I glanced up to see Sanjay hovering in the parlor doorway. "Was that Gil?"

"Yeah. He left. He wouldn't say where."

"Shoot." For a moment the young man seemed flustered, then he shrugged. "Oh, well, I guess we'll just go on without him."

From his comment, I assumed he would return to whatever he had been doing, but instead he continued into the room. As he did, I saw a bowed figure following in his shadow.

He gently pushed the woman out in front of him. "Lynley, I'd like to introduce you to Alice. Alice, Lynley."

"Hello, ma'am," Alice muttered, her eyes riveted to the parquet floor.

"Alice!" I rose and held out my hand. "So nice to

officially meet you—something more than relaying messages or texting."

She took the hand and gave it a brief and gentle shake. "Pleased to meet you too."

Now that I was finally in closer proximity, with the elusive housekeeper making no move to disappear into the woodwork as she had done on previous encounters, I took the opportunity to study her in more detail. I guessed her to be in her early forties, not nearly so young as I had imagined. But it wasn't just her waif-like appearance and her thin-boned structure that gave the impression of youth—her brown hair, pulled into a loose ponytail at the nape of the neck, was shiny and soft with natural curl; her face glowed with health. I had yet to see her eyes, the lowered lashes concealing their color, but in spite of her deference, she showed no signs of anxiety. Her hands, linked in front of her, were at rest.

"Alice has something to tell you, Lynley. I think you'll be interested."

"Oh? Would you like to go into the parlor and sit down?"

"No, ma'am. I have work to do."

"Alright, Alice. But there's no need to call me ma'am. I'm not your employer."

"Yes, ma'am."

Harrumph! "Call me Lynley… *please*."

"Yes, Lynley. If you say so."

"Now what was it you wanted to tell me?

Alice straightened her apron, then shoved her hands deep into the pockets. "I know about that place… the one up above the attic."

"The turret with all the Masonic paraphernalia?"

"Yes, ma'am… *Lynley*. Mr. Payne would have me clean

up there every third Thursday of the month. It was never dirty… Just a bit of dusting and vacuum. Took me no time at all."

"What is all that stuff? Do you know?"

"Not really. But I do know it was important to the mister, sacrosanct in fact. I asked him if it were a chapel, what with the altar and all that. He said no. Then he said it had to do with the *Order of the Masons*." She spoke the words carefully, almost reverently. "That it was a *Masonic Lodge*, and that I was to tell no one about it, ever. Not even Miss Whide or Cox."

"But Ida must have known, mustn't she?"

"I don't know. I did as I was bid and never mentioned the room to anyone, not a living soul. And no one ever mentioned it to me."

I thought for a minute. "A lodge? Isn't that where members have their meetings?"

"It can be," said Sanjay. "The term, lodge, may refer to either the meeting place or the organization itself."

"Alice, did Mr. Payne have people in? Did they go up to the room to hold meetings?"

"No, never. No one ever came."

"You're not here at night, though," I mused. "Maybe the meetings were held in the evenings."

She looked up from the floor long enough to roll her eyes, which turned out to be brown. "A housekeeper always knows, ma'am. No one ever came through these doors besides the caterers, the workmen, and us."

Chapter 21

Cats can get heatstroke when their body temperature rises over a certain amount. This is a medical emergency because a cat with heatstroke declines very fast. If it's hot and your cat begins panting, open-mouth breathing, becoming overly restless, salivating, stumbling, or vomiting, seek veterinary help immediately.

Sanjay returned to his photography project, and Alice disappeared into her kitchen. I sat back down on the bottom step which was fast becoming my new office and contemplated what to do next. I thought about grabbing my red journal and working on the *Mystery of the Murder of Roderick Payne*—maybe writing would help clear my mind. Then I thought about getting off my backside and going to assist with the estate auction prep—the other volunteers had been doing well, but they could always use another hand. Though it crossed my mind to sneak back up to the secret room, I squelched that urge—I'd given Gil my word. Finally, I considered going up to the apartment and taking a nap with Winnie.

But none of those things piqued my interest, not even the nap, and suddenly I realized what was bothering me—I was homesick. I'd gotten so wrapped up in the Payne drama that I'd begun to think of it as my life, but it was not. My life was back across town in an old Victorian home with nine cats and a generation of memories.

Frannie was gathering up the dishes from the

conservatory when I found her.

"I'm going to run home to check on Seleia and the cats. I talked to her this morning—Seleia, not the cats—and she said they're surviving the heat, but without air conditioning, it must be grueling."

"Poor kitties—I mean poor Seleia as well, but cats can suffer too if their people aren't careful."

"She knows what to watch for. She says so far they've just been melting into the floor like little furry puddles or hanging out in front of the box fans. She's given them ice in their water bowls. But I'd like to check, just in case she needs help."

I stood at the window wall, inadvertently tapping the table with a fingernail. Frannie began to load another half-empty tea glass onto the tray but paused mid-move, stuck there like a serving girl in a Dutch painting.

"Are you thinking about the turret?" I surmised.

"In a way. Actually, I was thinking about Gil. He was so vehement about not letting people go up there."

"Yes, that surprised me too."

She jiggled the glass in amongst the others on the crowded tray. "He's usually so..."

"Fabulous?" I chuckled.

"Something like that."

"He puts on a good act, but he's really very serious about his antiques. I guess it makes sense that if he doesn't know the value of something, he'd want to consult with someone who does."

"Sure, I understand that. But he didn't even go up to see what was there. He seemed angry about something, even before he got to the attic. Angry, or afraid."

I looked up sharply. "Afraid? Of what?"

She shrugged. "Fear often masquerades as fury. Just

sayin'."

Frannie hefted the tray off the table and sashayed out of the room. I watched her go, realizing she might have something there. Fear and anger can look very much alike.

But how did that apply here? Why would Gil be afraid of a room full of symbols?

* * *

As I drove home, I continued to mull over the possibility that something had got Gil scared, but I still couldn't reason out what. My guess was it had to do with the Masons. I knew nothing about the ancient fraternal order besides what I'd gleaned from the movies; according to those, the philanthropic society had spawned evil spinoffs that practiced a wide range of hideous secret rites. I doubted it was true in real life, but who knew? I decided to do a little research when I got back to the mansion where it wasn't so damnably hot!

I felt guilty as I pulled up to the curb in front of my house. There I was, living in the lap of air-conditioned luxury while my granddaughter suffered the terrible heat taking care of my cats. It wasn't right, but I didn't know what to do about it. I'd already tried calling a HVAC company to come install something, but they were booked through October. The nice man suggested I get a portable unit at a building supply store, but when I searched around, such items were out of stock for the foreseeable future, something the HVAC guy probably already knew.

Seleia was waiting for me at the door with a sly grin on her face.

"Come in, Grandmother" she beckoned playfully.

"What?" I asked, even before saying hello. Something was up.

She didn't answer, but the grin widened, and she stepped aside.

Doing as she bid, I warily entered, then stopped abruptly in the hallway. With a giggle, Seleia shut the door behind me.

"Notice anything different?" she teased, moving around me into the living room.

As a matter of fact, I did.

First off, it wasn't nearly as hot as I thought it should be. In fact, it wasn't hot at all! The air in the room was sweet and cool, a perfect temperature. But how? Even my grandmother's trick of putting a tray of ice in front of a fan had never worked that well.

The second deviation from the norm was something more tangible. Sitting on the couch, feet up on the ottoman with Tinkerbelle curled in his lap, was Fredric.

Fredric Delarosa was the embodiment of the cool young man. In his early twenties—he never would tell me his exact age—he was ready to take on the world. Dusky red curls and hazel-green eyes that always danced with mischief gave the impression of a tall leprechaun, and when he and Seleia had first started dating, I worried about that mischief. As time went by, however, I came to find him gentle, thoughtful, and kind. He treated her like a princess, and he treated me like a queen.

Still, none of that explained why he was lounging on my sofa like he owned the place.

"Fredric…?" I began.

Fredric beamed. "Hey, Lynley. Welcome home."

I looked at Seleia. She was smiling too.

"Well, Grandmother? It's like that game we used to play when I was a kid—*I spy with my little eye*. Except this requires spying with all your senses."

"I spy a man on my couch," I joked—sort of.

"Correct. But what else?"

Little had discovered my homecoming and was winding her soft body around my ankles. I picked her up and held her in my arms. Her fur was cool to the touch.

"It's..." I began tentatively. "It's... *C'est pas chaud!*"

Seleia and Fredric looked at each other. "Pardon?"

"Sorry. I've been spending too much time with Gil at the estate. It translates to something like, *it isn't hot*. And it's not! But how...?"

Seleia took me by the arm and led me into the kitchen where a boxy white robot hunched beneath the window. It was humming softly as it breathed cold air out of its middle.

"It only cools the downstairs, and I closed off your office and the room in the back where you keep the foster cats—this house is huge!" she said needlessly since I knew exactly how many rooms the two-story Victorian held. "But isn't it wonderful? Fredric installed it this morning."

"Why didn't you tell me?"

"He came over right after you called. The production company had to shut down filming because of the heat, and Fredric was able to wangle this unit from the set since they weren't going to be using it. Isn't it amazing? To be honest, I wasn't sure how much more I'd be able to take without roasting."

Seleia sashayed back into the living room and sank down on the couch beside Fredric. I stood watching, amazed at the peaceful scene.

"Well, all I can say is thank you. I'm so grateful to have Seleia here to look after the cats while I do this little job..."

"Not so little, so I hear," Fredric replied. "A live-in cat sitter for a dead millionaire? Sounds exciting."

"Oh, it is that!" I exclaimed before I could stop myself.

"Really?" Seleia commented. "I thought you said it was pretty boring."

I froze, then looked away.

"What?" It was Seleia's turn to sense a disturbance in the Force.

I sighed. "Okay, there have been some developments." I let Little jump down to the floor. "And I'll tell you all about them after I say hello to the clowder."

I found the felines in question scattered around the newly air-conditioned rooms. Accustomed to having the run of the house, they had found ingenious places to repose in their considerably smaller space. Dirty Harry was in the cubby by the television. Big Red reclined on the window perch soaking up the sun like a golden cat god. Mab and Violet had retired to the kitchen where they lay on the cool Marmoleum, their paws touching. They looked up at me briefly, then their eyes closed as they drifted back into their afternoon nap. I found Emilio and Hermione stretched long on opposite ends of the guest bed. Elizabeth came wobbling up from out of nowhere—who knew where she'd been hiding herself.

"Where's Solo?" I asked, coming back into the living room with both Elizabeth and Little in tow. "Did she go back under the couch?"

Seleia giggled and pointed to the white throw pillow behind her. On top of it, like a tiny queen, sat Solo. She opened her eyes and gave me a love blink.

"Oh!" I came over and touched her sideburn. "You are a sly girl, aren't you? Your pretty white fur blends perfectly with that pillow."

I took a seat in the armchair, at peace now that I knew all my family was safe. "She looks wonderful, Seleia!

Living with you obviously agrees with her."

Seleia reached around and stroked Solo's snowy back. "She's good for me too. I'm going to miss her when I go to live in the dorm."

I frowned. "Do you think your mother will take care of her…?" I caught my disapproval and tempered it. "I mean, I know Lisa's busy. Will she have time to spend on a cat?"

"You won't believe this, Lynley, but Mother has fallen in love." Again she passed her hand down the sleek fur. "She absolutely dotes on Solo. And I'll be home often. It's not like I'm going out of state. But you promised to tell us something—something I predict to be momentous."

"Oh, that." For a few moments, there in the company of family and cats, I'd forgotten about murders and murderers, about secret rooms and friends acting weird. I'd forgotten about the Freemasons, evil spinoffs, and how much I really didn't know about their truths and lore. Now it all came flooding back, a corporeal weight on my shoulders, and I suddenly realized, as with Seleia and the heat, I wasn't sure how much more of it I could take.

* * *

I laid out the tale as best I could, recognizing as I told it how bizarre it sounded. Thankfully both Seleia and Fredric were accustomed to my involvement in things not quite right and allowed me to go on without scoffs, queries, or interruptions.

"So you see," I said matter-of-factly, "all I need to do is catch this killer. Then the auction can go forward, the mansion can be sold, and I can come home." That last part came out as a sigh. How I wished that day were today, that I could just stay where I was, in my favorite chair in my living room in my house with my cats.

Then I thought of Winnie, the bright calico spot in a dark, convoluted saga. Winnie needed me, and I couldn't let her down.

Chapter 22

"Build a better mousetrap, and the world will beat a path to your door" is a phrase attributed to Ralph Waldo Emerson in the late nineteenth century. If he were currently alive, he might have changed "mousetrap" to "...litter box," for all the unique and inventive models on the market today.

I'd hung around my house for a few more hours. Seleia, Fredric, and I ordered Thai food from the local restaurant and ate take-out in the cool of the newly air-conditioned kitchen. I fed the cats, administered meds, and cleaned the litter boxes for old times' sake. Strangely, I found I'd rather missed that basic chore. Winnie's self-cleaning robo-box required only occasional monitoring, and that job was incorporated into Alice's schedule.

When I finally left for Payne House, Seleia and her beau were about to watch a movie, something from a comic book universe that Fredric recommended. I was glad he chose an action genre and not a romantic one. I kept reminding myself my granddaughter was no longer a child but a grown woman, and a smart one at that, but it didn't change my instinct to protect.

Both Fredric and Seleia had taken the news that I was sleuthing again with amazing poise. They volunteered to help any way they could. I thanked them profusely but insisted that caring for my cats was more than enough. I kept the offer in mind however—Fredric was extremely innovative when it came to thinking outside the litter box.

The mansion was vacant when I arrived, the volunteers gone to their various homes. A light twinkled in Cox's tiny house suggesting he was in for the night as well. There was a note from Alice in the foyer reporting that Winnie was asleep in the pantry cupboard in case I couldn't find her. The message was signed, *With Warm Regards*—a bit formal but a step in the right direction since this was the first time the housekeeper had initiated any sort of communication at all.

Winnie had quit her cubby and was now sitting at the top of the staircase, the mistress of all she surveyed. She rose, stretched, and meowed when she saw me. *Where have you been? I've been waiting.*

"I was visiting my granddaughter," I replied as I joined her and scritched her sideburns.

She enjoyed the contact for a moment, then recoiled. *Ug! You smell like cats!*

"Just my cats. Don't worry, I didn't bring them back with me."

Continuing into the apartment, Winnie trotting beside me, I was surprised how at home I felt there. Though I missed my own place, this little Winnie-world had gotten under my skin. So luxurious, so self-contained—an introvert's paradise. As long as the caterers brought food and the housekeeper replaced the used towels, I could live there forever.

I fed Winnie a packet of ahi tuna, then pulled out the fresh blackberry tart I'd ordered from the menu. I doused it with vegan custard, grabbed a prefilled glass of iced mint water, and took them both to the table by the window. It was later than I'd thought, the sun already down behind the West Hills, leaving only a slash of orange lingering at the horizon. The long twilit hillside was awash with purple, and in the distance, skyscrapers lit the city like a birthday cake. A single star, a planet, hovered in the velvet indigo, a reminder that we were not alone in this amazing universe.

As I was appreciating the nocturnal panorama, something hit the window with a thunk. I jumped, splashing my mint water and nearly toppling my dessert. The pane had been closed to let the AC do its job, but now I opened it. It didn't take more than a breath to discover the source of the disturbance.

A forceful gust of hot, dry wind ripped the sash right out of my hand. Like a blast from a giant oven, it swarmed into the room, shuffling papers and setting the cat wands to rattling in their custom-crafted stand. As I beheld the darkening sky, I could now see the outline of clouds moving, black on black. The one star winked out, leaving only gloom.

A summer storm! I thought with a combination of excitement and panic. As a child, I'd enjoyed those fast-moving tempests with all their untamed bluster. I loved the way they broke into the still heat of the season, and I'd stand on the front porch watching the lightning and sideways rain until my mother made me come inside again. But as I grew up, I learned the dangers of those gales. I still retained the childhood wonder, but now it was edged with fear.

What form would this storm take? Would there be rain? Thunder? Lightning? With the area so dry, lightning could be catastrophic. I thought about the wildfires that had devastated the Northwest in the past few years. Whole towns wiped out, families displaced. None of those fires had made it to the Portland city limits, though one had come far too close. This summer was hotter than ever, setting records for triple-digit temperatures. Were we in for another season of choking air and brown skies, the sun hanging above us like a blood orange mired in sludge?

It hadn't happened yet, but it could. It could happen tonight! Then what would I do, all alone in a mansion surrounded by trees?

Stop it! I told my overactive imagination. *There's absolutely no danger…*

But there was danger, wasn't there? Danger of another sort. A killer on the loose. Which would get me first—a natural disaster or a man-created one?

Me-row-row-row! *Yes, be afraid. You have reason to worry.*

I looked at the calico cat as she lay prone in her poof. "Thanks a lot."

I slammed the window shut and flipped the latch. I stared at my tart, then rose and put it back in the fridge—I'd lost my appetite. Taking the mint water to the bedside table, I began to get ready for bed.

After my bathroom regimen, I threw back the coverlet and slipped between the Egyptian cotton sheets. Winnie abandoned her poof to come up beside me, a soft presence. I set my glasses on the nightstand, then clicked off the lights with the remote control. For a few moments, I gazed at the ceiling, softly lit by the red glow from the clock on the bookshelf. Outside, the storm ebbed and flowed—tumult, then calm, then tumult again. The gusts pummeled the house like a boxer, and as I listened in anticipation for the next punch, I grew more and more on edge.

Finally I turned the light back on. Getting out of bed, I gathered Winnie's carrier, a portable bowl, and a bottle of water. I put the bowl and water in the carrier, added a few pouches of dry food, and placed it by the door, just in case.

* * *

I'd gone back to bed and must have fallen asleep, because next I knew, something woke me. I thought it might have been Winnie, but she was still curled up oblivious. The sound came again, a sort of buzz-chime sequence—my phone.

Gazing around the room, I saw it glimmering on the table by the window. I considered not answering but couldn't take the chance it was something important, at least not without checking to see who was making the call.

I glanced at the clock—twelve-forty-two. I'd been asleep for nearly two hours. I was surprised I'd slept at all, what with the chaos of the windstorm, but obviously I had. Now, as a new sort of panic caught hold, I was wide awake again.

In the short instance it took me to grab my glasses, jump out of bed, and cross the room, my mind laid out all sorts of scenarios for a call at that late hour. An emergency at home—with Seleia, with the cats! An issue with my mother—she was eighty-four after all! But the name on the screen was neither Seleia nor Mum. Instead, it read Jack Hess, the hospice patient.

Why would Jack be calling me so late? I wondered. Why would he call me at all? If it were health-related, he should be ringing the nurse at the hospice main number, not a therapy cat volunteer. But people get confused, people panic. Whatever he needed, I'd do my best to field his call.

"Hello?"

"Lynley? It's Jack. Remember me?"

The voice on the line sounded slightly breathless but not overly so, not that of a man in crisis. "Of course, Jack. Are you okay?"

"Yeah, sure. Sorry if I startled you. But I thought you'd

want to know."

"Know what?" I wasn't tracking. "Is this about your cats?"

"Naw, they're fine. It's that light in your tower up there on the hill. It's on again."

"Light?"

"The one we were talking about when you were here. You seemed pretty interested, and it is a weird thing. I checked my records just to be sure—this is the first time it's been lit since old Payne died. I figured you'd want to know."

"The light in the turret? And it's on now?"

"Yup! Beaming straight up into the sky like the one at that Vegas hotel."

There was a pause. "Lynley, you there?"

"Yes, I'm here. I was asleep, but thanks for telling me."

"Oh, sorry about that. I don't sleep much at night, and I guess I figure everybody's the same. Well, you go back to dreamland now. Sorry to have bothered you."

"No, no bother," I said quickly. "I really appreciate it. Hey, Jack," I added. "Did Hospice get back to you about sending a volunteer to help with your cats?"

"Sure did, Lynley, and I can't thank you enough. Turns out there's a nice little volunteer girl lives just down the street. She's coming in once a day to clean the boxes and anything else that needs doing for the Fantastics. Yesterday she gave them flea stuff and clipped their paw-daggers. She really knows her way around cats!"

"I'm glad. You take care. And thanks again for the heads-up about the light. I'll go check it out right now. And please," I added, "don't hesitate to call if it happens again, no matter what the time."

"You still there looking after Payne's kitty?"

I answered in the affirmative.

"Oh, okay." He hesitated, long enough for me to wonder if he had hung up.

"Is there something else?"

"Not really. It's just… well, you be careful, okay?"

Then he did ring off. I sat holding the phone, digesting that last comment. The man almost sounded scared.

A nice guy looking out for his fellow humans, I told myself as I readied to check out the mysterious light. From my window, I saw nothing, but then I wouldn't if it were shining straight up like Jack had described. I'd have to go outside for that.

"Want to go for a walk?" I asked Winnie as I threw a robe over my nightclothes and scooched into my slippers.

Winnie raised her head long enough to shoot me a sleepy look, then gave a kitty sigh and tucked her nose under her paw. I'd be doing this investigation alone.

The house seemed eerily quiet as I padded down the stairs and through the great rooms to the kitchen. I unlocked the back door, stepped outside, then listened for the click-thunk as the smart lock reset itself.

Moving quickly to the veranda, I turned and stared back up at the massive façade. A soft light shone from the kitchen. A few other illuminations were scattered around the building—night lights on timers. I picked out the window of my apartment, also aglow. Otherwise, naught.

Venturing out onto the lawn, I looked again. No radiant column beaming up into the sky, and no lights inside the turret. Had Jack been seeing things? Or had the phenomenon ended? Whichever, there seemed to be little reason for me to be outdoors in the middle of the night staring at nothing.

The hot wind still blew the occasional bluster, but the

storm itself seemed to have passed. In the black tapestry of sky, stars glimmered like crystals. A few tattered clouds floated across, obscuring their brilliance, then as if pulling back a curtain, revealing their splendor once again.

I was about to head back to my room when, out of the corner of my eye, I caught movement. Turning quickly, I thought I saw a shape, a shadow disappearing around the side of the house. I froze, my eyes fixed on the spot where the shadow had been, but it was gone now, leaving nothing to show for its passing. Unsure what to do, I listened, but all I heard was the rustle of leaves skittering across the pavers and the chirp of crickets in the bushes nearby.

For an indeterminate time, I waited. Then, with a rush of adrenaline so profound it hurt, I bolted for the house. As I crossed the veranda, I glanced up at my apartment. There was a cat silhouetted in the window, staring down at me.

My fingers fumbled the door code numbers, but I managed to get it on the second try. Once inside, I felt a bit safer, but I couldn't shake the sense that something was off. I double-checked to make sure the alarm had reset, then proceeded to tour the house, inspecting locks and latches. I'm almost embarrassed to mention I retrieved the signed Mickey Mantle baseball bat from the collectables room and carried it with me. *Almost*.

Finally I made it back to the apartment and locked that door as well. Whatever the shadow may have been—man, woman, or werewolf—they were not going to get anywhere near Winnie and me.

Not bothering to take off my robe, I lay down on top the bedcovers. Winnie was still in the window, watching the wild night things that only cats see.

Chapter 23

Cats have over one hundred vocalization sounds, but most of them are meant for us. Cats rarely meow to each other.

In my dream, I was in a department store, or maybe it was a library. It might have been a mirror universe version of the Payne House for all I knew. Great staircases ran between the many floors, and people were rushing up and down them, busily heading from one place to the next. The clatter of their hard-soled shoes on the marble made a drumbeat tattoo. How was I expected to sleep through such a racket?

I sat up, suddenly wondering why I was trying to sleep at all in such an obviously public place. Quickly I glanced down at myself—thankfully I wasn't naked…

I woke, breathing a sigh of relief upon realizing it was only a dream. There was no store, no library. I was in my little, very private apartment with Winnie beside me.

Winnie beside me, yes, but not curled in slumber anymore. The calico was sitting straight and tall, ears forward, whiskers back. Her mouth was slightly open as she tasted the air through her vomeronasal organ. Whatever phantom she perceived had got her fur standing on end.

Then I heard it too. Not the clattering of many footfalls, as it was in my dream—just a single set. It came from outside, but not from below. The clack, clack, clack was level with my room, and climbing!

I'd kept the Louisville Slugger after my manic tour of the house and now hoisted it again as I crept to the window and cracked it open. Peeking out, I could see nothing amiss—no moving shadows or shapes—but the sound of footfalls on stairs continued.

What stairs? I wondered in alarm. Not the grand stairway in the foyer with its antique carpeting, nor the kitchen stairs which were made of wood. These steps clattered like metal, as with a fire escape. But there wasn't one, at least none I knew of. Could I have missed such an obvious feature?

The wind was rising again, bristling across the landscape and obscuring all other sounds. I had two options: I could wait until the wind died down in hopes of catching another clue, or I could go back to bed, reasonably assured I'd been hearing things.

The choice was simple—bed it was. There had already been too many interruptions to my precious sleep cycle for one night. I was exhausted and at that point doubted my own sanity. Besides, if there really was someone doing a Spiderman up my outside wall—and the more I thought about it, that seemed a big "if"—the alarm would go off once they tried anything funny.

With a sigh, I turned back to my bed. I was ready to let it go as a bizarre offshoot of my dream when I saw Winnie. She was standing on my pillow, fluffed out in her Halloween cat mode.

Re-owww! she cried. *Danger!* Winnie had no intention of letting this go.

With a flying leap, she was across the floor and out the cat door before I could stop her.

Rats! I sighed. At any other time, I wouldn't have minded, but something about that last fear-filled meow gave me pause.

Winnie was unlike any other cat I'd known. Her meows produced actual words that I heard in my head. Was she speaking? I very much doubted it. I'd never quite decided whether the odd, vocal communication between myself and the calico was real or a figment of my fancy, but I'd played along. Up until now, her messages had been relatively benign, but her last one changed all that. Had the cat just warned me of danger, or was it all in my mind? Either way, my pins-and-needles nerves were one hundred percent real.

I had the overwhelming sense I needed to get Winnie back to the safety of the apartment. Though she wouldn't like it, it was the best place for her. But I had to catch her first.

Still in my robe and slippers, I unbolted the door and stepped into the hallway wondering where to start. She could be anywhere—bedrooms, parlor, kitchen, the pantry where Alice sometimes left treats. Then I heard a yowl from down the corridor. There were no words attached to this vocalization, yet I knew she was calling to me.

Seeing her hunched a few doorways along, I tried the *here, kitty, kitty* approach, hoping she would return of her own accord. Instead, she moved farther from me, stopping only long enough to give another demanding cry. Feeling uneasy, frustrated, and a bit sorry for myself, I followed.

The wind had ceased, and the only sound in the old house was the shuffle of my feet along the carpet and my breaths which I noted were coming far too fast.

"Winnie," I began, then cut off sharply. Something about the shrill of my voice breaking into the stillness wasn't right. I was *giving away my position*. The *psychopath would find me*, and then… *and then…*

I paused. What was I doing? There was no psychopath, at least not in the house. Whatever had got Winnie spooked, it couldn't have been human.

The long wail came a third time, beckoning me on. When I finally caught up to her, she was by the door to the attic, pawing at the panel.

Rowww! *"Let me in. Let me up."*

"Not a chance, you silly bean," I told her.

I went to grab her and ferry her back to our room, but stopped dead. In the action of leaning down, my ear came close to the keyhole. Through it, I could hear something strange. It was little more than a hum, though not the familiar buzz of the city; not the air conditioner; not a clock, computer, refrigerator, or any other household machine. This was softer and varied in tone like a song—or a chant.

Cautiously, I slipped the door open a crack. The gap was a bare two inches, but Winnie slithered through and was up the stairs before I could stop her.

"Oh!" I gasped in annoyance, mostly with myself. *Here we go again.*

Sure enough, there she was at the top, waiting for me.

Meow! *Come on! Hurry!*

I flicked on the light and started after her—what else could I do?

Nightfall had done little to freshen the stuffy space, and the air grew hotter the higher I climbed. I paused at the top. The hum was louder there, more well-defined, and I now picked out a rhythm like a group speaking in unison. It came, not surprisingly, from the back of the attic, the annex that housed the steps to the turret. Someone was up there—or to be more precise, several *someones*.

I crept across the room to stand directly under the trap

door. From that location, the chanting was intense. Suddenly it stopped, and I could hear people walking around on the floor above. There was the shuffling and scraping—chairs being moved—then absolute quiet.

Winnie hopped onto the pile of boxes, still toppled from our last visit. Picking her way to the highest point, she raised her paw toward the trap as she had done before, only this time she couldn't reach the rope.

Meow! *Open it.*

I frowned. Whoever was up there most likely didn't want to be disturbed by a cat and an old woman. It could lead to awkward, even hazardous, results. No, better to go back downstairs and call the police from the locked safety of the apartment. That would surely be the smart thing to do.

I'd almost convinced myself to let go of my curiosity when I heard a man's voice. He talked on for a bit, then another, younger voice broke in above the first. I couldn't make out the words, but as the exchange grew in volume, I realized it was an argument. If I knew what they were fighting about, maybe I could figure out why they were there.

Did it have something to do with the Freemasons and their Masonic Lodge? Could the light Jack called about have been a summoning signal? No one had come through the house, of that I was certain. Was there another way up, one known only to the Order? The footsteps in the wall—had they been real after all?

Those were questions for which I had not the inkling of an answer. And the biggest question of all—why would the Masons be meeting in the home of a dead man?—only plagued me further. What was left there for them?

Everything pointed back to the death of Roderick

Payne—that much I knew. For anything more, I'd need to hear what the men were saying.

I looked at Winnie who was looking at me. Her paw was still raised like a Japanese happy cat, although she didn't look the least bit happy.

Mew! *Up!*

Though contrary to my better judgment, I basically agreed with the curious cat. We'd made it that far; we might as well take it one step further.

I devised a plan. If I oh-so-quietly slipped open the trap door, leaving the staircase in place, it might be enough to get the gist of the argument without revealing my presence.

Cautiously I pulled the rope.

I never knew if my plan would have worked—the moment the trap was free, the ladder came down with a crash. This time I managed to jump out of the way without falling on my backside, so when a face glared down at me, I was caught red-handed.

"I'm calling the cops!" I yelled at the man above. "You're trespassing. You have no right to be here."

The man continued to stare. He didn't look like a burglar—in fact he was clean-cut and wearing a black tuxedo with a funny little apron tied around his waist.

"I'm doing it!" I shouted. "I'm calling them right now."

The man stared at me a few moments longer, then smiled. "Where's your phone then, little lady?" he said amicably.

He had me there. Standing in my bathrobe, hands at my sides, it was obvious I didn't have one. Plan B came into my mind fully formed—run away!

Before I could run, however, another face took the place of the first.

"*Mon Dieu,* Lyn-dear," chastised the familiar voice. "What have you done now?"

Chapter 24

Climbing is instinctual in cats. Is it the view? The feeling of aloofness? Or could it be the memory of sitting on the throne when they were queen?

"I should have known." Gil sighed. "I cannot keep anything from you, Lyn-dear—you and your curiosity."

"Gil?" I stuttered. His voice sounded strange, lacking most of the faux French accent that was his trademark. "What are you..."

"You might as well come up, now that your nose is stuck in our business."

He stood back so I could ascend, but I hesitated. Winnie, on the other hand, accepted the invitation with enthusiasm, taking the flight in two long leaps and disappearing from my sight.

I heard a round of jovial laughter. Whoever was up there, they liked cats—a point in their favor. If it was good enough for Winnie, I supposed it was good enough for me.

Still, I lingered, staring up at Gil. The fact I was dressed for bed was only one of my considerations. But then, as the antiques dealer had mentioned, my curiosity won out and I began to climb.

Step by step, I rose into the room. Taking in the small assembly of men, I recognized two more faces: Payne's lawyer Debon Kroll, and Cox the groundsman. The others were strangers, men of varying demographics, but all were wearing black formal attire and sported the strange and absurd-looking aprons. Some were standing but most were sitting in chairs lined up in front of the altar. Every single one of them was staring at me.

"What's going on here?" I asked Gil, since my mind couldn't grasp the group as a whole. Part of me was hoping I was still dreaming, still back in the busy library. Then Winnie meowed from atop a shelf of icons.

Meow-wow! *Snap out of it. This is no dream.*

"I'm sorry you had to see this." Debon rose from his place at the front and came over to me. Though his face was sympathetic, his height as he towered over me made me feel small and frumpy in my nightclothes. "We'd meant for this to be the final meeting. We never thought anyone would catch us at it."

"You never thought at all," another man exclaimed. I recognized the voice—Saul Baxter, Kroll's partner in the firm. I couldn't be sure, but he may have been one of the men who were quarreling, with Debon as the other.

Debon turned, his stance as stiff and formal as his outfit. "We all agreed it was the only way to determine what was next for our Lodge, Saul."

"That's not the only thing we need to determine." Baxter came forward, fixing his eyes on his partner.

I watched the two. Side by side, they looked like a pair of the most unlikely twins. Debon's tall frame and classically handsome features directly contrasted with the short man and his toad-like face, yet their body language perfectly reflected one another. Debon scowled, then Baxter scowled. Debon straightened his back and Baxter did the same. Finally Baxter turned away, a clear snub.

For a moment, I waited to see if Debon would mirror that motion as well, but he didn't so I returned my attention to Gil.

"How did you get here? I know you didn't come through the house."

"There is a stairwell that runs up the west wall. You would not have seen it, it is hidden. Only full members of our Lodge have the key."

"Of course," I grumbled with sarcasm. "Why wouldn't a secret room have a secret entrance? All very James Bond, isn't it?"

"I am so sorry, Lyn-dear." Gil went to put a protective arm around me, but I shook him off. I wasn't about to let him get away with the best-buddies routine until I had a lot more information.

Suddenly something clicked and I pulled back even farther. "You knew about this room all along! That's why you didn't want anyone to come up here. I don't know why I didn't think of it before." I paced a few steps. "When we showed you the trap door, you instantly declared it off limits. You said it was because you needed a Masonic expert to check it first. But you hadn't even looked. Sanjay mentioned the Masons, but it's not like you to just take his word for it. You couldn't have known what was in the room unless you'd been here before."

"Yes, I made the mistake. I was surprised you didn't catch me at the time."

"But why all the cloak and dagger? Why not just tell us what was going on? Is your group so mysterious as all that?"

"No, of course not, except…"

"Except," Debon took up, "there is the slight inconsistency having to do with Roderick Payne's will. In his will, he bequests all his worldly goods to Friends of Felines, which could also be interpreted to include the items in this room. We couldn't let that happen."

"But… you're the lawyer."

"The things here…" Saul took up, gesturing to the iconic pieces, "Belong to the Lodge, not to Mr. Payne."

"Okay, so what's the problem? I don't see FOF disputing such a claim."

"We couldn't take that chance," said Debon. "If you had decided to contest it, you would have won."

"We'd encouraged Roderick to add an addendum making the disposition of the Lodge items clear, but he never got to it. When the unthinkable happened, we were duty-bound to decide for ourselves. That's what we're doing now, figuring out where to move the Lodge, and how."

"Your figuring sounded more like a shouting match, Mr. Baxter."

The lawyer squinted light, browless eyes and looked away.

"Or was that about something other than relocation?" I pressed. Now that I was there and reasonably assured the Masons weren't going to kill me, I figured I might as well make the most of it.

Silence fell over the group, then finally Debon spoke up, but not about that. "I don't know how familiar you are with Masonic tradition, but Roderick Payne was the Worshipful Master of our Lodge. In the event of his unexpected death, I, as Senior Warden, have stepped into that position until election time."

"Not so unexpected," I mumbled.

"Pardon me?"

I looked up at the tall attorney. "Mr. Payne's death was not unexpected, at least not to him. The stipulation in his will proves that, as you well know since you're the one who oversaw the recording."

There was a sudden murmuring within the group, and I realized that detail wasn't common knowledge.

Cox lurched to his feet, looking slightly uncomfortable in his tux. "You're saying Roderick knew he was going to be killed?"

Debon gave a quick nod. "So it seems."

Cox began to frown. "Did he say who was going to be doing the deed?"

"No, of course not. No idea."

Was it my imagination, or did Cox look relieved at this news?

Suddenly something hit me like a two-hundred-pound seventeenth century cabinet. I'd already considered Payne's death might have to do with his Masonic connections. What if his killer were right there in that room? What if it was Cox, himself?

"Calm down, Cox," said Debon. "It's true there is a codicil that makes it sound like he suspected an attempt on his life, but that doesn't mean it's a fact. He was a suspicious old recluse who didn't trust anybody. You all know that."

Why was Debon making excuses? He knew better than anyone that Payne's fears were real. Could Debon be the killer?

"Payne was as sane as you or me," Baxter declared. "He knew someone was after him, and what's more, he knew the police would never find them. That's why he insisted Helen Branson and her shelter people join the search. Isn't that right Lynley?"

Gil turned to me, his face pale with shock. "Have you found something new? Something you have not yet told me?"

It made no sense for him to be surprised since he was

already aware I'd been asked to sleuth. Then another thought arose. What if Gil were the murderer? As far as I knew, he had no motive for killing Roderick Payne, but it was becoming more and more obvious I'd only just touched the surface of this crime.

The mood in the room took on a darker tone. Suddenly I felt the walls closing in around me, the black, mirrorlike windows compressing until all I could see was my own fearful reflection.

"No!" I cried. "No! This must stop. I don't care what you do with the Lodge, but I want you out of here right now! Go back down your secret stairway—tomorrow I'm having it locked and boarded up." I turned to Cox. "You're fired. You can stay in your house, but your access to the main house is rescinded as of now. As for you, Gil..." I faltered over the hurt and betrayal I was feeling. "You're fired too. Get out and don't come back."

"But Lynley..." he began, using my full name for possibly the first time ever in our lengthy relationship. I didn't want to hear it.

"Mr. Kroll and Mr. Baxter, I'll be speaking with your firm—the entire firm, not just you two who are obviously in on this... this farce! There's no way what you're doing can be legal, and even if it is, I think the police will want to know."

Suddenly I pulled up short. I'd let my anger get the best of me. Was I saying too much? If the killer really was there in that room, he might not be happy at being threatened.

I glanced around at all those formal figures, those eyes boring into mine, then without saying another word, I turned tail and rushed for the steps.

"Winnie! Come!" I called behind me. Surprisingly, the

cat obeyed.

Once down the ladder, I quickly leveraged it back into place and secured the trap so no one could follow, at least not right away. Hightailing it through the attic, Winnie and I skuttled down the stairs. I slammed the door, locking it with the ancient skeleton key that hung by a hook on the molding. We made the final sprint to the apartment in record time, and when safe inside, I shut the cat flap and locked that door too.

Dashing for my phone, I began to call nine-one-one, but then I hesitated. Maybe I was getting ahead of myself. Did I really need to bring in the SWAT team for a handful of Masons?

As I stood, out of breath from both exertion and fear, I wondered suddenly if I'd let paranoia get the better of me. What was the true likelihood that one of those men upstairs were Roderick Payne's killer? And if they were, getting them arrested for trespassing wasn't going to help matters. No, better to call the murder squad in the morning. I'd get hold of Detective Croft and tell her everything—absolutely everything—then let her sort it out.

I put the phone back on the table and looked over my shoulder. On my bed, Winnie was curled up in a perfect, circle, sound asleep.

Chapter 25

Cats know how to be present in the "here and now." In fact, they know no other way of being.

There was no point in my going to bed—I knew I'd never be able to sleep. For a while, I watched Winnie, curled up and snoring like a kitten. I was envious of that cat ability to live in the moment—to run when there was danger, then nap a few minutes later when the danger had passed. Did they just forget that moments before they had been nervous, threatened, or afraid? Or did they have a second sight telling them when they were safe? Most likely it was a little of both.

But I, poor human that I was, couldn't exorcize the image of those men from my mind, nor the distinct feeling that one among them was a killer. I had no real reason to suspect the Masons, but there was much I didn't know. What I did know was that something in that turret room was toxic, and instinct told me to beware.

Means, motive, and opportunity. If I were ever to unravel this mystery, that was the place to start. Pacing back and forth, I began to reason it out from the beginning.

Payne was a recluse and had been for decades, so the likelihood of his past suddenly catching up with him was minimal. He saw no one but his employees. Alice, Ida, Cox. The caterer. The occasional workman. I'd already hashed and rehashed that group many times, and since I had nothing new to add to the equation, I could write it off as a dead end.

But there was something new. Payne may have lived like a hermit in many ways, but there was one aspect to his life that I'd only just discovered—Roderick Payne was a Mason. And not just any Mason, he was a Master. I didn't know what that meant, but my guess was he hadn't risen to such status without putting in time. He could have been a member for years, in which case he would have met many men from all walks of life. Had he made enemies as well as friends?

I paused my pacing and sat down at the table, ready to record my revelation in the red journal, but as I picked up my pen and opened the book, I hesitated.

Why now? I asked myself. What would have changed between Payne and the Masonic brotherhood that could possibly drive them to kill? It made no sense. Unless Payne completed the addendum to his will, signing over the items in the turret to the Lodge, his death would only have caused problems for them. Besides, as a benevolent society, I assumed Masons frowned on murder. Sanjay said that to be a Mason, one must be of fine moral character—not the description of a would-be killer. Of course there might have been a more personal reason for one of the Masons to go after Payne, but since I didn't really know any of the players aside from Gil—who, now that I'd had a bit of time to think, I couldn't see as violent or conniving—that too was a dead end.

I circled back to the old conundrum: how did Payne know he was going to be murdered? Another thought came to mind, one I hadn't considered until now. If Payne thought his life was in danger, why hadn't he attempted to save himself? As far as I knew, aside from the lawyers and Ida, he hadn't shared his suspicions with a soul. He hadn't called the police, hired a private detective, or installed a bodyguard. Was he so resigned to his fate?

My thoughts kept returning to the turret. The place haunted me, though I didn't know why. Elusive as a wisp of cat fur, the more I tried to catch it, the farther it drifted away, leaving only a feeling I was missing some detail of the greatest importance.

I sighed in abject frustration. This line of reasoning was getting me nowhere. I had to face facts—I knew absolutely nothing about the murder of Roderick Payne. There was no way I could pick a killer out of the iffy suspect pool. And I shouldn't have to. It wasn't my job.

Then I sighed again. No, it was not my job, but if someone from the shelter didn't fulfill Payne's stipulation, likely Friends of Felines would forgo the grand inheritance, forgo the estate auction and the money from the sale of the mansion, forgo the new hospital wing that would help community cats and save lives. How heartbreaking would that be?

I glanced again at the sleeping Winnie. She was a smart one, and I would do well to emulate her wisdom. A little rest, and maybe I'd be able to think more clearly.

I went to the kitchenette to make myself a cup of chamomile tea, a proven soporific. I sorted through the box of teabags—Morning Thunder, Chai Spice, Earl Grey, Darjeeling—all black teas, fully caffeinated and guaranteed to zing me awake even more than I already was.

"Rats!" I declared out loud. Winnie flicked a furry ear and rolled over toward the wall, her patchwork back to me.

Mew. *Leave me alone! Can't you see I'm busy?*

I looked at the clock—two-thirty. Still time to get a bit

of sleep before morning. I knew Alice had a stash of herb teas in the kitchen for her personal use and figured she wouldn't mind if I helped myself to one.

This time I swapped my robe for real clothes, a summer dress and sandals, in case I ran into any more intruders. It was silly and indulgent, not to mention slightly paranoid, but the clothes gave me confidence, like a magic shield against the unknown.

I slipped my phone in my pocket and tiptoed out the door, leaving Winnie to get her beauty sleep. The house was quiet, only the hum of the refrigerator as I neared the kitchen. For a while after my confrontation in the turret, I'd heard the men squeaking and clomping down their secret stairs, but they'd been gone for some time now.

Tomorrow I'd find their outside entrance! I would get the contractor out to board it up! I would call Detective Croft! I would tell her absolutely everything…

I felt myself winding up again, muscles tightening, breath coming fast. I paused, took a deep inhale, and told myself to cut it out. Tomorrow would be here soon enough—my goal of the moment was chamomile tea.

I located Alice's tea tin shoved to the back of an otherwise empty shelf in the pantry. I took it down and lifted the flowered lid to find it did indeed contain the little yellow package I sought. I heated water in an electric kettle, rustled up an oversized pottery mug from a box of incidentals, and added a dollop of honey along with the stringless bag. Listening to the water come to a steaming bubble, I tried to concentrate on happy things—summer gardens, cats and kittens—but gardens reminded me of Cox, the gruff groundsman and possible killer, and cats led to the vision of Winnie perched on the Masonic altar like a goddess. So much for having a disciplined mind.

The scent of the tea alone was calming, sweet, and fragrant. I brought it to my nose and took a deep whiff. Life was not so bad, I had to admit. Though fraught with hurdles, this actual moment in time was perfect—quiet, gentle. I thought about going out onto the veranda but decided not to tempt fate. I didn't know why any of the Masons would be lurking around the grounds after my ultimatum, but the idea was enough to convince me I'd be better off inside.

I went instead to the conservatory with its plant shadows and peaceful surroundings. Greeted by the musty scent of mulch and soil, I sank onto a wicker chaise lounge, closed my eyes, and left all else to fate.

* * *

I woke with a start, not comprehending where I was. Overhead, huge filigree leaves played against green, winding vines. Something was poking me in the back. In fact there were several somethings.

I sat up, realizing I must have fallen asleep in the wicker chair, the source of the pokes. My mug of tea was cold, so I'd been there for a while. Well, that was the point of the chamomile—to help me sleep, though I would have preferred to have made it back to my own bed.

Instead of rested, I now felt logy and disoriented, that not-quite-real feeling that comes with interrupted slumber. Glancing at the wall of windows, I saw no hint of sunrise. Time to get to my apartment where I could remain undisturbed until morning.

I staggered back through the house, up the stairs, and along the hallway to my room. Zombie-like, I made for the bed and literally fell across it in a heap. For a moment, I basked in the comfort of a sleeping area not made out of little sticks. Then my eyes popped open as a thought struck me.

Where was Winnie?

Quickly I sat up again, completely awake. She wasn't on the bed or in the window. I thought back. When I'd come in, there had been no little meow of greeting, no sigh or purr. I lurched to my feet, looking around frantically. When my eye got to the cat door and found it wide open, I gave a cry of despair.

I was certain I'd closed Winnie's flap when I got back from the confrontation in the turret. I remembered reaching down and sliding the panel right before I locked the apartment door. No way did I want either Winnie or myself bothered by any stray trespassers.

Now the flap was open. Had I done it without thinking when I went for the tea? My mind had been all over the place. What other explanation was there?

Assuring myself that was the case, I strove to calm down. Winnie knew the house better than I did, and she would return when she was ready. But the feeling that something was amiss wouldn't go away. Exhausted as I was, I knew I'd get no rest until I located the wayward puss, so with a sigh, I picked myself up again and set out to search.

First I retraced my steps to the kitchen and then the conservatory, thinking she may have followed me on my quest for tea, but there was no sign of her. I searched the rest of the main floor, but most doors were shut and the ones that were open disclosed no cat. I did the same round upstairs with the same results. That left the attic.

As I once again approached the attic door, my heart fell. I distinctly recalled locking the door, but now it was ajar. In my imagination, I could clearly picture the flash of a calico cat slipping through the six-inch gap.

I ascended the stairs, dragging myself along with the aid of the handrail. My feet felt leaden as they heaved from tread to tread. At least I was getting my exercise for the day, I thought sarcastically.

Though the attic was dark, I resisted the urge to turn on the overhead light. Instead, I brought out my phone, ready with the flashlight app, but then I didn't switch it on either. For a few moments, I stood and listened. At first there was nothing, then directly above me coming from the turret, I heard a plop, a cat jumping to the floor.

"Winnie, you little creature," I huffed. Switching on the flashlight, I crossed to the annex. When I saw the trap door wide open and the staircase pulled down, I felt a jolt of unease. That meant at least one of the Masons had come through, come into the house. Gil? Cox? Someone else? Even so, it must have been a while ago. They'd be long gone by now. I paused to listen once again and was reassured. The only sound was the distinctive footfalls of a cat on the floor above.

Meow, called Winnie. *Come up.*

"No, you come down. I want to go to bed, and I want you to come with me."

Me-row. *You come up!*

"I don't think so," I declared, then I walked to the staircase and did just that.

Winnie was sitting tall at the head of the stairs.

"Come on, sweetie…" I reached for her, but she dashed away—only a few steps, but enough to make me chase.

I flashed the light beam around the room which, in the shadows, seemed almost ominous with its symbols, icons, and that imposing altar. When the illumination came back to Winnie, she'd moved even farther away. Ensconced on the desk in between the paperweight and the prayer bell, she looked exceedingly proud of herself.

"You know I can just leave you here if you're going to be obstinate."

Prrow. *Go ahead. I dare you.*

She called my bluff—she knew I wasn't going to do that. Since I had no idea where the secret staircase was located or if she could get outside that way, I had no choice but to bring her back down with me whether she liked it or not.

I moved slowly, my hand outstretched in a gesture of peace. She let me get near enough to touch her soft sideburn, then she leapt away, running halfway around the hexagonal chamber and scorching up a bookcase.

"Winnie!" I was losing my patience, what little there was left of it after the ordeals of the night. "This isn't a game."

But to her it was. Still, I understood cats well enough to know how to play: *Kitty runs, human follows; human gives up; kitty comes to see why the human is no longer playing.*

"Okay, have it your way." I turned and sat down in a chair. Sure enough, I heard a plop behind me, then felt her fur brush along my ankle.

"Purrumph?" she said, leaping into my lap to snuggle like a long lost friend.

I was about to employ the capturing clutch when I felt her body go rigid. Her head jerked up, and her ears flew forward. Though I sensed nothing, I tensed too on general principles.

Then I heard it—the clop, clop, clop of shoes on the outer staircase. The footfalls ascended until they came even, then a crack appeared in the western wall. Someone was coming through!

My adrenaline spiking, I shot a look around. Could I get back down to the attic before whoever it was made it inside? I didn't think so. Next best thing was concealment. Grabbing Winnie, I ducked behind the altar and prayed the calico wouldn't object to her capture with one of her signature screams.

From my hiding place, I heard the groan of a door being opened. Footsteps echoed across the room—a big person, I surmised; a man was the logical conclusion. One of the Masons, back for whatever reason? I didn't know why, but I had the strongest feeling this was someone new.

Winnie was beginning to squirm in my arms, but there was no way I was going to let her go. Gently I held her scruff as her mama had done when she was a kitten. She calmed down, but only for an instant. Then she set to howling like the diva I knew she could be.

The footsteps stopped.

"Winter Orange?" said a gruff voice. "Has my little kitty come to visit me?"

The steps took up again, then the room bloomed with a soft glow from the desk lamp.

"Come here, my darling. And quit making that infernal racket!"

Winnie wrestled out of my grip and hopped to the floor. Trotting toward the caller, she held her tail high as if greeting a friend. She moved out of my sightline, but I could hear purring from across the room so I assumed she was okay. This kept up for a minute, then I heard the galumph of cat feet running across the carpet. In a mad dash down the stairs, she was gone. *Smart girl,* I thought to myself, wishing I had some of Winnie's feline abilities.

I heard a sigh and the groan of Payne's big desk chair. Fingers tapping on wood. The pop of a can and the sour smell of beer. There was another smell as well—a fusty scent like that of unwashed clothes. The man seemed in no hurry. In fact, it was as if he felt at home there. The finger tapping continued, and he started singing a little tune. I recognized the words, a hoarse version of a song from the Wizard of Oz.

"Come out, come out wherever you are…"

The voice increased in volume as the singing continued.

"…and meet a poor being who fell from a star…"

Suddenly he hit the desk with his palm. "Come out now! I know you're there."

Slowly I uncurled from my hiding place. As I stood, I saw a total stranger glowering at me from behind the desk.

"Who… who are you?"

The stranger took a glug of beer and wiped his mouth with his hand.

"I, my dear woman, am Roderick Payne."

Chapter 26

History attributes the invention of the cat door to Sir Isaac Newton. When he tired of his cats interrupting his work by scratching to come inside, he had a carpenter cut two holes: one for the adult cats and a smaller one for the kittens.

For a moment, I stood in complete shock; then I burst out laughing. Granted it was more nerves than hilarity, but I did see the humor in the situation. Here we'd been going on the assumption that Roderick Payne was dead when obviously he was very much alive.

The man behind the desk didn't flinch, sitting as he had done when he recorded the codicil to his will. I applauded his audacity. He'd had us running around in circles from day one for an elaborate farce.

Then I faltered. Something was wrong with that picture. The more closely I peered at the newly resurrected Payne, the more certain I was of it.

Granted, the scruffy beard and long straggly hair concealed much of the man's head and face, and his shabby, dirty tunic contrasted sharply with the crisp, clean shirt he'd worn in the recording, but it was more than that. The shape of the head, the slump of the shoulders. In a sudden revelation, I realized this was not the same man.

"Who are you?" I repeated.

The man steepled his fingers displaying dirt-embedded nails of a darkish color.

"I told you. I'm Roderick Payne."

"No, you're not. I've seen pictures of Mr. Payne. I saw a video of him sitting right where you are now. You're nothing like him."

The imposter rose and came around the edge of the desk. In full view, he looked even less like the person he was claiming to be. This man was shorter. He was thinner as well, a thinness that came from years of privation, not days. Even if Payne had eaten sparsely for the weeks since he was proclaimed dead, he wouldn't look like that.

"Nonetheless, I am he."

I began to scoff, but he shot me a look so dark it stopped me mid-huff.

"You don't believe me? Then why should you?" he replied to his own question. "I've been gone a long time, long enough for the pretender to establish himself. And establish himself, he did!" The man touched the Remington bronze, then cast his eyes to the Thomson painting on the wall behind him. "Who would have guessed he could do all this in my name?"

"Wait—are you saying you're Roderick Payne and Roderick Payne wasn't Roderick Payne at all?"

He gave me a crooked smile. "If I understand that convoluted run of words correctly, then yes, that's exactly what I'm saying."

"Then who was the Mr. Payne who lived here? The one who collected all the beautiful things? The one who died?"

Payne began to tour the room, slowly and with no obvious destination. "His name was Jonah Winterbourne. He came from Syracuse, New York. We met by chance in a Marrakesh prison in… what was it? 1972?"

"Prison? What had you done?"

"Nothing really. I was caught with a tiny amount of marijuana, and he was said to have stolen a ring, though he claimed not. It was common for white boys to be arrested in those days, thrown in jail and given harsh sentences." He unconsciously rubbed his hand, and I noticed an old scar there. "It was no fun, believe me. Something I'd rather not dwell upon, if you don't mind."

"I'm sorry," I mumbled. "But you must have got out, right?"

He shot me a glare, and I instantly snapped back to reality—the reality of being alone with this stranger, this unlikely Roderick Payne. What was I doing trying to press him? I knew I couldn't trust him—an aura of danger clung to him, close as his dingy tunic—yet I couldn't stop myself. This man had the answers. All of them!

He glanced away and took up pacing back and forth. "Jonah was released. I was not so lucky."

He harrumphed into his beard, a grumble that I couldn't make out. Then he paced back toward me, and I heard it clearly: "My fault, all my fault."

"Pardon?"

He looked up sharply, as if he'd forgotten I was there. Maybe he had.

"Do you remember the seventies? You must—you're of that age. Wild times, those were. Full of fun and adventure and freedom." He paused, waxing nostalgic.

"Sex, drugs, and rock 'n' roll. Yes, I remember."

He turned a filmy eye to me. "I bet you were a cutie back then. Halter tops and miniskirts. Long hair and bare feet, am I right?"

"Well, not so much the miniskirts, but essentially, yes. I was a flower child."

"I would have liked you."

He leered in my direction in such a way that I again considered running, but the story had just begun. I could always run later. At least I hoped I could.

"I was a bit of a young buck myself. Hair down to my back and a mustache that beat out Tom Selleck. I had all the girls fawning over me whenever I came around."

This was getting nowhere. I needed to steer him away from his own self-appreciation.

"And what about this Jonah guy? Where does he fit in with your escapades?"

"Ah, Jonah. Well, to be frank, with our shaggy hair and furry faces, the two of us looked very much alike. We counted on that to make our plan work."

My mind jumped ahead. "You swapped identities?"

"Exactly. Jonah convinced me that his would be the lesser sentence. Possession of marijuana was a big no-no in those days, and as for his crime, they really couldn't prove he'd stolen the ring since it wasn't found on his person. He promised if I'd trade places with him, convinced them I was Jonah Winterbourne and he was Roderick Payne, he'd make it worth my while."

"And did he? Make it worth your while?"

Payne glared at me. He was rubbing that scar again, so I expected to hear him say no.

"Yes. Yes, he did. He promised me money and gave me a set of directions how to get it. A stack of American bills in a bus locker waiting for me when I got out." He whirled on me. "When I got out—ten years later!—it wasn't enough. Not nearly." His face took on an ambiguous stare. "But it was my fault too. The guy sounded so sincere, and the plan was simple. I was easily persuaded. From that moment on, I was Winterbourne, and he was me."

"What happened?"

"I was naïve, trusting. We all were in those days—it was part of the hippie creed. I never suspected he had ulterior motives, that he was a con man, and he was conning me."

Payne growled something unintelligible.

"Go on," I encouraged.

Again he cast me that dangerous glare. "I'm getting to it, woman. It's been a long while since I've talked to another human being, and even longer since I've told this tale."

"Sorry," I mumbled. "Take your time."

Payne was quiet, then he started up again as if nothing had happened. "The next day, Winterbourne bribed a guard into letting him go. I didn't think too much of it—if he could get out, more power to him. I felt assured I'd be out soon enough myself, since the crime I'd taken on was barely a crime at all. What Winterbourne had failed to mention was who had accused him of the theft. The prosecutor's wife! There wasn't even a trial before I was thrown into a dungeon and left to die. But first they did this." He shoved his hand out where I could clearly see the ragged white scar running from his ring finger all the way to his wrist bone. "A reminder of a theft I didn't commit."

"And Jonah Winterbourne knew that would happen when he traded places with you? How much trouble would be coming his—I mean, your—way?"

"Of course he knew!" Payne spat. "I doubt he realized the extent of it, that I'd spend the next decade in a Marrakesh prison, but he knew enough."

Payne coughed convulsively, then cleared his throat. "But it wasn't just that he'd tricked me into a bad situation," he took up once he'd recovered enough to speak again. "He destroyed my trust in my fellow man. As I withered in that dark place, I learned the lessons of betrayal. Everyone in that hole had a story, and all of them were bad. I hated him," Payne announced. "I hated that man. I hate him still."

He touched his forehead, then briefly put his hand over his heart, a deferential gesture that was not lost on me.

"But he's…" I was about to say dead when it all clicked into place. Here was a man who truly despised Winterbourne—for conniving him out of his own identity, for duping him into a terrifying situation, for ruining his faith in humanity. From the look of him, the real Payne hadn't fared too well in the years after his prison stint, while Winterbourne had amassed a fortune. Hate, resentment, jealousy, and quite likely a certain amount of madness—a perfect recipe for murder.

Suddenly it was obvious. Roderick Payne killed Roderick Payne!

Chapter 27

The technical term for a hairball is a "bezoar".

"You killed Roderick Payne!"

I stared at the man in shock. It was coming together now. I still didn't have all the pieces, but I had the one fact that made the others moot—the man in front of me was a murderer.

My curiosity evaporated in a poof of fairy dust as reality set in. I was alone in a house with a killer who had just confessed to me. Logic dictated I'd be next on his list.

Payne had come to the same conclusion. Crossing the distance between us in one long stride, he struck like a viper. Grabbing my wrist, he pulled me toward him. I could smell the stale breath, the neglected teeth. I tried to wrench away, writhing in his grip, but his hand clenched tighter. With a whiplike action that resonated pain all through my body, he twisted my arm until I thought my shoulder would burst. Maneuvering me over to the big chair, he shoved me down. It was the move of a pro and had taken less than five seconds for him to execute.

Once I was seated, he let go but loomed over me, a visible threat if no longer a tangible one. Though old and wiry, the man surely had me beat when it came to brute force. I'd need to come up with something outside the box if I were to get away.

I massaged my throbbing shoulder and tried to devise a plan. Meanwhile I began to banter and babble in the best nonchalant tone I could muster.

"So that's quite a story. Is it true? Did it really happen? I can't imagine going through such a thing. However did you get here from there?"

Payne's brow furrowed. "Huh?"

I'd indeed caught him off guard. Encouraged by his confusion, I pressed on.

"How did you get out of prison? What did you do then? How did you find Jonah Winterbourne? And why now? Why did you wait until now to come after him? Why didn't you do it sooner? What's the story? You might as well tell me… Please, Mr. *Payne*?" Why I added that last, I wasn't sure. Appeasement? Deference? Convoluted reasoning? It didn't matter—he seemed to react well to it.

Looming a bit less, he almost smiled. "You're a funny one. What's your name?"

I hesitated. "It's Lynley."

"Lynley?" He guffawed. "What kind of name is that?"

"It's *my* name," I shot back, taking even more of a dislike to this dodgy character. Since he'd manhandled me and was essentially holding me prisoner under pain of maybe-death, that was a step.

"I don't care for it," he spat. "It sounds like a surname." He regarded me, then spun away. "I'm going to call you Ellie."

Ellie? *Pshaw!* Wherever did he come up with that one?

It doesn't matter, my brain screamed at me. *His back is turned! Now's my chance!*

He stood between me and the attic stairs, but the door to the outside staircase was a straight shot. I bunched my muscles and was ready to dash when he returned his focus to me. The opportunity had passed.

"You want my story, Ellie?" His gaze took on a glassy

appearance. "I wouldn't know where to start."

But he started anyway, lighting into a tale that zigzagged from place to place, time to time, with no real continuity or destination. Though muddled and rambling, I did manage to glean bits and pieces as I waited for another opening to run.

Apparently he'd been much diminished when he was finally released from the Moroccan prison, in ill health and state of mind. He'd taken Payne's bribe money and continued to travel across Europe, though in contrast to his previous bold adventures, now he slunk in the shadows, bunking with beggars and thieves. He took many jobs, whatever he could find, including a stint in the French army where he learned what he called *l'art de tuer*—the art of the kill. After a time—he never mentioned how much time—he returned to the States. New York, Chicago, Dallas, Los Angeles, and eventually Portland.

"I looked everywhere for Jonah Winterbourne, but it was tough. I had his passport and he had mine."

"So you were really looking for Roderick Payne."

"I didn't know if he'd kept that name. I thought once he was safely out of Europe, he'd resume his own. That's what I would have done. That's what I still want to do..."

He seemed to seize in on himself, his face going hot with anger. "I found him. Here! Living like a doggone king!"

Payne slammed his fist down on the desk, making the paperweight jump and the cup of gold pens rattle. Then he went silent, but I didn't like the look in his eyes.

I needed to keep him talking. "Did you confront him?"

Those hate-filled eyes turned on me, flashing fire. Suddenly he blinked, and the glare reset to his normal watery gaze.

"Confront him? No. That wasn't how I did things anymore. I'd been a shadowman for too long. So I kept to the shadows."

Another piece in the puzzle! As I patched it together, I found what I'd been looking for.

"How long have you been living here, Mr. Payne?" I said softly, unsure I really wanted to know.

"Oh, a long time now. A year, maybe two? I don't bother with the clock anymore. Days, weeks, months, a lifetime—it's all the same between myself and God." He made the head-to-heart gesture again, and I had to guess its meaning was, at least in part, religious.

"For a while, I camped out in the gardens, but that wasn't safe. I swear that old codger Cox knew every blade of grass, every bush and tree. I nearly got caught a few times. That's when I moved inside."

"What about the alarm system? This place is set up like Fort Knox."

He waved a hand. "Not to someone with my experience. And once I was in, I made myself at home. I was content watching Winterbourne and living under the veil of his luxury… for a while."

"But then you got angry?"

He huffed. "Then I got bored. The man was a slug. Here he was, rich beyond measure, yet he never went anywhere or did anything besides meander around his big house looking at his things. Things! Things mean nothing. If I'd been him, I would surely have done more with such abundance."

"Is that when you decided to kill him?"

Payne's eyes shot to me, and he grimaced behind his beard. "Kill him?" he mused. "Yes. No. Yes—I wanted to wake him up, make him think, make him do something with his life, *my* life."

"You rigged the booby-traps?"

"Sure. Now that was fun!" Payne snickered. "And watching him squirm was even more fun. At first he thought they were mishaps, the results of living in an old and decaying house. He had the carpenters in, fixed room after room, but the 'accidents' just kept on coming." Another snort. "Finally he began to get the idea. I don't know what went through his head—poltergeists? karma?—but he knew it was more than a run of bad luck, and it scared him stupid."

"So you toyed with him like a cat with a mouse. Why didn't you come right out and kill the poor man?"

"I had no intention of killing him, Ellie—not at first. But as time passed and my incentives weren't working, I became desperate. I needed a reaction, a response. That's when I rigged those crates above his bed. I suppose that might have killed him if someone else hadn't got to him first."

"Wait... You're saying you didn't murder Payne—I mean Winterbourne? It wasn't you who poisoned him in the garden?"

"Certainly not," he huffed. "I told you, Ellie, I never leave the house."

If you didn't do it, who did? I wanted to yell at the top of my lungs, but I held back. Maybe Payne wasn't the killer after all, but he was still hostile. He'd tormented a man merely to get a rise out of him, and when that reaction hadn't come in what he considered a timely manner, he'd upped the ante by rigging a booby-trap that could kill. The real Roderick Payne was insane, and it was time for me to get my little self out of his presence any way I could.

My only advantage was that the chair where Payne

had unceremoniously dumped me was situated behind the big desk. The lower part of my body was obscured by several square feet of carved oak. If I could get to my phone without him noticing, I might be able to call for help. There was a problem, however. I'd need to unlock the instrument and click to my contact list before I could punch the speed dial for 911.

It will work, I told my overactive thought process. *Now shut up and do it.*

I slipped my hand in my pocket, stifling a groan as I extended my injured shoulder. I had luck with me—Payne had turned away and was fiddling with something on the bookshelf. Ever so slowly, I retrieved the phone and laid it on my lap. I paused, checking Payne once again. He was still engrossed with his find, a small dagger with Masonic symbols on the hilt. Cautiously, I pressed my finger to the print lock.

The phone came alive in a blaze of blue light. Payne's head jerked up, and he whirled around, on me in an instant.

Once again I felt his grip. With a vicious shake, he wrenched the instrument away. I cried out with pain and frustration, but he just glared at me. Then he crossed to the window and threw open the sash. In a violent move, he flung the little phone as far as he could throw, leaning out to watch it smash on the cement tiles below.

Without thought, I leapt up and bolted for the secret stairs. Payne was still at the window, and as I passed, I shoved him as hard as I could. It was an instinctive move, one I would question later on, but for now, my only thoughts were of my own escape.

Payne staggered, lost his balance, and went careening into the opening. Twisting at the last second, he caught himself, slamming into the frame instead. For a moment, he stood as if dazed, then with amazing alacrity, he came at me.

I was already across the room, zipping through the door and slamming it shut behind me. I'd never been down the Masons' staircase before, but it didn't matter. I knew where it led, and that was all I cared about. Without my phone, my only hope was to get to Cox's tiny house and have him call the police. And if that didn't work, I could make a run for the street and start flagging cars like the heroine in an old Perry Mason show.

I was about halfway down when I heard the door above crash open. My heart sank, knowing that Payne would catch up to me in no time. Even two floors away, I felt him behind me like a predator on prey. I sensed the hot breath, the bared teeth, expected that crushing bite on the back of my neck to come at any time.

I flew through the door at the bottom, a panel in the side of the house that, when closed, blended with the façade in a seamless manner. Running across the covered porch and down onto the veranda, I rushed by my shattered phone. I felt a jab of sadness—for the phone, for Payne and Winterbourne, but ultimately for me.

Once I'd passed from the house's motion sensor floodlights, I was enfolded by full dark. Somehow I got across the grass and to the tiny house without tripping and falling. Glancing back, I saw no sign of Payne, though I knew he was there.

I banged on Cox's door like a mad woman. "Cox! It's Lynley! Let me in!"

The door opened slowly, exposing a disgruntled Cox in an old-fashioned nightdress, hunter's vest, and gumboots.

"What you want? D'ya know what time it is?"

I shoved past him, into the little house, then turned, panting.

"Help...!" was all I could manage before collapsing onto a couch.

Cox flipped on a porch light and peered outside. He surveyed the grounds, then turned his attention to me.

"What are you on to?" he asked suspiciously.

I tried to think how I could explain everything I'd found out in the past hour—about Payne and the real Payne, about the booby-traps and the torments, about Payne's last crazy assertion that he wasn't a killer...

I snapped forward, my breath still coming in bursts, but suddenly it was less from exertion and more from fear. That question I'd failed to ask Roderick Payne—if he hadn't murdered Jonah Winterbourne, then who did?—now burned through my mind like wildfire. If it wasn't Payne, that meant it had to be someone else, someone such as...

"You!" I accused.

"Me what?"

I pulled myself standing and edged toward the door.

"Nothing, I..."

Cox frowned and cocked his head. It was a mannerism I'd seen him use before, but now it held a new meaning. There was a subtext to it, a demented intention.

"I think you'd best sit down again, Miss. You don't look so good."

He took a step toward me, and I screamed. I'd had enough for one night. I couldn't take anymore. If one more man came looming at me, one more murderer threatened my life, I'd fall to pieces. I couldn't fight. I couldn't run.

Still, there was one other thing I couldn't do—I

couldn't give up.

I screamed again. I assumed Cox would come and stop me, but until he did, I was determined to make as much noise as possible. My throat was dry, and my voice was failing, but I kept it up.

"Help! Murder! Police! Fire…!"

Strangely, Cox just stood there staring at me as if I were the crazy one. Then in between cries, I heard a door slam, not the one to the outside but from within the house.

Cox looked over, and so did I.

There, silhouetted in the glow from the room beyond stood Alice. In her hand she held a hypodermic needle.

Chapter 28

No one knows exactly how cats make purrs, but it has been proven that petting a purring cat relieves stress in their humans, which in turn considerably reduces the risk of stroke or heart disease.

Cox uttered an oath; I stood frozen to the spot. Alice? Were they in it together? Was she a killer too? I was surrounded by murderers, and I'd never guessed. Now it was too late. All I knew, all I'd found out, all the secrets I'd uncovered would be lost in one tiny prick of that needle.

But something else was going on. Cox had moved between Alice and me. His back was turned, but I could see the slump of his shoulders.

Then he spoke, so softly I barely heard.

"Alice, no."

The housekeeper huffed. "Alice, *yes!*" she spat back at him. "Get out of my way while I finish this one…" She nodded at me. "Then we can be free."

"What are you talking about, woman? I don't understand. Free? Free of what?"

Alice leaned close to the groundsman. "She knows, Maurice. She'll ruin everything. We have no choice."

"We? What do you mean, we? I'll have nothing to do with it! I'll have no part in more killing."

Cox turned to me, horrified. "She told me she'd done it, killed the Mister, but I never believed her. I figured it was just another bid for my attention—she'd tried that before, though not in such a morbid manner. A nutcase, not a killer, was what I figured." His attention returned to the syringe, and Alice. "Looks like I was wrong. You're both."

"But I did it for you." Alice gave a little pout, cute on her face if I hadn't known it was precipitated by insanity. "I did it for us, so you could get your inheritance like you deserved. Then we could be together, happy, rich."

"You're batty, girl. I was never going to be rich from Mr. Payne."

"But you said…" She gave him a confused look.

Cox became flustered. "I know, I know. I say a lot of things when I'm drinking."

"You said you loved me."

Cox gave a sigh. "Might have, I suppose. But truth is, Alice, I only put up with you coming around because you were lonely, and I felt sorry for you. Now put that sticker away and get your crazy self out of here."

I could see her mouth open, and her jaw drop as she digested his harsh and damning rejection, but she didn't move.

"Go on, git! I've got to think…"

He grabbed her by the shoulders and spun her toward the door. In her surprise, she went limp, but only for a moment. Then she began to fight back.

"No, You can't!" she cried, thrashing and flailing in his grip. "I won't go. I love you! I love you…"

Cox was by far the stronger of the two, but Alice still held the deadly syringe, which now in her anger, she was aiming at him. As the pair began to wrangle like Hercules and the lion, I took my cue to run.

And run I did—out the door of the tiny house, down the steps, and straight into the strong, grasping arms of a man.

It was my turn to struggle. Payne had been waiting, and now he held me fast.

"No!" I screamed at the top of my lungs. "Let me go!"

I gave a last great heave, then collapsed in my captor's grasp. I was exhausted, spent. My mind still cried for me to fight, but my body refused.

"Lynley!" The voice came through the deafening surge of blood that pounded in my ears—familiar, and comforting.

"Lynley, what's going on here? Are you alright?"

I lifted my eyes and stared into the handsome face of Special Agent Denny Paris. I blinked, almost sure he was an illusion born of terror and fatigue, that any moment he'd morph back into Payne. I blinked again. He was still there.

"Denny?"

"Lynley, it's me."

"But... How...?" was all I could manage.

"Jack called me. He said there was a strange light coming off the Payne mansion, that he tried to call you but all he got was a funny sound from your phone."

For a few more moments, I stared into Denny's eyes, still half-expecting him to disappear. When he didn't, I slipped my gaze to the house, the turret, and the blazing beam that shot straight up into the lightening sky. In one of the turret windows sat Winnie, looking very pleased with herself.

* * *

The rest of the night was a blur—or I suppose I should say, morning, because by the time Denny had called the police, the dawn was upon us. It came in stages—a soft, gray mist when the cop cars pulled into the drive, then timid tendrils that caught their dark uniforms as they swarmed across the lawn. The first rays caught Cox and Alice being escorted from the tiny house. When they took a cowed Roderick Payne into custody, the full sun was ablaze.

Denny had ushered me into the mansion, sat me in a comfy chair, and brought me a cup of very hot, very strong, very sweet black tea. Now I held it with both hands like a lifeline. Even though the outside temperature was rising by the minute, I couldn't shake the chill that had settled upon me like a shroud.

At some point, the police had taken a statement. I recall seeing Detective Croft's somber face rise into view. Her look was one of concern, and then she was gone again.

At eight o'clock, the volunteers began to arrive, all except Gil. I wondered if I would see him again—*ever*. I felt a pang of loss and regret. I'd fired him from the job, afraid he was Payne's killer. *How ludicrous!* I thought as I looked back on it. So much had happened between then and now. I needed to call him, to apologize, to ask him to forgive me. It was more than I could hope that he would come back to work, and more than I could do to worry about that now.

"Lynley!" Frannie came running into the room. "What happened? Are you alright?"

I stared up at her from my chair, then gave a little whimper.

"Of course you're not," she answered for herself. "Denny told me about Alice being the killer and Cox being a jerk letting her think they were in a relationship. And about there being a second Roderick Payne who was alive and living in the walls. My goodness, Lyn! What a mess."

She came over to me, took the cup out of my hands, and stood me on my feet. "I'm driving you straight home. Right now."

"But Winnie..." I blustered, waving at the cat curled up in the big chair next to me.

"Winnie will be fine for a little while by herself. Besides, Skie is here. I'll tell her to watch. They have a bond."

I nodded. It made sense. In my current condition, I wouldn't be much use to Winnie anyway, and more than anything, I wanted to flee that cursed castle. It may not have been haunted, but what had transpired in the last few hours was so much worse.

I don't remember the trip across town. I must have nodded off. When we got there, Fredric helped me up the steps and into the cool of the hallway. He and Seleia tried to guide me to the office bed, since my own room didn't lie within the air conditioned area, but I resisted.

"Bath," I exhaled. "I need to wash off..." Hot water was the cure-all for both fear and pain.

"Seleia, draw Lynley a bath," Frannie directed. "Warm but not too hot. Fredric, make a cup of chamomile tea. Fetch a glass of water, and a Motrin—make that two. Lynley, you relax here on the couch and pet your kitties while I make a call."

I looked at the drill sergeant who had taken my care into her hands, then sat as instructed. I was immediately inundated by cats—Little wasted no time in claiming my lap, and Big Red curled against my shoulders on the back of the couch. Dirty Harry hopped up on one side of me and Tinkerbelle on the other. For a moment, they glared at Little who just gave a slow blink and settled further into the warmth of my skirt.

I looked at Frannie. "How'd you get to be so smart?"

"Years of experience," she smiled. "And by years, I mean decades. But we're not going to talk about that, are we?"

She winked.

I knew exactly what she meant. At the moment, I felt every one of my sixty-plus years, and then some.

Chapter 29

Few shelters focus on senior cats because of the time, work, and expense involved. We who love all cats hold the ultimate admiration for those extraordinary few that provide comfort and hospice care for cats at the end of life.

The stifling, aberrant heat of August had given way to a perfectly lovely September. A few days of warm, quenching rain had re-greened the plants and reinvigorated the people. Everyone walked around without umbrellas, relishing the feel of cool droplets hitting their hair. They'd be sick of it soon enough as the gray drizzle set in for the winter, but for now, it was paradise.

After the ordeal at the mansion, I'd stayed at home to nurse my strained shoulder. I wanted nothing more than to disappear into the furry company of my cats and practice some reclusiveness of my own. Helen sent a gaggle of volunteers to Payne House to finish up with the auction prep, and Skie took over for me as official Winnie guardian. Skie and Winnie loved each other—I knew she would do a great job.

I'd called Gil and apologized profusely. I was all set to beg him to return as the lead of the auction team, for the cats' sake if not for mine, but it didn't take much convincing.

"Oh, *mais oui*. But of course," he'd told me. "I know you not mean it, Lyn-dear. Sometimes the crazy cat ladies can be a bit, well, *crazy.*"

I let the remark slide, being the one on the apologetic end. I was happy to see his faux accent was back in full force. That other Gil, the one in the tux and apron, was someone I'd need to contemplate at another time.

But that had been a month ago; now I was back on my feet and volunteering at the shelter once again. During my absence, production at Payne House had wound up, the photos and descriptions downloaded onto the online auction site, and the event itself had gone live. In a flurry of action in which I took no part, items were bid upon, won, delivered, mailed, and picked up on location. The auction house tallied up the take and sent a big, fat check to Friends of Felines. Now, all FOF had to do was sell the house.

"We sold the house!" announced Frannie as she sashayed into the volunteer room where I was spending my break.

"*The* house?" I remarked. "Payne House? I was just thinking about that." I sighed. "I hope it's someone nice. That part of Payne's bequest has always bothered me. I get why Mr. Payne wanted Winnie to stay with the property—it's the only home she's ever known and seemingly the only place she's happy—but what if it goes to someone who likes old mansions but doesn't like cats? What if they don't take care of her properly? What if they throw her out on the street? How would we ever know?"

Frannie was grinning like a cat herself, the grin growing wider every minute.

"What?" I asked. "Do you know who bought it?"

She nodded her head but remained mum.

"Well? Tell me before I burst with curiosity."

"I'd ask you to guess but you never would." She

laughed.

"Please, Frannie. Put me out of my misery."

"Alright, but we have to keep it quiet, at least for now. It was the Scarboro Trust, Sasha and Edward Scarboro."

"Scarboro—as in Skie Scarboro?"

"They're the ones. Skie's parents. Turns out they're among the wealthiest families in Portland, though they don't like to boast about it."

"Well, I never!" I exclaimed. "Then what was all her talk about minimum wage and the plight of the working classes? Skie always gave the impression she was strictly against capitalistic wealth."

"Oh, youth and rebellion, I suppose. She may be a socialist, but her parents sure aren't. They are conscientious people, however. They have plans to make over some of Payne House into a senior cat rescue and hospice—a place for old cats with no other options and for the dying ones so they can end their ninth life in comfort and ease. It was Skie's idea of course, but her parents are backing it. Skie will live there and manage the rescue. And..."

"She'll take care of Winnie!" I finished. "Oh, that's wonderful! I'll need to congratulate her and find out all about it, but right now I'm due at the foster office."

I went to rise, but Frannie stopped me with a hand. "Not so fast, girlfriend. This is the first time I've caught you when you weren't either incapacitated or running around, busy as a hummingbird. It's time to have *the talk*, if you know what I mean."

I did know. All those loose ends that people wonder about after something momentous happens.

"I've told you everything already," I sulked.

"Bits and pieces. And I didn't want to press you. I

could see you were still coming to terms. But now you're back and everything's normal again. It's time for you to tell all."

"Okay, fire away, but can we do it on the fly?"

I put my tote in my locker, and we headed out through the lobby to the other side of the building. As we approached the offices, we came upon Denny Paris leaning against the wall by the foster room. I'd always thought he quite resembled a modern-day Paul Newman, and that mixture of poise and nonchalance confirmed it.

"How are my two best girls?" he called up the hallway. He addressed us both, but his gaze was set on me.

"I'm good." I smiled. "Back to my old self."

"Who's old?" Frannie quipped. Then the three of us laughed.

"Lynley was just about to fill me in on all the gory details of her closing night at Payne House." Frannie winked. "I finally cornered her."

"Denny was there too," I pointed out. "At least for the last part. Why don't you corner him while I check in with Kerry?"

I ducked into the office but was out again in under a minute.

"Are you getting a foster cat?" Denny asked.

"No, just mentoring a new recruit, but he doesn't seem to be here yet." Taking a seat in the little waiting room I leaned back with a sigh. "Okay, Frannie. Shoot."

"Well," she began slowly, considering what she wanted to ask. "I remember everything you told me the morning after the... *you-know-what*... but you were pretty much out of it. What really happened that night?"

I knew there was no way to escape this friendly interrogation, so I went through it again, beginning with the surprise Masonic meeting in the turret and ending when my memories started fazing into fantasy, somewhere around the time I ducked into Cox's cabin and found myself facing a killer.

"So turns out it was Alice who injected Mr. Payne—I mean Mr. Winterbourne—with the potassium," I concluded. "She was under the impression Cox would inherit some big fortune, and the two of them would live happily ever after. I don't know if she was delusional or if he'd been leading her on. Apparently she'd told him she'd killed Payne, but he hadn't believed her until she came at me too. When he tried to stop her, they got in a fight, and I bolted. I have no idea what happened after that."

"The police arrived and took them away," Denny filled in. "Alice was arrested on suspicion of murder and attempted murder, and Cox was taken in for questioning. I'm not sure if he was charged as an accessory."

"I don't think so," said Frannie. "He was back at Payne House working in the gardens like nothing had happened when we were winding up the estate auction stuff. Grumpy as ever, I might add. I tried to talk to him, but he just walked off the other way."

I turned to Denny. "Do you know what they did about Mr. Payne—the real one? He'd been setting booby-traps all around the house, trying to get a rise out of Winterbourne. I don't think he wasn't really out to kill, but still, he was lucky nobody got hurt. He must have broken laws—attempted something-or-other."

"Yes, they found him hiding in the attic crawl space and took him in too, but then he was sent on to a mental facility."

"Hmmm," I muttered. "Makes sense that he was mentally ill. He said he'd been living in the walls of Payne

House for over a year." I shivered, recalling all those times I'd heard the inexplicable thumps and bumps. Now that I knew it had been a strange and possibly crazy man creeping around above me, I wasn't sure if I was relieved or more terrified than ever. And that awful moaning sound—had that been Payne as well? I decided I'd rather believe it was of human origin than a paranormal alternative.

"Who does that?" Frannie commented, bringing me from my deliberations. "Sneaks around in someone's house like a ghost?

"Someone who's been through unthinkable horrors and doesn't see any other way. He hated Winterbourne for stealing his life and leaving him to rot in a foreign prison. That's enough to make anyone a bit unbalanced."

"You sound very forgiving for someone who was chased and taunted."

Again I pictured the gaunt man standing in the turret window as I ran by. I'd shoved him, shoved him hard. Had I really meant to send him flying, a move which would surely have injured if not killed him? I kept telling myself it was reactive, not malicious. How much of a difference would that have made if the outcome had been his death?

"But I have a question as well," I put forth before I could get swept away in the torrent of my own uncertainties. "If the man we knew as Roderick Payne was really Jonah Winterbourne, what does that do to his bequest?"

"The auction's over and the house has sold. The moneys have been transferred to Friends of Felines," Frannie mused, "so I guess everything went as originally planned. But it does raise questions."

"Maybe I can help," came a woman's voice from

behind us. "Hello, Lynley. You look well." Helen Branson placed her hands on the back of my chair, her gray eyes shining. "I've been meaning to catch you, but it's been busy lately."

"Busy with a capital B," Frannie agreed.

I peered up at the strong, yet kindly face. "I got the card you sent, the one with the little calico holding a bouquet of flowers. Thank you, Helen. She looks just like Winnie."

"Skie Scarboro picked it out for me. I'm glad you liked it."

"So what about the name discrepancy on Mr. Winterbourne's will?" Frannie asked. "Is that something that could come back and bite us later on?"

"It could have if he'd signed his will under a false name, but thankfully Mr. Payne was thorough in his transition to his new identity. He legally changed his name to Roderick Martin Payne decades ago. For all intents and purposes, he was Roderick Payne."

"But now there's two of them. Do you think the real one—I mean the original—will kick up a fuss?"

"Not likely," said Helen. "Debon talked to him and had him sign a waiver pertaining to the estate of the second Mr. Payne. There shouldn't be a problem."

There was a glint in her eye when she mentioned the attorney. This time I wasn't going to let it go.

"Debon seems like a nice man, for a lawyer. Are you two close?"

At first, she gave me a blank stare, then her face dissolved into laughter. "You caught me, Lynley. Yes, Debon Kroll and I are close. He's my nephew."

"Oh," was all I could say.

"Anything else, Miss Marple?"

"No, sorry. I didn't mean to pry. Did your nephew say how Mr. Payne is doing?"

"From what he told me, I gather the old man is settling in nicely at his new facility home. They've cleaned him up and put him on a healthy diet. His mind may take some time to heal, but physically he's doing better already."

"I'm glad," I said. "He struck me as a good person at heart."

Frannie gave me a look of sheer incredulity. "How can you say that, Lynley, after what he did to you?"

"Well," I considered, "Winnie liked him, and that means a lot."

A round of nods and laughter ensued. "That's just how us cat people roll," Helen shrugged.

"Winterbourne, Winter Orange..." Frannie put forth speculatively. "Do you think Mr. Winterbourne named his cat to somehow honor his real family?"

I raised an eyebrow. "Interesting question. It would make sense he didn't want to lose all sight of his origins."

"Then again, it might just be coincidence," said Denny.

Helen nodded. "I don't suppose we'll ever know for sure."

The door to the foster room opened, and Kerry stuck her head out. "Lynley, your guy just called from the parking lot. He's on his way in. Do you want to come check his assignment before he gets here?"

"Sure, be right there." I looked at Frannie. "Well, I hope I've appeased your curiosity."

"For now, but you know that was just the first round. Let's meet up at the Pub and Pony for lunch tomorrow. I bet I'll have thought of more questions by then."

I said farewell to Denny and Helen and stepped into the office. As I passed the bulletin board, I glimpsed the notice that had caught my eye a month ago. The flyers that had been covering it were gone now, leaving a clear view of the headline, *Cat Sitter Needed.* Below were two photos—one of a clowder of cats and the other of a house. The house seemed familiar. If it was the place I was thinking of, it was in my neighborhood, less than a block away from me.

Cat sitting, I mused as I stepped around to Kerry's computer. *Now that sounds like fun.*

About the Author

Cat Writer Mollie Hunt is the award-winning author of two cozy series: the *Crazy Cat Lady Cozy Mysteries,* featuring a sixty-something cat shelter volunteer who finds more trouble than a cat in catnip, and the *Tenth Life Cozy Mysteries* involving a ghost cat in a small coastal town. Her *Cat Seasons Sci-Fantasy Tetralogy* presents extraordinary cats saving the world. She also pens a bit of cat poetry.

Mollie is a member of the Oregon Writers' Colony, Sisters in Crime, the Cat Writers' Association, and Northwest Independent Writers Association (NIWA). She lives in Portland, Oregon with her husband and a varying number of cats. Like her cat lady character, she is a grateful shelter volunteer.

You can find Mollie Hunt online:
Blogsite:
www.molliehuntcatwriter.com
Amazon Author Page:
www.amazon.com/author/molliehunt
Facebook Author Page:
www.facebook.com/MollieHuntCatWriter/
Sign up for Mollie's **Extremely Informal Newsletter** and get a free Crazy Cat Lady short story!
https://tinyurl.com/5yx4x56d

Praise for Mollie Hunt, Cat Writer:

"I know Mollie as a true, dyed-in-the-wool cat person, as a cat guardian and a foster parent and, most importantly, as a human being. One thing I can spot a mile away is true passion... and Mollie Hunt has it. People like Mollie are rare in this world because they infuse their own curiosity… with true empathy… the recipe for not only a quality person, but, in the end, a great artist as well."

—Jackson Galaxy, Cat Behavior Consultant

Praise for the Crazy Cat Lady cozy mystery series:

"I knew this novel was about cats, but its theme is cats! Cats are as much the main characters as the main character is!"

—Sharon from Goodreads

"…an outstanding amateur sleuth mystery that will delight cat lovers and mystery lovers alike. ***Cats' Eyes*** *has so many exciting twists and turns; it keeps the reader fascinated until the final thrilling scene. I liked the addition of 'cat facts'" at the heading of each chapter. I learned a few fascinating tidbits that I didn't know."*

—Readers Favorite 5-Star Review

A NOTE FROM THE AUTHOR

Thanks so much for reading my ninth Crazy Cat Lady Mystery, *Cat's Play.* I hope you enjoyed it. If you did, please consider leaving a review on your favorite book and social media sites. Reviews help indie authors such as myself to gain recognition in the literary jungle. Thank you in advance for your consideration.

Want more cozy cat mysteries? Look for more books in my **Crazy Cat Lady** series. Don't worry—the books need not be read in order. Just pick a plot that interests you and start reading.

> *"...Each book drew me right into the story and kept me intrigued and guessing all the way. They're as cozy as can be for cat enthusiasts, but there are also some real scares..."*
> —Catwoods Porch Party

Or check out my **Tenth Life** paranormal series.

> *"Superior read; colorful characters in a delightful cozy. This is the sort of cozy mystery that you like to curl up with on a rainy day with a cup of tea."*
> —Amazon Verified Purchaser

For sci-fantasy fans, there is my **Cat Seasons Tetralogy**—Cats saving the world! So far there is **Cat Summer** and **Cat Winter**, but **Cat Autumn** is on its way.

"Mollie weaves a story that blurs the lines of mythology, spiritualism, mysticism, science and reality that took me into

another world. The continuous struggle of good fighting evil, well, it's frightening—not in the least because so many of the things she's written are real."

— Ramona D. Marek MS Ed, CWA Author

"A genre-bending fantasy, **Cat Summer** *carries the flavor of Warriors and the author's own contemporary Cat Mysteries, together with Arthur Clark's 2001... Tolkein and other dark fantasy. For cat-lovers and earth-lovers, a cool and fascinating tale."*

—Sheila Deeth, Author

For poetry lovers, **Cat Poems: For the Love of Cats**.

"This collection of cat poems touches on the joy of becoming acquainted with a newly adopted friend, the heartbreak of saying goodbye to an old one, viewing life through a cat's eyes, and celebrating those who foster and advocate for cats... Every one will touch your heart."

—Mochas, Mysteries, and Meows

Not cat-centric? A stand-alone mystery thriller, **Placid River Runs Deep.**

"...A thrilling combination of menace and pastoral beauty. After reading this book you may want to rethink your summer holiday." —Lily Gardner, author of **Betting Blind**

Books are available from Amazon, Smashwords, Draft2Digital, Powell's, and Barnes & Noble.

Made in the USA
Coppell, TX
30 October 2022